Chill Factor

Linda Iris Willis

Published by Clink Street Publishing 2023

Copyright © 2023

First edition.

ISBN:
978-1-915785-07-7 - paperback
978-1-915785-08-4 - ebook

Into the light...

And somewhere in this nightmare darkness
There must be light
Some way out of the tangled barbed wire manacles
Of confused corruption, grotesquely masquerading
Calling itself – 'The Law' Presuming, accusing –
Whose Law is it anyway?
Whose life?
Who will pay?
Who has the most?
Of course! – Not!
Who can afford it least?
Yes – my dear innocent you must… pay the price–
Trounced by trust
Floored by fools
Grounded by geriatric dwarfs
Mean-spirited, mind bending maniacs

And somewhere there is peace
And tranquillity
And happiness – a reason –
A reason to go on – living
A reason to go on – loving
A reason to go on – caring

And someone does – care
And so through bleak and dark
Despair and cruel deceptive discovery
I reach through bloody thorns
And place my bruised and bleeding fingers-
In safe hands-

Someone will kiss them better
And heal them, and me –
And one step at a time
One breath at a time
I will stand straight and strong –
And smiling yet –
So much I can't forget –
But somewhere in this nightmare of darkness –
You take my hands –
And lead me safely back into the light.

Chapter One

A chill wind blew me to this lonely place to recover. Savagely eastern the windwhipped up the slate grey sea. An angry sea under the stern stone-coloured skies. Unremitting. I pulled my blue woollen scarf tighter around my head, sheltering my ears against the bitter, biting, cold. Sanctuary for my thoughts in the numbness that this hostile iciness was inflicting on my senses. I trudged along the shore in well-worn Wellingtons wondering how on earth did I get here? Perhaps the rugged red rocks once so familiar and friendly would help me to find the answers I craved. Perhaps if I thought long, enough – hard enough – the pain would go away.

The sheer joy this hidden cove in deepest Devon had showered me with since my dad had abandoned two wheels and moved on up from a motorbiketo the four-wheeled luxury of his first Ford – a real car! And, although the journey took us longer than it did to reach sunsoaked Mediterranean beaches - and still does -, it didn't matter. Time meant nothing to me. I fell in love instantly with its unspoilt and natural beauty, safe in the knowledge that when I fall in love with anyone or anything that love lasts a lifetime.

Could this be the smuggler's cave that once seemed so big when I was so small? Covered in black shiny mussel shells and grey, gloopy bits of fungus, smelling of sea salt and ozone, bright gleaming bronze seaweed dangling down the slippery rock surface. I stood still for a second, breathing deeply, inhaling like a reformed addict; scents once so familiar and gratifying. Brine, sweet sea salt on my lips and tongue. Urgent, sudden freshness uncoiling suffering from which the mind recoils.

Disentangling the man-made mess. I gazed out to the horizon, focusing through my foggy thoughts as I remembered the tales my dad told me long ago. Stories of the sea. Of smugglers and pirates lighting up the bay, using secret coded messages which glinted from black lanterns with tiny golden candles flickering inside. Skulking across the shingle in thigh-high leather waders as the inky blackness of the night engulfed them. Despatching cargoes of brown wooden kegs reeking of brandy, rum and whisky. Contraband. All the delicious and forbidden things we shouldn't and couldn't have, whichonly feeding the fickle flame of desire, making them appear to be more exciting than they actually were. Fleeing the excise men who chased them routinely along the cliff tops in their red livery coats and gold braid. Breaking the law every day of their lives, nonetheless, for some inexplicable reason, had always held a special place in my heart. An unexplained and rebellious affection for these rogues. The smugglers. The buccaneers – like Robin Hood and Dick Turpin, stealing from the rich to give to the poor. I never wanted these dubious fallen heroes to be caught! They needed no licence and heeded no man-made law. Yet liberty, freedom and independence were the badges of honour I graciously bestowed upon these fearless, reckless pirates!

No matter how turbulent the tales of terror were, I listened to them with awe. Wondered at them, and then put them safely away like jewels in my 'imagination box', happy, confident that these were the only secrets I had locked away! Digging up the rest of the beach with my bright yellow plastic bucket and spade in the gentle warmth of English summertime absorbed all my attention. But I did sometimes look out to the misty horizon, wondering if that pink brushed lemon haze was actuallyskilfully concealing a black and white skull and crossbones fluttering defiantly from the mizzenmast of a sturdy oak pirate ship! I had not a care in the world. No need to worry about thieves and pirates or anyone toharm me. Totally secure in the knowledge that I was loved. And can love ever spoil anyone? Can we ever have enough? I slumped down on the biggest rock I could find.

Smooth from constant years of sunbathers sprawling across it during the summer months, worn and wearied by the wind that whipped across the pale grey, peach and cream pebbles in the wintertime. I picked up a flat stone, with no curves in it, holding it in my hand like a talisman. I let go of it, flinging it into the stormy breakers. My dad could skim stones, my husband used to be able to do it, and my son was skilled at sending a pebble halfway across the Channel if he felt like it. Why I could still only manage a sad 'plop' as it landed in the murky water sending out slow half-hearted grey circles like a broken wedding ring was a mystery to me still. But the ripples go on. My dad told me once long ago, "If you look at a lake or the sea, it can appear to be very tranquil and calm sometimes. Until someone comes along and throws a stone, or even a rock, right into the middle. Instantly it makes a deep hole. Right there. But the ripples! The ripples are endless. And life itself is no different. It only takes one person to throw that stone into the centre of your own little world. Maybe a momentous business decision, an act of betrayal, cowardice, or cruelty. Whatever the reason, the repercussions are as endless as the waves upon the shore. And they will continue affecting completely innocent people who had nothing whatsoever to do with the decision to toss that stone in the first place. Maybe for the rest of time. Yet, it is others who are left to pick up the pieces. You – who has to pick up the pieces and rebuild your own life. Make it better."

My dad was not a University graduate. He went to school in London's East End just before the War and had a hard life in many ways. But he never ever complained. His philosophy was simple, based on truth, instinct and old-fashioned common sense. Total honesty and integrity were some of the greatest gifts he willingly shared with me.

I stuffed my freezing hands into my jacket pockets. As usual, I'd left my gloves somewhere safe – so safe I couldn't find them. My fingers were beginning to turn a vivid shade of blue. But, as I got up slowly from the sturdy rock and began to walk steadily, carefully back across the windswept beach, white crested rollers beginning to bang across the shingle, sending sprays of bleached foam skyward like sparkling fireworks, I knew I had reached the crossroads and was about to make the most momentous decision of my whole life. At last, it was time to dig down deep and find the courage to move on.

When I got back inside my cosy hotel room with its king size bed cosily covered with a thick comforting duvet, crisp white cotton sheets, complimentary wrap-around terry towelling bathrobe, and matching slip your feet in and snooze slippers, warmth engulfed me just like the blast you get when you step from a plane, landing somewhere exotic. I pulled off my scarf and sand-encrusted wellies and ran hot water into the bathtub, pouring generous dollops of Crabtree and Evelyn summer flower scents into the bubbles. I felt curiously reassured by doing something so very simple. One of those small but precious 'be good to yourself moments'. I climbed in. Relief embraced me as I lay back and allowed myself to reflect properly on all that had happened to me. Why did it happen? Could I have reached out and stopped it –said, hey – not this time – it's my life you're playing about with here? When exactly did I lose control of something only I should have been in control of? My own life?

Getting slowly out of the bath I wrapped the towel carefully around me, pulling down my hair from the tight-bunched scrunchy held messy top knot. Running my fingers through it till it fell in floppy loose, damp curls around my face. I knew I had to relive it all again. Just one more time. I slowly poured myself a chunky tumbler full of chilled still mineral water. Took it with me to the small floral print-covered armchair by the large picture window. I don't know how long I sat there. Completely still. Watching the deep peach glow of the setting sun across the bay. Till I became cognizant of a sense that before I could begin looking towards the future, I had to go back to the past, one more time.

And that began with my childhood. Which was truly carefree. When we are privileged by complete protection, sheltered from the harshness of the dark places, we take it for granted. Why would we not? We know nothing else. Just as a nine-year-old child has no idea how it feels to be starving living in Africa, consciousness fails to connect with the notion that some people are living a very different sort of life indeed. And not as far away as another continent. And not where you would expect to find it.

So, we try to protect our children with the love we generously shower upon them. We shield them from things we despise because we do not want them to suffer – or be hurt. But the deadly danger that creeps up like a cancerous weed is that it is our very protective instinct that makes us eventually vulnerable. Weak. It makes us gullible and trusting and naïve. Like men going into battle armed with wooden sticks when the enemy are armed with machine guns, the outcome cannot fail to be ugly and gruesome. For only the strongest survive. And that is a bitter lesson it's taken me a lifetime to learn.

Chapter Two

Television studios are magical places. Massive arc lights with perfect round faces like full moons hanging on to steadfast lighting grids, lined up above shining white floored studios, scattered with sets, dotted with cameras, booms, and technicians. Each time I walked past a gleaming, bright red 'on air' light stuck to the studio wall, I felt curiously alive. Like a shot of adrenaline had just been injected into me. My dad had worked in TV since the early days and therefore I knew a lot about it already. And I loved it! When I was small, Christmas parties with Santa dressed in a big red fluffy red outfit with snow white fur, sitting inside a massive golden sleigh complete with bells and real reindeer was the stuff of fantastic fantasy and beautiful tinsel-covered dreams. I was the luckiest kid on the block. Now it was my turn to embark on the first firm step to a career I had always dreamed of. In the world of the mini silver screen. Still very much a male environment, fiercely protected by all the 'men in suits in charge. They fully intended to keep it that way! Camerawomen simply did not exist, or female Lighting Directors, or even Heads of Department, unless it was a 'safe area for the fairer sex – like Wardrobe or Make Up.

I had a burning desire to be a designer. "Forget all about that! It's a man's world!" I was unceremoniously informed by the Head of Personnel. A small wiry man with greying wispy hair and a very serious expression. Always carrying a clipboard. Containing what, I had no idea. Maybe he thought it made him look like David Frost. It didn't. Nondescript sweatshirt and grey flannel trousers. His uniform. Clothes as uninspired and insipid as he was. But if he said, 'no' then you simply did not get a second chance. So I didn't give him the opportunity of saying, 'no' to me. I took the 'female option' instead. I wasn't too unhappy. I had a career in television, surrounded every day by creativity and colour. "Just get your foot in the door, and work it out from there!" my dad said. That's all I'd ever wanted to do. I had longed for the day when I could chuck out my dusty School books with battered covers, and revolting bottle green hockey shorts and head for a world of full-time fantasy in the entertainment industry. My school had been built next to MGM's back lot. I had watched through the windows during countless boring Geography or Chemistry lessons while splendid film sets appeared. Oriental pagodas, red and gold pointy tips piercing the bright blue skies. Strangely surreal appeared above the boys' cricket pitch. "Stop daydreaming out of the window, Lesley!" I was constantly reprimanded. But you have to follow your dreams sometimes. There were war films with night shooting, the best and noisiest special effects bombarding the neighbourhood during the filming of US blockbusters with mega superstar heroes. A torrent of complaints would fill the local paper the next day. But only from those who didn't work there, and never would. Jealous of those who were fortunate and talented enough to do so. Envy is the root cause of so much pain and evil. And it never goes away.

"Lesley?" I looked up into the glare of the spotlight above me, as Dean Jones, one of the young whiz-kid Directors, temporarily blocked my vision. Like many little men, he had a tendency to overcompensate by behaving in a brusque manner, taking instant control, and establishing authority. Always trying to have the upper hand even in the banalest of conversations. Dean was wearing scruffy blue denim jeans with worn-out faded patches, and a checked shirt. He sported what he thought made him look, 'intellectual and clever' – a small beard. "Oh, Lesley, I thought you were the latest newscaster for a moment – as you were sitting in her chair!"

Derision was tempered with discretion as Dean was well aware that my boss was not somebody it was helpful to upset. I had no intention of losing 'my cool', so I swivelled off of the black leather chair with as much grace as I could muster in such a short skirt, and left the impressive chunky glass and chrome newscasters' desk to its rightful occupant. "I wish!" I thought. But instead, I laughed and told him, "I was just waiting for some paperwork from Ainsley!" I looked over my shoulder at him, as I made my way across to the plastic gun metal grey seats with flip-up tops that constituted 'audience seating'. I sat down on one of them. Waiting for Ainsley to arrive.

Ainsley Logan was a designer. And boy did I want to be like him! "You have a brilliant sense of colour!" he had told me the first time we met. I had fallen for him instantly. From the very first moment, we got on like a house on fire. Throughout my whole life, I had always enjoyed the company of men, very much indeed, but Ainsley Logan was somehow different from other men – set apart. I believed he was gay. So I felt very 'safe' whenever I was with him. I could be friends with him. I could flirt with him, and tease him. But I knew that he wasn't about to make a pass all the time, and I knew that way our friendship would last. I think Ainsley felt safe with me too. He was wonderfully appealing. Seriously goodlooking with a mop of long black, straight shining hair. He had a glossy fringe that flopped across his deep brown liquid chocolate-coloured eyes. I could have written a whole book of poems about Ainsley! He was amazing company and fun. We shared the same stupid irreverent sense of humour. He treated me like an equal. A buddy. And that's what we were.

And although he was content to wear jeans just like all the other guys, Ainsley's Levi's were 50ls and golden, never faded blue with threadbare bits on the knees! His shirt collar was always casually turned up just the right amount on his white Italian shirts and his hair curled tantalisingly over the back of his neck, in a perfect curve. Tempting you to stroke it tenderly like some kind of exotic Siamese cat's fur. He was gorgeous, and I loved Ainsley to bits.

All at once, he came crashing through the studio doors looking like an Anglo-Arab long-legged stallion, all arms and legs. Making his gangling way towards me, sunglasses perched on top of his head, he stopped abruptly, and started pulling out sheaves of papers from a massive, well-worn, forest green leather binder. "Look at these for me, Les – I need your opinion!" White papers were partially concealed beneath the cover, suddenly becoming visible, shining like some kind of hidden treasure. I couldn't wait to unearth it and see what multi-coloured wonder he'd created with his felt tips today! Ainsley's sense of colour co-ordinated completely with his sense of humour. Exciting, unpredictable, extraordinary, and extreme. Like some kind of richly woven tapestry suddenly leaping into life. And for no explainable reason, you simply ended up feeling good. I gazed at the intricate patterns eagerly.

"Ainsley!" I gasped. "These are fantastic!" he smiled a little sheepishly, thanking me, pushing back his thick fringe with one hand. Hiding – could it be a blush?

"Thanks, Les," he replied. "I needed to hear you say that! I know if you really like them that they're OK. Because one thing you always do is tell me the truth. And if you think they're OK…" Well, if that's how he wanted to describe his miniature masterpieces. I would have chosen a much more colourful superlative. Ainsley, it appeared, was typical of the truly talented. He didn't brag. He didn't need to!

Television is a glamorous world. And during the 'golden years' the rewards were rich. Our Studios were like one big family. Sons and daughters followed in their father's footsteps to become young cameramen, floor managers, stagehands, and even secretaries. Christmas parties lasted for the whole month of December. In a protected world, we were safe from the reality that existed outside of our little corner of creativity. It was also a free-spirited world. But I had no deep-seated desire to drift too far down that path. My dreams of a career in television were dashed before they had even had a chance to get into first gear? I had no wish to be dubbed a dipsy bar-fly, falling in and out of bed with a variety of sweet-talking technicians with a chat-up line mere mortals would kill for. So I made a pact with myself to go out with as many boys as possible, steering well clear of the dangerous waters too much intimacy can drag you into. I could always walk away when I felt things getting too hot to handle.

No hiding place for what was considered, 'politically correct', we just got on with it, and if one or two wolf whistles came along, so much the better!

"Guess who's coming in tomorrow?" said Ainsley, plonking himself lankily down beside me in the canteen with a full cup of steaming black coffee in his hands.

"Dunno," I replied, my mouth half-filled with jam doughnut.

"Elton John!" I wasn't quite so enthused as my pal as I had already seen Elton rehearsing at the film studios, when I worked there, but nevertheless, I gave him what I hoped was an encouraging smile.

"That's great, Ainsley. I'll keep my eye out for him!" When Elton came into Studio D as a guest on the Muppet Show he seemed to be smaller than he is now. He still had his own hair. And when he passed by in a tight-waisted green velvet suit, he looked pale and drawn. Enveloped by a cloak of sadness. Eyes staring into the distance. He took no notice of me at all. He seemed troubled. Ainsley was besotted.

"Isn't he fantastic?!" he cried, as Elton pounded out 'Crocodile Rock!' on a dazzling white mini baby grand, wearing huge rainbow-coloured glasses and purple feathers. He looked more exotic than Kermit, Fozzie and the rest of the gang all put together.

Like living inside a huge box of chocolates with all your favourite centres in one cellophane wrap, that's what it was like working in television in those days. Tom Jones, Paul McCartney, Andy Williams, Barbra Streisand, John Wayne. A never-ending stream of stars. "We're doing the Royal Variety Performance at Drury Lane this year!" said the Head of Light Entertainment, as I walked down the corridor with him carrying a box of files. A very tall and distinguished extrovert, he favoured pastel-coloured cashmere sweaters. I thought he was very clever and talented.

"Can I come?" I asked cheekily. He stepped back in mock shock.

"Why?" he boomed, pulling a comical face.

"You know very well why! Cliff Richard is appearing isn't he?" I replied.

"Oh, for heaven's sake – you're not a Cliff Richard fan are you?!" He attempted to look dismayed. "It's only big wigs, Lesley. Directors and all that. You understand don't you?" I nodded.

Two days later there was a loud banging sound on my office door. He put his head round the edge of it making sure I was there and then walked over slowly, clutching two lemon and white pieces of card with golden royal crests on top, and swirling writing which was embossed. "Here you are – you brazen hussy!" He smiled, as he tossed them onto my desk. Oh, wow! Long dress, designer glitz, fur coat – and Cliff – there is a heaven!

I stood in the wine velvet sumptuousness of the Stalls Bar at the Dominion Theatre, surrounded by celebrities and cigar smoke that circled the air in puffy pale grey wafts, acrid aroma blending seductively with the most expensive perfumes on the planet, thinking, "You have arrived – definitely!"

Film premieres, first nights, end of production parties. A string of glittering occasions, filled with high glamour, high spirits and high expectations. Living in the fast lane of a bubbling world of champagne and compliments made it seem as if anything were possible. Understandably, I loved every moment. I looked forward to getting ready for work, each morning sitting in front of the dressing table mirror adjusting my make-up, before leaving for the studios and reminding myself how lucky I was to be doing this job that I cared about so very much.

Ainsley was my constant source of comradeship. And although I went on lots of dates, with lots of good-looking guys, I was in no hurry to swap my happy-go-lucky lifestyle for anything heavy and serious. I had kept in touch with my girlfriends and we went to clubs, restaurants and the movies. We were young. Carefree, with money of our own to spend. The future was a distant blob on the grown-up horizon, that we didn't need to talk about, focus on or even really give much thought to. On Saturday morning we would get up early, dashing off to Miss Selfridge or Kensington High Street Boutiques like Bus Stop and Biba. We had to be the very first to get the very latest look. Sometimes we ended up being thrown out of the shops when the ever-helpful shop assistants wearily replaced the 'closed' signs on the doors. We intrepidly trekked from one end of Oxford Street to the other and back again, like explorers in the jungle, seeking out and tracking down a rare species of designer suit with a swirly skirt, or a pretty pair of patent leather platforms, or white boots.

One day there was an abrupt and unexpected shift of gear from full speed ahead in the fast lane in top gear to slowing down and spluttering to a halt in first. A bright spring morning.

The crocuses had already started to bloom in blue and white clumps like tiny bouquets, and the first daffodils were sticking dazzling yellow heads out of murky brown mud, smiling up into the chilly pale blue vernal equinox skies. "Lesley! It's Lucy!" she cried down the phone, almost hysterically. My best friend. Older, and supposedly wiser, than me. She had just turned thirty, and she had just decided to do something we'd all avoided like the proverbial plague, up until now. "I'm getting married!" she squealed down the phone like some kind of demented seagull. I heard the words that jangled and tangled themselves in my head, clattering down the line, thumping into the quiet orderliness of my neat and tidy office.

"What?" I echoed. Dumbstruck. My free-spirited loony friend Lucy, is always ready for a laugh and a joke. Always there, to see me through everything, from getting sloshed in West End wine bars to getting my wisdom teeth removed under general anaesthetic. Getting married? The 'm' word wasn't part of our lives, was it? We were career girls. Independent. The young female voices of our age. And we didn't need all that old-fashioned 1950s vacuum in one hand, husband in the other stuff did we? A man to make us complete?

"I'm thirty!" She was laughing now.

"So what?" I replied.

Lucy suddenly sounded all grown up and serious. "I've got to settle down some time!" I didn't even know Lucy had been seeing anybody that special.

"Who to?" I heard myself begin to gabble, a bit like a deranged duck.

"Trey!" she replied.

"Trey?"

"Yes, Trey Williams. You remember. The American guy I used to work with. He's come over for a short holiday. He's divorced now. It's been so frantic – like a sort of whirlwind! And we've talked about it a lot and we've decided to get married. In September! Will you be my bridesmaid? Oh, and do my flowers for me?" I gasped, trying to take it all in. Astonished. We were headed into completely unknown territory here, like Peter Pan whirling back at top speed from Never Never Land to North Watford.

"Of course," I replied. I didn't know what else to say.

"Oh – and something else, Lesley – we're going to be living in New York – America!"

There was a loud and defiantly audible 'click' as she put down the phone. I was losing my best friend. And all of a sudden I could feel the draught of time's chill moving forward, creeping up my spine like quick growing clematis, wrapping itself around me, uninvited. Nature sure is female. A victim, yet at the same time an aggressive instigator of change. Every day that Mother Nature faces a new challenge, women do the same. Like the circle of the Moon linked to the tides, so our cycle drives us, like a restless spirit that refuses to be hushed. Pulling and pushing like the waves. Instinctively aware when it's time to move on. We don't always listen to her though. A sudden chill breeze blew through my open window, blowing my new net curtains aside and knocking my glass vase of fresh white freesias onto the floor.

I helped Lucy choose her wedding outfit. Not traditional white long and flowing. "I'm too old for it!" she insisted. "Also, because it's Trey's second marriage, I will wear a long pale grey dress with a tailored jacket. But with a flouncy hat!" To be fair, Lucy did let me choose whatever colour I wanted for the bridesmaid outfit. Which was nice of her considering the 'theme' was palest silvery grey. At least she didn't inflict that cheerless non-colour on my jaded senses and drooping and doubting shoulders. I chose gold. Simple. Discreet. Classy. I felt like a candlestick.

Chapter Three

I helped Lucy to stuff endless amounts of carmine-coloured chrysanthemums into clear plastic bowls that were supposed to look like glass but wouldn't break. They stood like guardsmen in the centre of each oval table at the reception. But by the end of the evening, the once pert petals were sagging as they flopped and dropped down despondently over the misty containers. When Lucy walked into the grey walled ivy covered church, she stood in the arch of the doorway, for just a brief second, silhouetted against the bright September sunshine playing outside on the grass behind her. She glanced back over her shoulder quickly. "Still time, Lucy!" I thought. "Still time to run away!" How irrational was that? This was Lucy's wedding day for goodness' sake!

A baby's piercing cry suddenly, unexpectedly, echoed around the walls of the old church. Reverberating from the hushed congregation, like a herald. Lucy gave no impression of having heard. Looking straight ahead of her she determinedly picked up the front of her long silvery grey dress with one hand, and marched briskly down the aisle on her dad's arm.

The reception in a local hotel with brown fading folding seats and crumpled table-cloths was tedious. I had a dull throbbing headache. Midsummer humidity hung in the air like damp fog and I just wanted to go home. "Look after her!" I begged Trey.

"Yep." He had a faraway look as he absent-mindedly answered.

After Lucy left for the States, things were never quite the same. The chill of Autumn set in early. She wrote from New York, phoned a few times, and then the calls tailed off as she got on with her new life. The first frosts took a firm, relentless grip. And it snowed in October, leaving my car stranded in the car park.

"Ainsley?" I said, looking at him across the top of a big china mug of frothing hot chocolate smothered in whipped cream. I'd given up worrying about whether it would end up adding extra inches to my hips. "Do you fancy coming to the pictures?" A flicker of – could it be alarm? Traversed his mobile features momentarily. His usually smiling brown eyes, shifted direction and looked uneasy.

"Why?" he asked. As if startled by my request. Like a six-year-old boy suddenly being ordered to eat their greens. "Do you mean – like a date?" he was beginning to shuffle about a bit in the hard-edged canteen chairs, looking even more uncomfortable.

"No – it's just that there's this new blockbuster on at Leicester Square and I thought you might like to see it with me, that's all – just as a friend…" I was beginning to wish I'd never started this dubious conversation in the first place. But I had started. So I carried on.

I began to scrape the cream off the top of the cup with an unused white paper sugar wrapper. "Just as a friend," I continued, softly. It was a pretty lame attempt to salvage something that was sinking faster than a submarine in a hurricane, but I did it anyway. Ainsley stared down at his cup of weak lemon tea, for what seemed like an eternity. Saying nothing. I could hear the loud, 'tick tock' of the clock on the studio canteen wall above us. White-faced, with hard black numbers stuck to it like accusers. Very, very slowly he moved his head, and looked up at me, pushing his thick silky fringe back from his eyes with long, sensitive fingers.

"Lesley." Hesitation and the tone of his voice told me everything – yet nothing. I didn't want to hear what he had to say to me. But I knew he was going to say it anyway. "We've been friends for a long time, Lesley. I don't know how to tell you this really. I've been putting it off because I didn't know how you would react. I've been seeing someone. And at first, even I didn't know what was going to happen. But it's so special. We just seem to click and it just feels right – you know? We just want to be together forever, really. I've found the love of my life, Lesley!"

I gazed back at him submerged in disbelief. "Who is he?" I asked.

"No – Lesley! It's not a bloke!" I am not sure if he squirmed. Maybe he did. But I'm still not sure. I had sat and listened to his emotional outpourings and now I felt a sickening wave which threatened to engulf me. Like I'd just been punched in the stomach. I did not want him to continue. All I really wanted to do was to drop my hot chocolate and head for the double-sided glass doorway, out of the stifling confines of the studio's canteen, and into the fresh air. "Her name is Emma. She's a film editor. We've been seeing each other for a few months now. She is gorgeous Lesley. I know you would like her!" No – I wouldn't!

"But, I thought..." I began to speak, feeling very foolish suddenly. Like a little girl lost, trying so hard to be part of the sophisticated grown-up world – and missing the point – completely. Yet still, he was talking.

"Emma has made me realise just how happy I can be! I feel so alive! She is a real woman!" Oh, great – so what about me? Ainsley could obviously read my mind at that point. "Well – no hard feelings, eh, Lesley. After all, we have never ever had that kind of relationship, have we? We have always been, well – mates!" Mates. Like a bloke. Only I wasn't a bloke! I took a gulp of the chocolate, which was now tepid, and tasted horrible. I started to get up, my chair made a scraping sound across the vinyl floor. "You don't have to go..." his voice trailed off, because he knew as well as I did, that it was too late. A sudden chill between us after all the years. I heard the 'clink' of a broken window lock as it swung open abruptly behind me.

Or was it the fractured, splintering sound of yet another one of my carefully constructed safety chains?

I couldn't sleep at all that night. Lying alone in the darkness listening to the incessant ticking of the tiny golden bedside alarm. But there is another clock that ticks even more loudly. The one inside. I was already in my mid-twenties. Did I want to be a career girl? Yes indeed! Did I want children? Yes indeed! But did I want marriage and all that? Not really. It wasn't something

I had even thought about seriously, or for very long. I wanted to be like Peter Pan and stay young forever. Frozen in time. Stop all these damned clocks ticking away and shove them down the throats of the alligators, just like Captain Hook. I tossed and turned all night long.

***

When you don't have the luxury of brothers and sisters you take it for granted that the love of your parents is total and unequivocal. Freely given. Freely accepted. I thought everyone was so blessed, but, like many things, it is sometimes not until they are taken from us that we begin to realise quite how very precious they are.

I sat on the hard pebbles, watching benign waves gently lapping against the seashore. Bright, autumnal sunshine was illuminating the auburn-coloured rocks glued to my favourite bay with a dusky, amber glow. The last dying embers of what had been scorching summer sunshine. Still warm and golden. "I don't know what to do, Dad," I had told him as he sat beside me. Sturdy and safe. My dad was not a glamorous dad. And I was so thankful for that! He was a real dad, cushioned and cuddly with twinkling sincere blue eyes, and a smile that could light up a room, the moment he stepped inside it. Always able to make me laugh. With one bear-like hug from him, and whatever else was happening in my life, I would have been able to take on the Spanish Armada single-handed! My mentor and guide, it was to him I had always turned whenever I was troubled. My fortress.

When I was a little girl I felt that I lived in a castle, not a house! And my dad was the castle walls surrounding us, protecting us from the perils that lurked beyond the boundaries of the front gate. My Knight in shining armour, guardian and guide. "Everything happens for a reason," he used to tell me. "You don't always know at the time what that reason is. But eventually, it will become clear. Your life is planned. And although it is sometimes very difficult to understand or to see ahead – you must always go forward – never go back!"

My dad didn't go to Church every Sunday, but his simple belief in the Almighty was deep and strong. "You'll be alright," he assured me. Putting a comforting arm around my shoulders, gently squeezing them. "Everything will work out. God will guide you. In the meantime, don't worry about what might or what might not happen. Enjoy what you have!"

I looked across at the sparkling sea, as it splashed about around the strong, ruddy rugged rocks, just as I had splashed about when I was a little girl. I was content to believe what he said.

Not long after that, I met Paul.

Chapter Four

It's a small world – television. Full of families. And Paul Pearson's family was no exception. His father was one of the first Directors to be asked to work on the opulent, prestige, no-expenses spared American shows. His flair for all things technical impressed me. Well, I was not a technical person – what did I know? His only son, Paul, had left behind him a privileged private school, with no qualifications, heading off to be a hippy on the windswept salty surfers' beaches of North Cornwall.

Riding the wild surf on Fistral Beach instantly appealed to one who craved self-indulgence, self-satisfaction, a hedonistic lifestyle, answering to no one. Doing exactly what he wanted to, whenever he wanted to. No questions asked. No replies given. If his parents, or indeed anybody else, said, don't do it, he would go ahead and do it anyway. He was a rebel. He owned two cars. One, a custom-built banana yellow vintage sports car, the other a sleek silvery blue Lotus Elite Coupe. Blown back from the beach at the behest of his father, he was now working as an Assistant Director. A job his dad helped to secure for him. He was my new boyfriend.

Paul Pearson wasn't at all like anyone I had ever been out with before. He was very tall, and that made me feel surprisingly safe. He had a dark beard, which made me focus my attention on his piercing steel blue eyes. He had a startling lack of dress sense: his wardrobe consisted of Playboy bunny grey and black T-shirts, woollen fleecy jackets and bright yellow sports shirts. He had memorised a staggering assortment of painfully excruciating jokes. He had a flat in Kingston-on-Thames, overlooking the river. His family owned an apartment on the quiet bit of Majorca near Formentor and a huge country house in Hertfordshire. My first impression of Paul Pearson was that he was blatantly posh! But that didn't matter. I liked him for who he was. Did I know who he was? I thought so.

We didn't have a 'routine courtship' if such a thing exists. If indeed, that is what it was. For weeks we would not even see each other and then get together and have a great time. Uncomplicated. Like I'd planned. "I don't want to get too serious!" he told me. Fine. Usually my line, but whipped away from me by Paul, just like one of Fagin's lads stealing leather wallets from an unsuspecting punter's back pocket. There was something else that was different, too. On our first date, Paul did not rush to kiss me. Made no attempt. Just said, "Goodnight!" and whisked off into the darkness revving up the engine of the Lotus, as he sped off down the road. He's a gentleman, I thought.

On the third date, I stood on tiptoe and tried to kiss him. "What are you doing?" He looked startled.

"Kissing you goodnight!" I replied.

"No, no – I don't do that straight away! I don't really like kissing!" was his extraordinary reply. But I kissed him lightly on the cheek anyway. And off he went.

Now, whenever I was invited to a film premiere or a party, I was able to take Paul along too. One day we left the Lotus precariously parked on a double yellow at Leicester Square, as we flew across the road to an opening night at the Odeon. "Don't give me a ticket!" he turned and yelled to a passing policeman.

"You don't have to worry – with a car like that – you can afford it!" the policeman retorted with a smile.

"You're kidding – I can't even afford the petrol!" joked Paul. Anyway, I thought he was joking.

And so really our relationship jogged along happily in a haphazard little way. With me not thinking too much about it. Getting on with building my career like a complicated piece of Lego. And Paul driving us around in his Lotus. We started to spend more and more time together without seeming to realise it. Long lunches on the banks of the Thames on bright Saturday mornings, in an assortment of trendy wine bars, and plush new pizza parlours. Fashionable American burger bars were sprouting up like summer flowers all over the place and we sat happily people-watching as we munched our way through homemade burgers and the latest line in relish. That part of south London was upwardly mobile. It suited our lifestyle. It suited me at the time. We bought flashy roller skates from a shop on the Kings Road and tried them out, whizzing up and down the hill and along the river banks. On lazy Sunday afternoons we would browse slowly round the antique shops in the High Street or we would take long, bracing walks in Richmond Park, chasing the golden-coloured reindeer with their massive, big, brimming shining brown eyes. So trusting. So vulnerable. I was falling in love with the place. I was slowly falling in love with Paul. My work was clicking away almost like clockwork.

Sometimes I would catch the tail end of a whispered conversation in the studio corridors, or in the canteen. Curious looks behind my back. "They are jealous of me – that's all." Paul would say, vaguely. And I had no reason to doubt what he said. I was concentrating on my own job. Wrapped up in my world. How often do we pull down the shutters firmly on what we refuse to hear or see? Wearing massive blinkers that blind us to the truth? Allowing us to make momentous decisions with our eyes wide shut. It would not be the first time I did so.

Cold winds of change were about to blow through my comfortable life, disrupting it forever. But on those balmy summer evenings when Paul and I would stroll up to the top of Richmond Hill, and share a bottle of bubbly while watching the setting sun over the Thames, I had no idea how much.

Strikes were something miners did or students. Or firemen even. But television crews? Never. So when the powerful ACTT Union voted for a walk-out plunging TV screens across the nation into darkness, pulling the plugs on all transmissions the result was catastrophic. My dad, and everyone else, was forced suddenly to find part-time work anywhere and everywhere they possibly could. It was very hard. The Studios were officially closed, except for a skeleton staff, including me. I was non-Union at that time. I had no choice. Anyone who has ever had to endure the harrowing experience of the 'white knuckle ride' that constitutes driving through the middle of an angry picket line will understand. Most of the men I had known since I was very young, and had watched me grow up. They smiled looking a little bit embarrassed. But others did not. Angrily thumping their fists on the roof of my little red car till it ended up dented, and I ended up shaking with fear inside.

In the middle of this anarchic turmoil, and the steamiest midsummer heatwave for years, Paul got down on one knee in the middle of Richmond Bridge – and proposed to me. And from that moment my world did not stop spinning. For Paul wanted us to be married as soon as possible. Once he had made up his mind it had to happen straight away. "We have somewhere to live. We both have good jobs," he reasoned. "And – there is something else too – I love you, Lesley!" I was completely overwhelmed. This was so unexpected. Like a bolt out of the blue water in the river beneath us. Paul had discovered an intoxicating love potion like nothing I had experienced before. I was simply swept off my feet. For a girl who had spent a lifetime being oh, so very carefully in control, I suddenly wasn't. And I felt happy.

I felt loved. And I felt uneasy. I had been thrown a curved ball and I didn't know whether to catch it and hold on tight, run with it – or throw it straight back again!

All things considered, my parents took things very well. "Is it some kind of joke?" asked my bewildered mother.

"Congratulations! I knew this day would come!" smiled my dad warmly, finding a bottle of champagne from somewhere and handing us all a glass full.

My life was about to change forever. I was now engaged. I was getting married. I would be respectable and I would officially join the "I am grown up" brigade. OK. I could handle that. I laid down on my bed thinking about it. My feet suddenly felt very chilly. I pulled the duvet tighter around me.

Chapter Five

Someone very famous, whose name I don't recall, once said, "You cannot go to Richmond without falling in love." That's true. I fell in love with the place. I fell in love with a man. I think I fell in love with being in love. It's a heady cocktail that makes you feel completely alive. The grass becomes a vibrant shade of green, the river is always blue, not muddy coloured and murky. You smell the first blossom on the trees intensely when they start to burst into bud and then bloom in palest pink and white froths as you wander through the gardens leading down to the Thames. And the warmth of summer nights when jasmine and honeysuckle surround you, shooting sweet fireworks of fragrance up your nose. It's all of that – and more. You feel wanted. Needed. Suddenly special.

Sitting on a wooden bench at the very top of Richmond Hill became one of my favourite places. The view of the Thames as it snakes its way past the islands and winds its way towards Ham and Kingston is one of the most beguiling and stunning in London. Especially at night time when a million twinkling fairy lights flicker like fairies clasping candles in the wind. The landing lights of Heathrow Airport to the right, the golden glow of Twickenham and Roehampton ahead. Wonderland – and all for free. No wonder that the members of the Rolling Stones, The Who, and John Mills and his family chose this land of enchantment to be their home. Paul and I would sit together, holding hands in the moonlight, looking out at this magical place. Perfect. Like a scene from a movie.

One peaceful Sunday afternoon, just a few weeks before the Banns were being read out, we made our way to the top of the hill and sat down on a bench warmed by the sun. "I have something to tell you," said Paul.

He looked suddenly serious and I clutched his hand a little tighter. "What?" I asked him.

"Something that happened when I was a little boy."

"What happened?" He didn't look at me, just continued looking straight ahead out across the treetops.

"My parents sent me to see a psychologist." The afternoon sun was warm on my bare arms. Sunshine glinted on the sparkling water as the river boats and pleasure boats cruised leisurely by. Small rowing boats full of young boys trying to impress their girlfriends as the wooden craft swayed precariously from side to side. Their giggling laughter spiralling up to us. I looked at Paul, but he was still staring straight ahead. A fixed expression in his blue eyes.

"Psychologist?" I echoed.

It jarred. Oddly at variance with the bright summer day and the carefree mood of the moment. Strangely disconnected. Why was he telling me this now? What on earth did that have to do with us?

"I was about six. It was for my behavioural problems. My parents said they couldn't handle me!" He laughed then, a short burst which flew off into the air. And that's all he said. He never ever mentioned it again. If there was a sudden chill breeze blowing right across the top of the hill, I didn't feel it. Perhaps I should have.

Whirlwind romances are definitely the stuff of fairytales. Cinderella, Sleeping Beauty, Snow White, miraculously meeting Prince Charming. All the Disney stuff little girls are spoon-fed like maple syrup from the first time a baby doll is placed into their chubby little hands. When I was small, my cousin Danny was given a state-of-the-art bright blue pedal replica of a Ford motor car. My grandmother bought it for him. And he guarded his prized new possession like gold dust as he raced up and down the park in it till the wheels nearly dropped off. He wouldn't even let me sit inside it. Which was a shame! Because I was given a gift too. Which I would have been more than glad to share with him if he'd asked. I got a state-of-the-art four-by-four brown and beige version of a Silver Cross pram, with big shiny silver wheels. Now – I would have been more than happy to let him sit in that if he'd wanted to! Instead, I deposited my rosy-cheeked plastic baby doll inside it and set off to see my grandmother, who lived at the very top of a very tall block of flats. And in my attempt to push the pram up the steep steps leading to her front door, I came unstuck. And so did the wheels of my pram. The whole weight of it fell onto my tiny fingers, which were crushed beneath it and the doll flew off into outer space.

Oh – the pain! My mum carefully wrapped my battered fingers in crisp white bandages. With bows on the end. "They're dollies!" she proclaimed. No. They were not dollies! They were sterile dressings covering my wounded hands and, from that moment onwards, I had the sneaky suspicion that had I been offered the chance to race around in the Ford instead – well – I would probably have been a whole lot safer!

Now I was grown up I had a car of my very own. Not a Ford. A Fiat. Bright tomato red. With shining white and silver alloy wheels. Black leather upholstery. I loved her. I loved driving around all over the place. Most of all I loved the independence she afforded me so willingly. She was always there for me. Whenever I needed her. Uncomplainingly taking me anywhere I wanted to go – like a magic carpet. I simply adored her for my freedom on four wheels. So when I was planning my wedding my car and me travelled backwards and forwards in a continuous loop, from Kingston, to the studios, to my parents home, to Paul's parents, and all around the West End searching for the special and precious gifts that we stuck on our list.

The intensity surrounding a whirlwind wedding is arguably even more exciting than a whirlwind romance. Just as unpredictable, and baffling. The speculation involved in choosing the right dress, and photographer, and the proper church, cars, the reception, the music, the cake and the outfits for the wedding party. It's total 'bling' from the moment that the date is set. Wandering around Hatton Garden, gazing into shop windows searching for wedding rings, and an engagement ring. Finding out in a single moment all about precious gems. Diamonds. What was a carat? Nothing orange or crunchy! The sparkle of a real diamond is unequalled. It twinkles, it flashes in a second, while caught out unexpectedly basking in a sudden burst of sunlight. It glitters and winks at you from a distance flirting with you from its twenty-two-carat golden holster. Try me. Try me. Buy me. Buy me! Blinding brilliant. I could have chosen anything. Modern designs, antique with filigree. Blue diamonds. White diamonds. I opted for a classic solitaire. In plain gold band. Traditional. Unchanging. A diamond that would be timeless, never going out of fashion. After all, you know what they say – A Diamond is Forever!

My wedding day was frantic. Most brides confess that they cannot remember much about their big day. Oh, but I do. I do. I got up early and had a hot bath. Looked for my car keys, and couldn't find them – anywhere. My darling little four-wheeled freedom seeker had decided to be capricious today. So I ended up running at full pelt down the road, with sweat pouring down my face like raindrops. All the way to the local hairdressing salon in the centre of town. Why I didn't call a cab, I just don't know. I kept thinking that a bus would come along that I could jump onto, or my dad. But they didn't.

So by the time I collapsed in a heap into the hairdressers' imitation leather chair, I was already dangerously behind schedule. "Have a cup of tea!" urged Moira, my stylist, attempting to calm down both me and my curls at the same time. I did. "Do your nails!" she advised. I did. "Don't get nervous!" she cried after me as I slipped out of the door with my hair all beautifully coiffed, spritzed with unfamiliar spray, even my errant floppy fringe flicking back just the right degree over my right eyebrow. I did!

Lucy would have been my first choice for a bridesmaid. "I can't come over!" she had wailed plaintively down the phone. "Trey is working so hard, and me too, and, well, we cannot really afford the plane fare at the moment." Her voice trailed off.

"It's OK," I assured her, feeling curiously let down and disappointed. We had always promised each other we would be there for the 'big day'. But I was getting married now, it was the end of an era and the beginning of a whole new life. I had Paul. I didn't really need my girlfriends now, did I? It's hard to ask people you work with to a wedding. Difficult to decide who to invite, and who to leave out from the guest list. I asked my boss and his family. I asked Dean Jones and his new wife Wendy. I didn't ask Ainsley.

Children are great at big occasions. Rising to the occasion in a way that shames most adults. It's more often than not the mature members of the wedding party who end up doing stupid things, saying stupid things, falling down drunk or getting overly emotional. So being a Peter Pan sort of person I decided to do it my way. My attendants were tiny tots. Little people with personalities all their own. There is an innocence and guileless quality that children contain. And you just cannot bottle it. More is the pity!

So when I walked down the aisle in my full-skirted, long white chiffon dress, with a bodice made from finest French lace, and a train and veil that trailed half a mile behind me, it all felt a bit like being in the fairytale that all little girls secretly dream of. Even if they don't admit it. My parents had skimped on nothing to ensure that they provided the most perfect of weddings for me. I still thank them from the bottom of my heart for that.

I had always envisaged getting ready for my wedding, if indeed I ever had a wedding like they do in the movies. Just like all the glossy magazines dedicated to 'Brides' and 'Wedding Day' tell you. All serene and relaxed with a face full of Max Factor, and a tranquil, yet beguiling enigmatic smile. Pampered. Floating about like a Princess in some kind of romantic haze. It wasn't quite like that! Four days before my wedding day I caught a humdinger of a heavy head cold. My face wasn't so much 'Translucent Beige' more 'Frosty White, with a Bright Red Nose'. My bemused boss took me out to dinner, in a very plush local restaurant called The Swan. All my working colleagues turned up without me knowing they would be there at all. "Surprise!" they yelled in unison, as I sat there sniffing and stuffing damp Kleenex into the pockets of my black velvet blazer. They bought me bunches of flowers. They gave me gifts. They were lovely. I was supposed to give a speech but my throat was so sore, I simply couldn't speak. I went home. Drank fresh orange juice for the Vitamin C. I drank Beechams powders to bring down my temperature. I drank enough tea to re-float the Titanic! My cold got better.

I arranged armloads of fresh flowers, balancing them precariously on the kitchen table. I struggled out of bed at an hour I thought only came around once a day.

I headed off with my folks to Covent Garden Market, very, very early in the morning. As pinky peach dawn was breaking over the grey silhouette of Vauxhall Bridge, making it look like a beautiful Turner watercolour. We arrived at the huge granite-coloured doors. My dad pushed them open. Oh, I never tire of the sight and smell of fresh flowers in such profusion. Every single bloom is like a smile. And there was an ocean of smiles greeting me that morning. Cheerful and merry the friendly Cockney salesmen – were so lively – so awake! "I want coral pink – for my wedding. I'm getting married on Saturday!" I told them. Piles of petals were heaped into my open arms. Long stemmed roses, with blushing tips, and glossy green sharp-edged leaves. Chrysanthemums, snow white gypsophila, long-stemmed candy-coloured stephanotis. And the overwhelming perfume, knocking your senses for six like a thousand cricket balls heading out from the Oval. I have always adored flowers. I chose roses for my bridal bouquet and the top table arrangements. Peach, pink, plump from the fertile plains of Holland. I selected a perfect rosebud to stick into the buttonhole of Paul's silver-grey morning coat. After all, roses mean love, don't they?

"You've all got to go!" my mother's voice was uncharacteristically shrill, rising above the noise of hoards of photographers, friends, family members, and tiny bridesmaids, who had suddenly descended on her usually calm and peaceful home like an invading army. Not like her at all! Face turning bright pink above her bronze-coloured silk dress, auburn hair gleaming like a well-worn copper kettle.

"Mum," I began. But even I could see, something had to give – or was about to! My cousin Stephen came to the rescue.

"I'll take Chloe, Celeste, and Hannah to the church," he volunteered.

Deftly, he gathered together the straggly crew of tiny pirates in their cochineal organza frocks, clutching pale wheat wicker baskets brimming over with pale pink and white flowers. A sea of satin ribbon, golden curls, pastel net and the heady smell of Johnson's Baby Shampoo, shot past me as fast as they did – like a bunch of renegade rabbits. And suddenly they were gone. "Come on, Rose, you're coming too!" Stephen took her firmly, gently by the arm and led her out into the waiting chauffeur-driven Rolls. She looked, what exactly – distraught? Distracted? Upset?

Whatever it was I knew I couldn't deal with it. Not then. I was grateful when the bedlam calmed and peace and quiet descended in tranquil lucidity.

I was left with my oldest and my most trusted ally. My dad! I don't know how he managed to straighten my headdress which had slid over to one side, stop the veil from tumbling off of my silky curls, patting it down on top of my head with big paw-like hands, rather like a baker putting a pastry cross on top of a bun, put his big comforting arm around my shoulders to give me a reassuring hug, and pour a glass of Cinzano, all at the same time. But my dad could do anything!

"Alright?" He smiled. And suddenly I felt the panic that had risen steadily through my body, miraculously start to drift away again.

"Yes!" I smiled back at him gratefully. "Yes, I think so. But I'm so late. I won't be on time at the church!"

He shook his head, still smiling. "It doesn't matter!" He laughed. Then he said something I'll never forget. Taking my small hands in his big ones he held them safe and secure in his grasp, and he looked right into my eyes. "You don't have to go through with this if you don't want to. It's not too late," he told me gently.

"But everyone's at the church! It's all arranged!" I needed guidance. Help me, Dad.

"It's only what you think that matters! But if you truly love Paul and this is what you want, then I will take you to the church. Take your time, though! And finish your drink first!"

We had a glorious Indian Summer that year. Autumn's dazzling mantle of russet, gold, and deepest amber covered the tree-lined road to the church in the sometimes quietly spectacular splendour only Mother Nature can provide. Splendid treasure. It costs nothing at all. I felt the oak trees and beech trees were lining my route for a reason. Like Dick Turpin and his highwaymen riding out from the bluebell woods, wishing me luck, saluting me in their gold and crimson velvet cloaks.

I descended from the Rolls Royce and stood for a moment under the archway of the stony-covered doorway of a country church that had been there since the beginning of time almost. My tiny bridesmaids flicked about behind me, tripping over my train in a well-meaning attempt to straighten it before I took the journey down the aisle to meet Paul waiting for me at the altar. I was late. So nothing unusual then! I could make out blurry faces watching me as I drifted past them. Smiling, encouraging. We made our vows to each other, and I was shaking so much with emotion that all the rose petals on my bouquet started to quiver, shivering in my freezing cold hands. I was about to promise to spend the rest of my life with this tall, dark, handsome – stranger.

To love, honour and cherish, in sickness and in health, forsaking all others, for better or worse, for richer or poorer. Till death us do part. Till death us do part. The Vicar, who had gently admonished me for my late arrival appeared to have forgiven me now.

Placing Paul's big hand on top of my small fingers, he bound them together with deep blue velvet, trimmed with gold brocade. "Those whom God has joined together let no man put asunder!" he said meaningfully. In his deep voice. I remember that. Yes – I still remember that.

We sat down to sign the register, and as I seemed to have momentarily stopped shaking, I braved it by glancing up quickly to see what was happening on the other side of the altar. All my aunts, uncles, and friends, were smiling back at me. I felt as if they were probably thinking to themselves, "Yes – at long last!" Walking back down the aisle was altogether more enjoyable. I was married now and I didn't ever have to worry about going through it all over again. A bit like passing a driving test! I didn't have to be concerned about fluffing my lines, falling over my feet in their specially designed white high-heeled shoes and Christian Dior stockings. I'd done it. We stood framed in the doorway looking over our shoulders while the photographer took pictures, and then we moved off to the tree-shaded quadrant where it seemed all at once anybody and everybody had produced cameras – all shapes and sizes. Click! Click! Rolls of Kodak were despatched down the lenses in seconds.

"I wish they'd hurry up! This photographer's getting on my nerves," Paul announced loudly. "I cannot wait to get inside out of the cold!" I carried on smiling at the cameras lined up in front of us. I hadn't felt cold. But all of a sudden I felt a chill in the blustery breeze that blew my veil from the paving stones where it had been anchored behind my dress by an anxious little attendant, and it flew up crazily into the air behind me. I got it back.

Chapter Six

I don't know who dreamed up the name 'honeymoon', combining honey and moon for whatever reason, but it is a unique experience. A holiday that affords the newly-weds a chance to recover from the rigours of a traditional white wedding, or indeed any kind of wedding. Anyway, whatever, the dopey name stands for, if it is supposed to paint a portrait of romance, we produced our own little masterpiece with tender strokes of the brush and a palette that was vivid. Paul whisked me off to the Canaries and the moon in jet black skies sprinkled with tiny sparkling stars was as big and round as any studio arc light I had ever seen.

Sipping Tequila Sunrises through luminous turquoise straws, we watched as the huge scarlet and burnt–sienna sun slid slowly down into vermillion seas. Palm trees blew softly, waving their branches into silhouettes along the seashore. It was just what a honeymoon should be. We held hands, exploring the orange volcanic mountainous interior of Tenerife, which sometimes resembled a lunar landscape. Paul spoke 'parrot talk' to the exotic birds with emerald and scarlet feathers more luminous and dazzling than anything Elton had stuck on top of his head.

On my birthday, we went to the rooftop restaurant of a local 'hot spot' hotel. Zooming up the outside of the building in a glass lift, looking out over the whole bay as we did so. When we reached the gleaming crystal cocoon at the summit, we found that the roof pulled back to reveal the stars. Flame-coloured flamenco dancers sped across the floor. Pounding, passionate rhythm. As Paul and I danced cheek to cheek, I felt him press something tiny into my hand. Wrapped in sparkling silver paper. A golden chain with a diamond heart perched in the centre.

"Happy Birthday – I love you!" he whispered. And I thought, life just doesn't get more perfect.

When we returned home, we were treated like celebrities. We had tans when everyone else had just been celebrating Guy Fawkes Night. Two brown faces amid a pallid sea. The strike had ended. Everyone was back at the studios working. The local paper printed a large photograph of us and wanted to know all about our wedding because we both worked in TV, and then we settled down to enjoy the rest of our lives – together.

Finding a reason – pinpointing a moment – is impossible. We think that if we treat people the way we would wish to be treated, then they will afford us the same respect. Idealistic. I was naïve and I believed it. For it's always the good guy in the white hat, who wins in the end, isn't it – overcoming any kind of adversity. But I had never stopped to wonder, what happens if we cannot always distinguish who the good guy actually is. If he is disguised. Wearing the wrong colour hat. Concealed so carefully in a cloak of secrecy that hides hideous betrayal, immorality, corruption and deceit. Evil visits us from unexpected places. In many guises. It sneaks up on the defenceless in ways that are truly terrifying.

Just when I thought my life couldn't be more perfect, three things happened in the space of a week. Lucy rang me long-distance from New York to tell me she was pregnant. Paul's father rang to say his wife Christina had been taken ill, diagnosed with Alzheimer's Disease. My boss phoned in the early hours of New Year's Day. "It's good news really, Lesley." He sounded distant – unconvincing. "We've been awarded the new franchise. A licence to continue broadcasting. But not under the same terms and conditions. It means that the studios here will be forced to close down. We've all got to move northwards, or take redundancy. I'll ring you later."

The cream-coloured phone in my hand suddenly felt like a brick. I replaced it heavily onto the receiver. "We're going to have to move up North, or risk losing our jobs," I told Paul quietly. Without saying a word, we put on thermal gloves and après ski boots, heading out into Richmond Park, where we plodded silently through deep snow drifts and the icy chill of a freezing cold, thickly frosted January morning. Someone had just thrown the first pebble, that my dad had warned me about. Deep into the heart of all our lives. And the senseless, resounding ripples from that would last for eternity.

Chapter Seven

Mental illness is something people shy away from. Still. It shocks us. We shudder when we think about it. To be confronted with stark cold reality so early on in my uncomplicated, happily married little world was the first of many hurdles I would be forced to confront and find a way of struggling to the other side of. Whittington was a name I had previously only associated with a bloke called Dick, and a furry black and white cat, who wanted to be Lord Mayor of London. Dick, that is – not the cat! The Whittington Hospital in Highgate was about as far away from a fairy tale as you could get. When Paul's mother was admitted for tests, I felt a weird mixture of incomprehension, frozen fear – and pity. For any one of us could be the tragic victim suddenly struck down. Few things are more terrifying than the psychiatric ward of a decaying Dickensian bleak black turreted monstrosity of a place like this. Yet I agreed to go along with Paul when his mother was admitted for tests. I hate hospitals. Always have.

The smell of disinfectant and disease; trolleys full of instruments of torture; the bleak, blank faces flanked by crisply starched nurses in control. They simply scare me to bits. But still, I went. "Lesley," her voice was thin and frail. She smiled up at me, clutching a wedding photograph of Paul and me in her hands. "I've shown it to everyone!" she said. I tried to make light-hearted conversation. Made a very feeble attempt to make her laugh. Tried so hard not to cry. Or be afraid. But I was. Alzheimer's Disease had not been given an official name, one of those new designer diseases that nobody really understood, even the doctors. No one wanted to admit that it had afflicted a member of their own family. That someone so close had been smitten by this terrible taker of brain cells and reason. Plunging innocent victims into a deep well of incurable pre-senile dementia. Confusion ran riot plaguing the medical experts and loved ones, and most of all the ordinary man or woman affected who craved nothing more than a normal life. With dignity. And the promise of a future.

What future for sufferers? Pretty grim. Diminishing memory, fading awareness, and eventually complete lack of control of everyday bodily functions. So I sat on the edge of Christina's hospital bed. Paul's glamorous, lady-like blonde mother, who had never harmed a fly. Never swore. Never caused anybody any trouble. Who was capable of singing like Julie Andrews on a good day, and I thought – why? Paul refused to accept what was happening. Like so many things, he chose to shut it out of his mind. Running away faster than a competitor in the London Marathon. "She is merely crying out for attention," he said. "It's her own fault All she has to do is to snap out of it. If she gets a headache, I've told her she should stand on her head – it will soon go away!"

I stared at him, unable to believe he could speak to his own mother in such a way. Then I thought about it some more, and realised it was a heavy weight to handle.

Maybe I was the one being insensitive here. But what I didn't realise at the time was that it was just the tip of a deeply frozen and unforgiving iceberg. There was more to come – oh, so much more.

Work has always been my saviour in stressful times. So I plunged myself back into mine with renewed zeal and intensity. 'Real life' was becoming a bit too real and hard to handle right now. I found the security of my tidy office, my ordered pile of correspondence – my things – an ordered pile of work heaped on top of my wooden desk curiously reassuring. Coupled with the company of my good-natured, even-tempered and down-to-earth boss. But still, the threat of imminent closure of the studios hung over us all like a cloud full of poison gas waiting to discharge its deadly cargo.

"I've got to move up north soon, Lesley," he told me one bright sunny morning. "And you will have to decide if you're coming or not. Have you made up your mind yet? Are you?"

I gazed back at him in a semi-stupefied way. "Em, can I let you know... later?" I asked.

"Of course," he replied, re-adjusting his reading glasses and sorting through the stack of papers on top of his ruby red leather and mahogany desk.

I didn't want to go. That was the truth. My life was based in the south, near to London. My family, my friends, everything I understood and had always been familiar with. But my job meant everything to me. My lifeline. My security. And somewhere in the darkest recesses of my mind that relentless little time clock was still mercilessly ticking away. Ever so loudly sometimes. Children! Children! It cried out when I slipped into Studio D to watch The Muppets rehearsing on my way back from the canteen with a cup of tea in my hand. Oh shut up! I told the voice inside my head.

Soon after that, Lucy phoned to tell me she had lost the baby. For once I did not know what to say to console her. She had just lost the one thing that I knew she wanted more than anything else in the whole world. "What happened?" I asked her.

"I was in the kitchen... I fell from a chair," she replied quietly. She sounded so far away. Well, she was far away. But Lucy's tiny broken voice might have been transmitting from the Moon.

"Oh, Lucy!" I said. "I am so sorry." I stopped trying to talk to her then, as I heard her softly muffled weeping at the other end of the phone.

Just when I thought I had my fill of shocks and surprises, I unexpectedly bumped into Ainsley, as I was absent-mindedly trailing along down one of the corridors, carrying a clipboard full of production notes, and a half-empty white plastic cup filled with half-cold lemon tea, with a curled up piece of lemon, stuck to the inside. "Hello, Les!" He grinned at me. His heart-piercing smile that, surprisingly, still managed to slice through me like a pirate's dagger, in swift seconds. Pushing his fringe from his dark eyes, he rested his arm lightly around my shoulders. "I've got some news!"

He bent his head forward so that for a moment we were locked together like collaborators. He grinned at me and winked and I just knew that I really did not want to hear what he was about to tell me. I also knew with no shadow of a doubt that Ainsley Logan was about to ruin the remaining peace of mind I was holding onto as tightly as the clipboard in my hands. "I've been offered a brand new job, in the West End. I leave next week! They want me to start straight away!"

He was gabbling excitedly now, like a wayward child. "I'm so thrilled, it's for a new company called Images which is being set up to do mostly commercials. All over the world, so there will be lots of opportunities to travel. Lots! It's what I've always wanted to do. And the best thing is that Emma has just got a job there too. They need editors desperately apparently. Well, in fact, they are taking on all kinds of staff, really. And you'll never guess what else?!" I could see my artless amigo was bursting at the seams of his tight leather jeans to tell me what else. But at this moment I didn't want to guess what else. My world was suddenly drifting apart in disjointed bits like well-worn, well-known leaves falling from an oak tree. I really didn't want to hear the next bit. But Ainsley made sure I heard it anyway. "Emma is expecting our first child! I can't believe it!" Neither could I. "I've been telling everyone! I never knew that I could be this happy! It's all working out so wonderfully isn't it, Les?"

I stared straight back at him, and for some inexplicable reason, all I wanted to do was to smack him – hard! But why should I feel that way? Why this terrible ache inside and something painful in the pit of my stomach like I'd just eaten something that violently disagreed with me? I held on tight to the clipboard, placing it in the 'comfort zone' between us, spilling the rest of the lemon tea all over the pale blue carpet beneath my feet. "That's great, Ainsley!" I lied. "Really great. Fantastic! I am so pleased for you! I wish you all the luck in the world!" Only I didn't. I really didn't. And for a wild moment, all I really wished was that it was going to be me and Ainsley who were about to produce the tiny tot. My head was beginning to throb.

"Have you decided what you are going to do?" he was still talking, with a stupid grin smothering his face. Oblivious. Come on, Ainsley, surely you know me better than that? Why couldn't this dimwit see what was right before his bleary brown eyes. Maybe he could. Who knows? I was defeated. I didn't know how to react or what to say to him. Speechless. "You and Paul, I mean." He continued speaking in rapid bursts, like he was high on some kind of miracle drug. I couldn't tell him the truth.

But I couldn't lie to him, either. "No," I replied flatly.

"Oh, well – suck it and see then, eh, Lesley?" Laughter rang around the walls like pealing church bells as he turned to make his way back down the smokey gun metal blue corridor. I could hear the disjointed, discordant twangs of instruments being tuned up, filtering through from the band room, where musicians were warming up for the evening's live studio show with Lulu and Shakin' Stevens. "Oh – by the way, Lesley – I nearly forgot!" he shouted back to me. "You and Paul must come along and have a farewell drink with me next Friday. That's when I'm officially leaving! It will be my last day!" I nodded. "I'll see you in the bar at mid-day then. Everyone will be there! Just follow the crowd, and you will find me!"

I am not sure how long I stood there, staring bleakly after him as I watched him disappear in a haze of deep brown leather and Armani aftershave. "Oh, I am going to miss you, so much!" was all I could think. Stabbing pangs of pain took hold of me, shaking me hard, till my regrets fell into a heap on the floor with the rest of the lemon tea.

Not many full-grown men can get away with wearing white. All white. But Ainsley could. Tight Levi 501s hugging his small bum, crisp white Italian cotton shirt, cuffs rolled back, collar turned up, top button undone revealing lightly tanned skin from the sprinkling of summer sunshine we had enjoyed and the early spring break he and Emma had grabbed in Cyprus. He looked so cool. Casual. Controlled and completely content. "Cheers!"

he raised his glass as we all saluted him with fluted glasses filled with Hock. I was losing my best friend, yet again. Hang on. That couldn't be right. Not now. Paul held up his glass, putting a restraining arm on my elbow. Of course, Paul was my best friend now, wasn't he? Wasn't he?

I didn't realise quite how much I would miss Ainsley. I missed seeing his customised shiny black and white Mini Cooper whizzing crazily over the speed bumps into the car park at about one hundred miles an hour. Like me – always late. I missed waving across the canteen to him, as he perched nonchalantly on a bar stool, drinking pints of lager. But I discovered that what I missed most were our long, laughing intimate heart-to-heart conversations. I really missed them.

"Do you want children?" Speech spilt from my mouth like random strips of spaghetti.

"What?" Paul looked up idly from the TV programme he was preoccupied with. About outer space and aliens.

"Children," I repeated. I watched my words fall into the dimly lit lounge like pebbles into the sea.

"Maybe," he replied distractedly.

"Do you?" I carried on. Paul turned to look at me, briefly averting his gaze from the 22" screen.

"What is it now?" he asked, just a hint of irritation on his face.

"Well, I really think I do, and I've been wondering, well, with everything that's going on at the moment… Well, I just wondered… that's all." I stopped speaking. Paul turned back to concentrate on the sci-fi fix.

"Yes – one day, perhaps," was all he said.

A chilly draught had begun to blow fiercely through the French windows leading onto the small balcony overlooking the gardens. I got up, closing them quickly. And went to bed.

Chapter Eight

Sometimes life is determined by us. Sometimes life is determined for us. Sometimes life is determined – and that's it.

Paula Watson had always been a very good friend of my boss. The Head of her Department, she was ferociously protective of her job. An ex-dancer who had been abandoned by her airline pilot husband and left alone to bring up her young son. One of the only females to be admitted into the 'higher echelons' of television management, she possessed a ferocious temper, a whiplash tongue that could dish out biting insults like acid drops, and a deliciously wicked sense of the ridiculous. She could shout at the top of her voice. She could drink any man under the table and still be left standing sedately at the bar in her perfectly tailored suit and immaculate high heels. I was still quite young, but unlike many of her contemporaries, I had never been afraid of Paula. She respected that. I respected her. When Paula held a soiree I was always invited. Intimate, full of fun and wonderful juicily irreverent anecdotes and gossip about famous people she knew. I looked forward to Paula's 'dos' with great pleasure.

The food she served was always fabulously individual. Lots of intricate little surprises. Her wine was the best. Her stories were superb. I liked Paula – very much.

For the first time, Paul was coming with me. "I'm not sure about this," he complained petulantly as I tried to persuade him that it would be fun. Knowing deep inside it was an evening Ainsley would enjoy every bit as much as me. And to share things with someone who appreciates them doubles the pleasure – always.

"I would rather stay in and watch TV quite honestly," moaned Paul. He would always rather watch TV than have a conversation, I was beginning to realise. Nevertheless, I was determined. "Come on – you'll enjoy it!" I smiled, swirling a lipstick wand over my mouth and grabbing my best jacket.

On the way to Paula's I sat in the car and started thinking about my dad. He was worried for the first time in years about the future. "I'm too young to retire, and in any case, I enjoy my job too much, I don't really want to do that!" he had confessed. "I'm too old to get a new mortgage and start all over again. I don't know what to do for the best."

I had never seen my dad so worried. My dad had always found the solution to absolutely anything. Anything at all. So I shared my concerns with Paul. For he was now my husband, and that is what husbands and wives were supposed to do weren't they – share? "But, whatever happens, tonight, please don't say a word about what we're doing," I begged him as we got out of the car and trotted up Paula's pebbledash path to her perfect little cream-coloured cottage with hawthorn thatch and yellow roses around the tiny oak door. "Because I've not told anybody." Paul had never been told what to do. He wasn't about to start now.

The evening was merry. Filled with laughter and witty repartee. Naturally, as things relaxed, talk came around to the franchise change and how it was going to affect us all. My boss knew more than anyone. So did I. We were both being very cautious and circumspect with our replies. We didn't offend. Didn't pretend. Didn't give anything away. Paul was sitting beside me on Paula's pink floral chintz sofa, his legs spread out in front of him. He picked up a smoked salmon sandwich, stuck it into his mouth and then suddenly I heard him speak. Words spilling out like sawdust.

"Lesley's not going!" he announced in a loud voice. The room went quiet.

I felt as if all the studio spotlights were aimed straight at me, like Robin Hood and his outlaws lined up with bows and arrows before me. The hum of laughter fell silent. Everyone looked slightly uncomfortable and embarrassed by Paul's unnecessary outburst. They shifted about on their seats, looking at me. I looked across the room at my boss. His silent face mirrored my own thoughts. "Oh, Lesley!" I had trusted him, and he me. He had asked me so many times to give him an answer. And I truly couldn't, wouldn't, didn't. Now he had his answer. An answer. Paul's answer.

"What will you do, darling?" Paula's husky voice came out from the shadows, reassuring, rescuing me.

"I don't know yet," was all I could manage. Because I didn't know. That was the truth.

I looked at Paul in disbelief. He carried on eating, drinking Paula's fine wine. Not a care in the world. I had just resigned from my job. In front of everyone I knew. Not in confidence, with my boss. Paul had high-handedly done that for me. I felt cold suddenly.

Chapter Nine

I got up early for once, deciding to walk along the cliff top. The sun was out. The wind had changed direction and crisp, cool breezes were blowing in refreshingly from the West. Early spring. As I made my way down the well-worn cliff path, so familiar, I slid easily over smoothed red earth-worn glossy with ceaseless trudging walking boots, flippers and bare feet en route to the tiny sandy and pebbled cove beneath. How I loved this place. The air was truly sweet, filled with white May blossom. Pure fragrance, never overpowering. Uplifting. Dappled light flickered though the bright green and yellow shoots that were beginning to burst forth from the bleak, stagnant weathered brown dusty twigs. Nature was on the move once more. Coming alive. Eternal optimist that she is. Ever hopeful for the future. Never giving up.

I sat down on the warm wooden bench. I had sat here so many times before. I gazed out towards the sea. Tranquil. Perfect. Still and calm like a painting. Azure and palest powder today, glittering here and there as the sun caught sparkling waves like a match lighting a candle. A smuggler's candle in an inky black lantern perhaps. Last one racing back to fling themselves back aboard the pirate ship hiding on the hazy blue and lemon horizon. I still had an awful lot to think about.

***

When the studios closed I was still in denial, really. For right up until the moment it happened I still believed that somehow, they could miraculously be saved from closure. And all our jobs alongside them.

The Head of the Company came down to address every single one of us. To reassure us. We all shuffled into Studio D, gathering together like a flock of geese. "It will never happen! Never," he told us emphatically. "Not while I am Chairman of this Company! I give you my word – and my word is my bond!" We all knew that. We never doubted it. And as he stood before us, tubby, confident, smiling broadly at us, huge cigar in one hand, we had no reason to disbelieve him. Maybe we had no reason because we didn't want to find one. We all wanted to remain right where we were.

So I stood bleakly, weakly in the redundancy queue with first-class cameramen, Lighting Director, and secretaries. An endless line snaking right down the corridor on the third floor, and all the way down the stairs behind it to reception. "What will they do without you, Princess – how will they manage?!" said Sam, one of the laughing-eyed cameramen, smiling at me, with thick black eyebrows and curly black hair.

"I don't know what will they do without you?" I replied rue-fully. I tried in vain to smile. What on earth would I do without the studios? That was more to the point.

No one knew that Paul and I had been trying for a baby. Already many of the girls had made the big decision. If a ca-reer break was inevitable then why not go with the flow, take a natural pause rather than wait until you had another good job? But nothing was happening. "It's stress," said the Doctor. So we booked a holiday to the South of France. Lots of fine wine and seafood and sunshine.

On our last day, everyone ended up in the bar, as usual. Last goodbyes, fare-wells. It was like waving goodbye to my family. Some people had decided to move northwards, afraid of staying behind in the place they knew so well and not being able to get another job. Not least of the problems confronting everybody was the fact that two new production centres had been built. One in the west and one in the east. My dad was offered the east, Paul also. My boss and I were offered the West. Paul's dad decided to take early retirement and head off to the south coast with Christina. The pebble had been tossed and its ripples had only just started, reaching far and wide.

I promised myself I would be alright. I could handle this. Drinks were coming in full and fast. Decibel level of chattering was enormously loud. I turned round. That's when I saw him. Ainsley had been standing still at the end of the bar watching me for – how long? I didn't know. He looked bronzed and fit. Camel-coloured suede had always brought out the best of his dark good looks. He didn't avert his gaze from mine, as he started to push his way through the jumbling crowd towards me. Glossy black fringe flopping as usual. Suddenly he was there right in front of me. A glass of lager in one hand. Me in the other. "Are you alright, Lesley? Are you happy?" was all he said. That's when the tears came. Streaming down my face, An uncontrollable waterfall of grief.

"Yes! I am!" I ran off to the Ladies, and wept, and wept, and wept.

Chapter Ten

The South of France is beautiful. Full of celebrity, gloss, glitz, glamour, beaches and winding coastal roads clawing through the flower-covered cliffs. Like a movie. Lots of dazzling sunshine. So much, in fact, that in August when Paul and I drove down in the middle of a scorching summer it was indeed truly sizzling. Masses of forest fires were ablaze as we neared the coast. One by one the roads were closed off behind us as the trees turned black, and the forget-me-not blue skies were filled with voluminous clouds of charred, acrid smoke and cinders. You could see the orange flames flaring up through the middle like a knife, with reckless and deadly intensity.

And you didn't know from one moment to the next where the deadly burning stain would savagely appear. Each time we pulled through a toll station, they told us no more cars would be let through after we were. Helicopters and planes flew overhead, dousing everything in sight with oceans of water, but still, you could smell the burned timber, burned wood, burned to a crisp.

We were unaware that the fires had made headlines back in the UK. My parents watched the *News at Ten* in horror every day as the fires began to become more uncontrollable. We carried on heading south. Driving into them, through them, and mercifully, safely out the other side when we eventually caught sight of the bright blue Mediterranean sea. Our hotel was perched on the Promenade des Anglaises. Right opposite the beach in Nice. Very French. Very chic. With lots of wrought iron on the balconies. Vivid scarlet geraniums spilling over the top, cascading down. I fell in love with France, instantly. Driving to Monte Carlo was just as I had imagined it would be. I'd seen it in the movies now let's see if it's true – indeed, it was.

Long winding coastal roads, and tunnels cut through the mountains, taking you from searing heat to the cool inside of the cliffs. Bursting out into dazzling sunshine on the other side of the tunnel. No wonder Grace Kelly chose this as her fairytale home. No wonder she was beguiled by its beauty, not seeing the hidden danger. We all do that sometimes. The pink palace perched on the hillside was like something you would buy for a wealthy child in Hamleys at Christmas time. Perfect little soldiers standing outside just like the tiny wooden ones you buy in boxes on the first floor.

Monte Carlo reeked of money. You could actually smell it in the air. Restaurants spilling onto the pavements. Burgundy and gold awnings, ginger and cream with French names written across them in scrawling writing. Tasteful. Discreet. Expensive. Yachts in the glittering harbour. White, azure, silver, clinking, sparkling. The old razzle-dazzle. The Casino was just as we'd seen it in so many James Bond movies. We entered its plush ruby red interior with crystal chandeliers dangling from the ceiling and played the tables and even the slot machines.

So the dream of having a baby didn't need to be a dream any longer. Full of the very best seafood, Soave and sunshine, we drove back happily through the lavender carpeted mountains of Provence, smothered in sweet smelling and astonishingly aromatic lilac coloured drifts; a warm blanket of heady scent wrapping itself intensely around us. Stressless at last. Completely free. Ending up in Paris was the icing. I'd been there before, but surprisingly, Paul hadn't and I eagerly showed him all the places I had discovered: Montmartre, the Left Bank, Eiffel Tower, Arc de Triomphe, the twinkling white lights all along the Champs Elysees, even the McDonalds sign; the only white example you will see! Like strings of diamonds. A fabulous glittering necklace strung out along the street.

Magical Bateaux Mouches sailing serenely down the Seine under a perfect half crescent moon and skies scattered with stars; Paris had seen it all before, so many secrets. The grand old mademoiselle of romance, intrigue and desire, in love with love and lovers. A uniquely beautiful city. Huge trays of fresh croissants, orange juice and hot steaming piquant fresh ground coffee greeted us first thing in the morning. Delivered by the friendly French hotel waiters. "Bonjour!" they would chorus, as they buzzed about nimbly in black and white striped outfits. It was wonderful. "How Ainsley would love this!" I thought fleetingly. Bizarrely.

When we got home Paul was working in the West End at the studios for a while, and I popped in to pick him up from work. By coincidence, Ainsley had also dropped in at the same time. He was having a drink in the bar. Spreading the good news he had just received. Emma had just produced the brand new baby. A little girl: Emily. "She's gorgeous, Lesley!" he told me in a voice filled with hushed wonder. "The most beautiful little girl you've ever seen! Quite simply – she's the light of my life." I never forgot the look in his eyes when he said that. Never.

I sat in the garden that night drinking Coca-Cola from a can. Ainsley had a daughter. Lucy had lost her baby. And me? I was still living in limbo vaguely wondering why Paul and I could not conceive the one thing I now found myself longing for more than anything. A child of my very own. It was becoming an all-encompassing obsession, that swallowed me up and the longer it went on, the worse it got. I found myself looking longingly into prams at the screwed-up pink and cream tiny faces, surrounded by random pink and blue bits of rabbits and ribbon. I truly envied all the friends I had who seemed to produce offspring like shelling peas. I yearned for a baby of my very own. So much that it actually hurt.

I could never have dreamed that I of all people would feel this compulsion. The little girl whose doll's pram had unceremoniously fallen on top of innocent little fingers.

But I did. Mother Nature again, tugging relentlessly at my maternal sleeve.

There is no easy way to hear devastating news. That I have found out the hard way over and over again. So when Paul reluctantly agreed to go for tests we set off together to get the results from Dr Jones. "It's not good news, I'm afraid." He peered at us over the top of his glasses, looking small and mean. Filled with authority and knowing things I didn't want to. "Paul – you have a very low sperm count indeed, it appears. You had an accident while surfing years ago. Is that right?" Paul nodded.

"Well, that's damaged the scrotum and it means that the sperm level is so low, there is every likelihood that you will never be able to have children." There. He had said it. It was out there in the air like a nuclear explosion. He looked straight at the two of us. Uncompromising. Chillingly, icy cold. I couldn't take in what he had just said. I went numb. Frozen. I just wanted to run away out of his surgery as fast as I could. I wanted to go home where it was warm and get my dad to put his big arms around me and cuddle me and tell me everything would be OK. I could not look at Paul.

"Is it anything to do with me?" I asked quietly. Assuming in fact, it wasn't.

"No," replied Dr Jones, in a matter of fact doctor's voice. "It's Paul who has the problem."

"Is there anything we can do?" I asked him.

His reply chilled me to the bone. I started to shiver. "Yes – have you considered adoption?"

My insides were turning inside out. Empty. Hurt. Destroyed. I had just been informed I could never ever have a child of my own, simply because I had married a man who couldn't. Robbed of the right of every woman. No highwayman or pirate could have stolen something so precious. I went home in a daze. Made a pot of tea. Hot. Sweet. Comforting. Only it wasn't. Paul had sat in stony silence all the way home. Now he stood by the copper hooded fireplace drinking his cup of tea, with his back to me. He turned around. I'd been dispossessed. It wouldn't be the last time.

"I'm devastated, Paul." I started to cry. "I wanted children so much. That's one of the reasons you get married isn't it?" I was distraught. Paul wasn't.

He was calm, cold, icily angry. I was in agony. "It's all your fault!" he started to shout at me.

"What?" I couldn't believe what I was hearing.

"You must have tests! It's all your fault!" his voice was getting louder and louder. This was just too much on top of everything else. I was upset enough.

"Tests? But there's nothing wrong with me, Paul. It's not me that's got the problem – the doctor said so." I stammered. "He said it's because of the injury you sustained while surfing and the damage – well, you were there, Paul – you know what he said!" My words spilled out like the tears that were raining down my cheeks. "I'll stay with you, Paul – I don't want to adopt."

Paul was furious. In a blind rage, he pointed his finger at me accusingly. "No! No! It's you! You don't want children! That is the truth of the matter! You just want your career back don't you? And you are using this as some kind of excuse! It's all your fault! I can never forgive you! If you wanted children – you would have tests!" His icy blue eyes were filled with pent-up fury as he carried on pointing the finger of blame – like a Judge.

I was shaking. In an instant, he had succeeded in turning everything around. Unable and unprepared to confront the truth. Take responsibility. It was so much easier just to make me believe everything was my fault. Yet it wasn't! I had just been mugged by him. Having my chance of children of my own swiped away from me in swift decisive slices. And I was being expected to take the blame.

Cold, hard reality had once again shoved its unwelcome jackboot into my open door. I had a feeling it was there to stay. I didn't know what to do. I felt desperate. I rang my dad. He didn't have a magic wand. He had a magic way. With people. Paul actually did sit down and listened to him. He was the only person he ever did listen to. Over hot cups of tea and glasses of beer, my dad talked to him. Men's stuff.

In deep voices. Paul listened. And so did I. I bought Paul cotton boxer shorts, instead of skin-tight Y-fronts. He started wearing baggy tracksuits instead of tight jeans.

I took my temperature every day. Paul had a healthy diet and cold showers.

One morning I woke up feeling sick. I never felt sick. And then I was sick. I just didn't feel like me at all. What terrible kind of disease had I picked up? I was worried.

I told my mum. "You might be pregnant!" she told me. I laughed, a hollow sort of sounding noise.

"I don't think that's very likely!" I said. After Dr Jones imparted his devastating news, I started applying for jobs. At the BBC and other TV and film companies; I had even been in touch with Ainsley's new bunch of TV executives. If I couldn't have children of my own, then I would be a dedicated career girl. That was all there was to it. Maybe it was fate. The way it should be. Our life is planned. I had never had much to do with babies, anyway. Didn't know one end from the other.

Lucy was the same. She even put her nephew's baby grow on upside down and inside out. That's how clueless we were.

I had two interviews on Thursday. One in the morning at the BBC and one after lunch at Dr Jones' Surgery. If I was going to get a splendid new job, I had to rid myself of this mystery virus. Get some pills or something.

I went to the BBC first thing. Bright and early. "We're very interested," they told me. "We'd like to put you on the shortlist, and see you again next week!" I was delighted.

Four hours later I slumped into Dr Jones' leather patients' chair. "I feel awful," I told him. "So sick."

"You could be pregnant," he replied in an even voice.

"But that's not possible, is it?" I replied. "After what you told us… it can't be that can it?"

"We'll do some tests," was all he said. "Ring up on Friday morning for the results."

I went home feeling icky. Maybe he would give me some kind of special medicine.

"Lesley Pearson?" The receptionist's voice was shrill and well-spoken at the other end of the telephone.

"Yes," I replied.

"We've got the result of your test."

"Oh – yes, OK." I leaned against the radiator by the open window.

"It's positive! You're pregnant, Mrs Pearson!" I heard the words, but I couldn't connect – couldn't believe it could possibly be true.

"Are you sure?" I asked her dumbly.

"Yes," she replied. "That's alright – isn't it?"

Alright?! "Yes!" I exclaimed. "Yes! That's absolutely wonderful isn't it?!"

I could hear relief creeping into her voice as she relaxed and said, "Yes – of course." I slid down the radiator ending up sitting on the bedroom floor. I felt happy, elated, and really scared. All at the same time. I was actually going to have a baby. I couldn't believe it!

Some women sail through pregnancy like a yacht in all its splendour, billowing around in white clouds of floaty frocks, smiling, unperturbed and completely composed. I didn't. I was sick – constantly. Throwing up anywhere and everywhere within the slightest sight or smell of food. So a job at the BBC was out of the question. I went along. Explained to them. They were very understanding. "We'll see you in ten years' time – or so!" they said.

Paul was working at the studios in the north east and rehearsing in London. We decided to move to a new house in the area we both agreed we liked best of all and let the future kind of take care of itself. We stayed in the place we knew best. The south.

Paul's father believed at first that taking Christina to live by the sea would help her. Also when the time came for her to be hospitalised permanently they would put her in a brand new one, not something old and horrible like the ones near to their home.

For a while, it seemed things were improving. Then she had to go to hospital all the time. She slipped rapidly away. The last time I saw her she took my hands in hers squeezing them tightly. "Don't go!" she pleaded as her eyes looked right into mine. Wild. Searching. Abandoned and desperate. That was the last time I saw her.

Paul went to Christina's funeral alone. "I don't want anything else to happen. I don't want you to lose the baby," he told me. I agreed with him.

I think I handled being pregnant quite well, all things considered. Still wearing tiny belts around my gradually disappearing waistline till they ended up practically beneath my bustline and I came to the conclusion that maybe I wasn't so much looking 'cute petite' as 'Dawn French – on a bad day'. So I abandoned the belts and chose outfits with big white Peter Pan plate-like collars instead. To focus attention on the face. Not my non-existent waistline. Didn't work, but at least if I concentrated on the top half of the dressing table mirror I looked remotely normal. We didn't fly that year. I introduced Paul and my 'bump' to the pretty Devon cove I'd played in so happily when I was a child. I knew that we would come back again. And again.

It took three days for my son to be born.

When they laid him in my arms, pink-faced and indignantly yelling at the top of his voice, I felt as if I was the only woman ever to have given birth to a baby boy. I was elated. Instantly besotted. Not just because we were both safe and OK at last but because he was mine. A boy! A boy! Sheer joy! We called him William. William Paul. The midwife took his tiny body from me, handing him to Paul. "It's a boy. Here he is, Paul – say hello to your son and heir!"

My mum and dad were over the moon, understandably. So relieved. So proud. So delighted with their one and only grandson. Paul's dad came to see me. Alone.

I sent cards to everyone telling them we had a son and his name was William. Lucy rang me. "Lesley! I'm so pleased for you! How absolutely perfect!" Ainsley and Emma sent a 'Congratulations on your New Baby' card. I didn't recognise the handwriting, in pale blue turquoise ink. Must be Emma's, I assumed.

I took William home from hospital happy to see the back of the Maternity Ward. Happy to see the back of any ward for that matter. I just hated hospital. When I got back to the warmth and security of our mock-Georgian home I settled down content with our new little fellow. Now we were no longer a couple – we were a family. I had no clue about babies. So I read the books. I got the nappies, the feeding stuff, the cot and the pram. A whole new world. And a whole new wardrobe of tiny clothes. Plus some for me as I'd thankfully shrunk back rapidly to my size ten.

Paul was working long hours and weekends. My parents came over to see us while he was away. Helping me. My dad cuddled William with such tenderness although he was such a big man.

The tiny bundle lay protected and safe in his caring arms. Paul arrived home, very late. "I'll talk to you tomorrow!" I called after my mum and dad as they got into their car, and pulled away.

"Yes – 'bye!"

They were gone. I turned back to William who had gone through yet another box of Pampers. "Come on, William, let's get you cleaned up!" I said as I trotted off to his room with him.

It was unusual to get a phone call so early on Sunday morning. I'd just finished feeding William. The sun was shining brightly outside the window. Blinking through net curtains. Paul opened the door quietly. And just stood there. Frozen. Still.

"Lesley – it's your dad…" I'd never heard that tone in his voice before. Never seen that look in his eyes before. I never wanted to see or hear it ever again. "He's had a heart attack, Lesley. I'm afraid he's passed away."

***

I pulled my fleece jacket tighter around my neck, as the chill wind blew up from the beach. I got up from the bench and weaved my way through the little track of pathway that led down to the cove. When I got there, it was warmer. Morning sun bleaching the stones and rocks. Shining fondly on the smuggler's cave. I walked slowly over to it. Smelling the fresh salt in the air. Touching the hard rock which crumbled ever so slightly between my fingers. "I miss you, Dad." I said out loud.

***

I don't recall how I struggled through those early days, all I know is that I could not have done it without William. Tiny and helpless, he was my saviour. Paul was away working much of the time, so as often happens, I was the one left to bring up William, more or less by myself. Taking responsibility for the childhood complaints and worries and tantrums, along with the playfully happy times. Motherhood is fraught with a disturbing mixture of joy and anguish coupled with pure worry. Plus exhaustion. I didn't know it was possible to feel so incredibly tired. So tired that I could hardly stand up when I returned from hauling the trolley and William all around Sainsbury's and he immediately started yelling for something the moment we returned home. And although there were times when I felt sure I could have fallen asleep on the spot, I didn't mind, because his merry little smiling face greeted me every day, morning, noon and night. When he wouldn't or couldn't sleep I would dance with him, singing to him. Cliff Richard songs! And at least I had worked out which way the baby grows went!

I hadn't heard from Ainsley for some time. One day, I decided on the spur of the moment to get out of the house and take William with me on a shopping spree to Brent Cross to get some cool new baby outfits. My hair needed washing, but no matter. I didn't have time for that. I tied it back quickly with a velvet scrunchie. Applied a little lip gloss. Left my old blue jeans on: in case, William decided to throw up after lunch. No one I knew would see me after all. What did it matter?

I bumped right into Paula Watson outside the front door of Fenwicks. "Hello, darling!" she kissed me on both cheeks, flicking her hands from side to side. "Come and have coffee!" she purred, delighted to have someone to chat to. And to show off her new palest pink Chanel jacket and perfectly fitted silver grey trousers.

We made our way to one of the more 'buggy friendly' coffee shops and while we took charge of large white china cups filled with frothy Cappuccino, William happily settled for a straw and freshly squeezed orange juice. It was nice to be out in the world of fashion and focus on non-domestic chores for once. And as Paula's throaty voice rattled away like a steam engine eagerly passing on all the latest gossip I watched in fascination as the endless stream of ladies who know how to lunch, and mini execs, trotted back and forth in the latest creations from Alexon, Donna Karen and new young American designers I didn't even know existed. I was trying to work out whether I could justify the extravagance of maybe buying myself a new spring suit from M and S, or perhaps something with a designer label – like a bottle of perfume – when I realised guiltily that I hadn't really been listening to what Paula had been saying for at least the last five minutes. Paula had gone quiet. Looking at me with speculation sprinkled across her perfectly painted pink lipstick smile. "So what do you think about that, darling? I suppose we'll miss him, won't we?" Her eyebrow had arched ever so slightly, like Vivian Leigh in *Gone with the Wind*. Questioning. William was gurgling about in his buggy, destroying the plastic straw in swift bendy strokes. I had no idea what she was on about. I had no choice but to own up.

"I'm sorry, Paula," I confessed. "I was day dreaming. I didn't quite catch what you said It's all the broken nights – sleep deprivation! You know…!" I finished lamely.

"Ainsley Logan!" she repeated brightly. Sharply. Hearing his name spoken like that, out loud, had the same effect as a hypnotist clicking his fingers, suddenly tugging me out of a self-imposed trance.

"Ainsley?" I repeated dumbly.

"Yes, darling. He's gone to Sydney! Australia! With work. You know what he's like. Always chasing rainbows. Seeking something exotic. All those colours! The aborigines and all that! He's wanted to go for such a long time. You of all people must know how he's always longed for adventure. Searching for something – shall we say – different?" her eyes were questioning, knowing, daring me to admit – what?

"Yes," I stammered back.

"Anyway, they left just after Christmas. It's so romantic – quite thrilling isn't it?"

I couldn't take in what Paula was saying. Surely Ainsley wouldn't go all the way to the other side of the world – and not even tell me where he was going? Without so much as a 'good bye'? "Has Emma gone?" I asked her bleakly. Knowing the answer, but somehow feeling the need to make my suffering even worse, by hearing it confirmed.

"Yes, of course, darling. And the little one – the daughter. What's her name – Emily isn't it? Such a pretty little thing. Long dark hair – just like her daddy! I'm sure they'll be so happy. Such a wonderful and exciting place to bring up a young family. A golden opportunity. Don't you think so, Lesley?" Was she doing it on purpose or had Paula suddenly really become so dim-witted and insensitive that she didn't realise the effect her careless words were having? In any case, why should they have any effect at all? After all, I was happily married, wasn't I? I had a brand new son who I adored. What on earth was I worried about Ainsley Logan for?

"Yes," I said thoughtfully. Suddenly, I didn't want coffee any more. Or the yucky, mucky, frothy stuff swimming about on top of it, with melting, soggy, tired chocolate sprinkles. I just wanted to grab hold of William's buggy and run with it. Away. Away. No designer suit or heady perfume could console me now. Momentarily I felt lost and empty. Ainsley was on the other side of the world. I'd never see him again. I had no idea.

Chapter Eleven

"My father is getting re-married," Paul announced out of the blue. We were walking down Oxford Street in the middle of a chilly December looking for Christmas gifts. William was safely snug with my mum, at home. So we had peace and quiet in which to browse and sift our way through the goodies piled up on display in West End stores filled with twinkling merry Christmas lights, artificial trees and fairies with bent wands and coloured cellophane. Father Christmas beaming down at us from every street corner market stall, and inside all the stores. Is Oxford Street ever peaceful and quiet? Despite the Salvation Army giving a rousing chorus of 'O Come All Ye Faithful' on the corner by John Lewis, for a moment it seemed as if it was. I was shocked.

"So soon?" I replied. "Who is she?" I asked him as if it really made any difference.

"A woman who was working at the hospital. She looked after my mother. They've been seeing each other for some time, apparently," was all he said. Paul had never spoken of his mother since she had died. Even when I tried to persuade him to tell William about his grandmother he was wary. Skirting around the subject like a hockey player on the outside wing. Anxious to pass the ball to the centre forward as soon as possible. Away. Out of sight – out of mind. Not to be mentioned again. Forgotten.

I had no burning desire to meet Paul's father's new wife – Clara. When I did she turned out to be the total opposite of Christina. She was divorced, with five huge sons who looked like they would be only too willing and able to beat the living daylights out of you at the drop of a hat, and a daughter who looked suspiciously like one of the sons.

Clara was an ex-nurse, and maybe it was my built-in aversion to all things clinical, but I really didn't hit it off with Clara and she didn't care. As for Paul's father, he had become a distant figure as far as William was concerned. When they did meet, Will had to constantly be on his best behaviour for fear of offending. Paul's dad was a very autocratic man. Always believing he was right – about everything. Clara just nodded, and said, "Yes – of course – you're right!" agreeing with him to keep the peace. He seemed to look down at people, for some reason. I had no idea why, especially given the family he had just got involved with. However, life is hard to understand – constantly.

Paul's career was getting rocky. Or at least, his attitude to it seemed to be heading that way. "I'm fed up with the travelling, being on the road half the time. We will have to move north!" Paul unceremoniously informed me just as I was about to put William to bed. He stuffed a handful of leaflets from estate agents into my hands. I put them on the sofa.

"But that's crazy, Paul," I replied. "We've only just moved into this house! The rehearsal rooms are in London, you are working either on location or all around the country half the time. It doesn't matter where we live we would still always be in the 'wrong' place. What's the point in moving?"

Throughout our whole lives we prevaricate, argue, spend sleepless nights worrying about what will happen to us, and then the decision is suddenly made for us. Paul applied for a job with a television news company based in central London. They offered it to him. He took it. He hated it. "It's not like the kind of productions I'm used to! It's a very different ball game. I don't like it at all!" he moaned. "They keep asking me to go for a drink, get involved, be more sociable. I'm not interested in all that!" I wasn't sorry to hear that he didn't want to drink away all our hard-earned cash but still I was very concerned because we had just taken out a big mortgage to help to pay for our new home.

"Stick with it, Paul!" I urged him. "Please just give it a chance. See how it goes. Give yourself some time to re-adjust. Things can only get better!"

Six weeks later Paul came home to tell me he had lost his job. "Good!" he exclaimed with glee. "Best thing that's ever happened to me! Now I can do the one thing I've always wanted to do. Work for myself. No rules and regulations. No one to be answerable to. No one is going to tell me what to do – ever again!" I had already accepted the fact that Paul would never be told what to do. He even seemed to resent being asked to do the most simple of things. As if somehow it was demeaning and beneath him. Like washing up or taking out the rubbish. He had a 'superiority complex'! I was beginning to discover the depth of his appalling arrogance, which I was finding increasingly hard to accept.

I didn't have my dear dad to lean on any longer. My ally and sturdy support. My confidante. To make things right. I took my courage in both hands and decided to tackle Paul's father. He knew him better than anyone, I figured. He was his only son, after all. I waited until we were invited to spend the weekend with him and Clara in their brand new bungalow in the middle of the New Forest. A deadly dreary place full of pensioners. The only teenage faces to be seen were those of the grandchildren who were carted in to visit at holiday time and weekends. The dull characterless clean inevitability of 'retirement property'. I tolerated Clara. I was always polite because it was my nature to be so. Friendly almost – almost. I always came away with a stinking headache. I always felt a bit like I was acting being me, rather than actually being me. I seemed to be doing that more and more.

William came up to me, putting his arms around my leg, crying. "Those boys have just told me he isn't my grandpa, any more!" he wailed.

"What boys?" I wanted to know what on earth was going on. No one had the right to upset Will like this for no good reason. No one. Clara's Nike clad grandsons had told Will that from now on Paul's father was nothing to do with him. He was "our grandpa now – not yours!" I was very upset. I attempted to tackle Paul about it to resolve this situation once and for all.

Up came the barbed wire fence just like something in *The Great Escape* stopping Steve McQueen from jumping across it on his motor bike to freedom in neutral Switzerland. "I can't help what my father says. It's his opinion. And it's nothing to do with me!" he retorted angrily. "You're making a fuss about nothing. " He flatly refused to mention it to his father.

Clara smoked like a chimney and so did Paul's father. Paul offered to take Clara to the local off licence to stock up on Benson and Hedges and whisky. Instantly, I seized the opportunity to speak to him about Paul. I told him about William. I voiced my concerns about Paul's behaviour and the chilling characteristics I was discovering. His terrible, often violent temper over the most mundane of slights or grievances.

His unsympathetic reply was curt, crisp – almost hostile. "I don't think you have anything to complain about. Paul's always had his own way. He has always spoken his mind. He is used to that. And as for his temper – well he has one – so do I! Always have. Christina was so afraid of me she used to run away and lock herself in the bedroom! Or she would take herself off to stay with her mother till things calmed down. Yes, she was terrified of me sometimes. So there you are." He held his arms out wide – hands splayed like bats. "He takes after me!" Just as his son had learned to do, he had turned the situation around. Something evil was being made to seem virtuous. As if the women were in the wrong, not them. We had somehow 'brought it all on yourself – overreacting – Making a fuss about nothing.' The blokes who should have been wearing the white hats – protecting me – my husband and my father-in-law just weren't wearing them.

A sudden abrupt rumble of thunder outside in the garden warned me a storm was about to start. Thunder and lighting echoing across the distant trees, all the way back to the sea. There was much worse to come.

***

Lucy phoned out of the blue. "Hi Lesley! How are you, babe?" It never seemed to occur to Lucy, or indeed to matter, that however long we'd been apart, not spoken, she always chattered away instantly, freely as if she'd only just replaced the receiver from our last heart-to-heart. "What's your news?" she asked in her breathy, familiar friendly voice. I filled her in. "I've got some news too, Les." A moment's hesitation, then she said it very quickly. "I've left Trey. I flew back home yesterday." She went silent again, yet I could feel imperceptible intimacy deflecting down the line as she calmly confided. "I'm getting divorced."

Why? I had to ask why? For some strange reason, I didn't feel surprised. Just overwhelming sadness. "It's a long story, Les. Lots of reasons, really. Don't want to dwell too much on it now. You understand, don't you? Anyway, hon, I'm moving back in with Mum for the time being. She's on her own now since losing Dad and well – it's going to be different! But for the best in the long run, Les. For the best! Things happen for a reason." Lucy being Lucy then rapidly changed the subject ending up telling me a string of filthy but funny stories. Making me laugh out loud till the tears were rolling down my cheeks. I hadn't laughed like that in ages. Why is it that when faced with disaster we find so much comfort in such simple things?

Two days later I got a post card. Addressed to me. In big, bold, solid hand-writing, immediately recognisable. Thick black ink. On the front was a multi-coloured photograph of an Aborigine man wearing full tribal costume. Zig zag woven headband and vivid orange and lime green feathers. A spear in his right hand a brown and cream furry shield over his arm. "How do you like the new outfit?" he had written. Then just four little words. "I miss you, Lesley." No kisses. No love or slushy stuff. Just four words. But they told me everything I needed to know.

***

It was peaceful and quiet on the beach. Still early in the season, it was free of the clutter and clatter of noisy holiday makers. Lonely perhaps? I didn't feel it. My cherished cove was re-charging her batteries just like me so that we would be ready to face the challenge and onslaught that the coming season would hurl our way. Recover from the debris that had already consumed us. Flotsam from the winter's high tides and vicious storms. The beach, the tide, the rocks and me were standing still, standing straight, reflecting, taking a deep breath to taste the salt on my lips, smelling the fresh sea air still cool, but reviving my senses. Just enjoying being. Sunshine was beginning to break through the palest blue and grey of the hazy horizon. I could see more clearly. The clouds were slowly beginning to move away, at last. Out to sea. To overshadow someone else's bay.

Chapter Twelve

Right from the start, Paul insisted that I be the one to stay home and look after William. I offered to go back to work when he lost his job. He was having none of that. "No, no! I am the one who will go out to work. Your job is now to look after William and the home!" he insisted. Arguing that it didn't need both of us to go to work. I would be lying if I said that saddened me because in truth it didn't really. I adored my little son, and would not have wanted to leave him for the world. He was my son, and as far as I was concerned, I was the best-qualified person to take care of him. Not that I had any preconceived ideas of how to do it. I just knew it felt right and natural. Instinctive, like a duck sitting on her nest hatching baby chicks and then feeding them and taking care of them. Like the lioness in the jungle fiercely guarding and guiding her cubs. Mother Nature again. Pure and simple. I found myself rarely thinking of Ainsley or Lucy, or indeed much else apart from my complete and utter absorption with William. For when I do something it's with true Scorpio intensity and one hundred per cent commitment. No messing. No half-measures.

So the dedicated career girl who everybody had assumed was completely clueless with kids, who hadn't even been trusted to hold anyone else's baby when the girls had proudly produced offspring and paraded them around the offices purring with self-satisfaction. Had one of her own. And I did it my way – Miriam Stoppard baby book in one hand, William resting on my hip in the other, Cliff on the stereo – we survived in a world of Brio, matchbox cars and Heinz baby food.

When William was sleeping I would thumb through Paul's thick navy blue production manual of everyone in TV and film.

Writing letters for him, and ringing up production managers to get him freelance work. Very successfully. It never even occurred to me that I could have been putting all my efforts into re-building my own career. Paul was now the principal earner. The bread winner. I was the 'elected home maker'. All the trappings of a traditional marriage. I supported Paul completely. William and I would go on shoots with him when we were allowed to. Packing plastic blue and white striped baby bags and the buggy and the massive assorted paraphernalia that accompanies the pint-sized.

Brighton was one of my favourite places. And so, while Paul was working on a film for a local television company, we went to stay with him during shooting. It was great to have the stony grey and pink beach all to ourselves so early in the morning. We were up and out even before the young deck chair attendant, who soon got to know us, remembering our names. William and I created our own little world and while Paul was assisting the Director on his film, we walked down the wooden planks on the white Victorian pier, gazed at brightly coloured fish in the Aquarium, wandered around antique jewellery shops in The Lanes, stuffing our faces full of cream cakes and orange juice every time we found a pretty little coffee shop. Happy times.

Early one morning Paul received a letter from HTV in Wales offering him six months' work on a television series. "We could come with you…" His abrupt reply startled me.

"No!" he retorted. "I don't want that. It's too long to be away from home." I didn't know at first if he was referring to me and William, or him, or all of us. I assumed he meant all of us.

"William isn't at school yet. It won't matter." He was determined.

"No!" he retorted. "I don't want to do that. It's too long to be away from home."

The more I tried to persuade, him the more defiant he became.

Two weeks later Paul dropped a bombshell. "I'm leaving television!" he announced out of the blue as we were having Sunday lunch. We hadn't even discussed this possibility. "I've had enough. I want to try something else. I've got an interview with a local company next week. An insurance company."

I knew nothing about the insurance business. Financial protection? I had once been out on a date with a man who worked for an insurance company. Never again, I had promised myself faithfully. He was conceited, pompous and full of his own self-importance. That's all I knew about insurance. Oh, yes and the fact that nowadays it wasn't called 'insurance' any longer. An insurance salesman had a slightly self-conscious seventies-style time warp title – Financial Adviser. Nevertheless, I wished Paul luck. I couldn't imagine he would ever settle down in a job like this but I told him. "It doesn't matter what you do for a living, Paul. As long as you're happy. You can sweep floors for all I care, as long as we are together. A family. That's all that really matters at the end of the day – that we have each other." He looked at me. Squeezed my hand. Said nothing.

"Insurance?! It's the last thing I ever thought he would do! He'll hate it! It will be the worst job for him!" Paul's father told me bluntly.

"Insurance?" said my mum. "Won't that be really long hours, dear, and the evenings as well, and weekends? You and William won't see much of him, will you? You won't like it, Lesley – not one bit!"

William wanted to know why his dad was leaving the Police Force.

I had to patiently explain that working as an assistant director on *The Bill* wasn't the same as being a real policeman. But, at four years of age, the policemen rushing around on the tiny TV screen looked pretty real to him. Paul took to the insurance business like a duck to water.

At first, he attempted to assure me that the endless, interminably tedious hours would decrease as business picked up. "I'll have evenings off with you and more time to spend with William once I've got set up. I'll be able to have time off and still do some freelance television work. You'll see. Just be patient for the beginning of it. Things will only get better. I've listened to the forecasts of potential earnings, and I'll be making loads of it! We'll be laughing!"

Pipe dreams. I'd heard Paul's piecrust promises before – as easily broken as made. "I won't be an assistant director forever,

Lesley. What I really want to do is… direct! I want to show my father and everyone else. Then they'll have something to talk about! Just watch their faces. People will have to do whatever I tell them to do. It'll be on my terms My terms only. No one is going to tell me what to do again – ever!"

Yet in this rambling appraisal, he never was specific about exactly what kind of programmes he actually intended to make. Perhaps I had overlooked an unquenched yearning deep inside him to make documentaries with subject matter that would shock the world. Confront reality. Make a difference. No. Did he want to make musical programmes that would bring opera and ballet to the masses? Not just elitist entertainment purely for the rich, but making it accessible to everyone. No. Did he long to make hard-hitting drama full of incisive reasoning on current crises and political correctness? No. Paul simply and solely wanted his name to appear on the credits as director. To be the man in charge. Paul Pearson.

The insurance business is a totally different creature to television production. It is probably impossible to find two industries more diverse. Deadly snakes from the jungles of South America may as well attempt to co-habit with a team of playful polar bears from the Arctic. I tried to get on with them. I really did. It was hard going. Very. I found myself seated next to Paul at dinners and social functions organised by Allied Investments. The 'little wife at home'. With a daft imitation smile on my face as I listened half-heartedly to an assortment of unattractive men in ill-cut suits in the new shade of 'greige' – greyish/beige – and gold-rimmed glasses drone on and on like boring bees settling on a non-conforming hive.

"What do you do, Lesley?" Goodness at last someone had actually addressed a question to me – they wanted to know who I was and what I did! Not just treating me like part of Paul's cufflink.

"Well actually, I used to work in television…" Before I had a chance to carry on, John Simpson, Paul's Branch Manager, turned his head away from me, idly puffing on an ill-smelling short stubby cigar, and began to talk to the grey-haired man on his left. He'd cut me dead. I had not experienced that kind of rudeness in a social situation like this before. But there was plenty more where that had come from. When he eventually turned back to me he rested his arms on the table, pushing his fingers in between each other like a pack of playing cards. I opened my mouth to speak. Not quickly enough.

"Yes – I was saying, we went on a convention with the Company last year to San Francisco. Allied Investments are marvellous people to work for. We were all given ceramic eggs with 'San Fransisco' and Allied Investments printed on it and the date! It's something I'll always treasure. We keep it in pride of place on the sideboard at home. It's the first time we've been and I cannot wait to go again. Neither can my wife. There were a few hundred of us – from all over the country! Every branch of Allied Investments was included. Simply fantastic!" I said nothing. "Of course, if Paul ever makes the grade he'll be able to take part. The wives are sometimes invited – if they promise to behave! You get a week away with the Company. It's to make up for all the weeks you've spent on your own while the men have been out prospecting for Allied Investments. Pretty generous isn't it? You'll just have to push Paul to work harder. That's what all the other wives and girlfriends do!" His mouth had adopted a slightly twisted, contemptuous sneer as he vaguely looked at my non-designer dress.

I looked back at him levelly, with probably ill-disguised disgust. "I don't want a free holiday," I replied evenly. "I don't want a 'free' anything. I just want Paul. And if I want to go on holiday with my family I will earn the money to pay for it. As for pushing Paul into an early grave by piling on the pressure to perform – no way! That is not my style I'm afraid. I want my husband – nothing else!" I could feel my face beginning to flush as angry redness crept up my neck, covering my décolletage, beneath the black taffeta evening dress I had chosen with such care. "Excuse me, I am going to the Ladies." I got up, tripping over my handbag which I had left on the floor underneath my seat, almost running past the gigantic frozen ice sculpture of the Allied Investments dragon plonked right in the centre of the buffet tables.

When I reached the Ladies room I stood in front of the large gilt-edged mirror, applying coral-coloured lipstick, and tried to put powder on my flushed front to tone down the pinky 'rash' that had appeared, and not get it on the delicate black fabric.

"It's no good you know. They all end up the same way!" The woman beside me's voice was slightly tipsy. Softly spoken.

I turned round to see a small blonde woman with rabbit-like eyes, and a pale pink dress. "My husband was the same when he started. Coming home very late each night, full of big ideas and how all the financing works, and everything. Borrowing from the Company to subsidise their business and getting deeper and deeper into debt in the process. The Company get a hold on them you see. Gradually they tighten their grip until the men are so trapped by the financial constraints and the contracts they've signed up to. They are duped. Beguiled. Bought. They are never the same again." I looked at her miserable face.

"How do you stand it?" I asked her quietly.

"Well, it's either grit your teeth, sit it out and put up with it… or do the other thing."

"Other thing?"

"Yes," she replied, quietly. Calmly. "Divorce. Didn't you know? They call Allied Investments the Divorce Capital of the World!"

Tom Cruise once starred in a movie called, *The Firm*. He was a young lawyer taken in by promises of wealth and riches beyond his wildest expectations. Bought. Promised pleasure and luxury. At a price. If you conformed. Played the Corporate Game. His horrified wife stood back helplessly watching as her once happy life began to disintegrate around her. Allied Investments was to become Paul's 'Firm'.

And my torment.

***

I heard Judy's voice behind me. Calling. "Lesley? You're up and about early this morning!" Soft Devon vowels, must be all the scones and clotted cream that made them so delicious. Squinting in the early morning sunshine she put her hand up to shield her eyes, the sleeve of her grey jumper rolled momentarily back down her arm. There, just above her swollen wrist, was a vivid purple and yellow bruise.

"Judy." Instinctively I reached out to take her hand. She swiftly drew it away from me. Out of sight. "Sam's done it to you again, hasn't he? When?"

"Last night," was all she said. Then. "Coffee?" Brightly, smiling again. Putting on the Ritz, tidying up the mess. Sweeping up the shame with invisible brooms. We looked at each other for a few seconds. Understanding everything. Yet understanding nothing. Sisterhood of subterfuge. We share secrets, don't we? Sweet secrets, naughty secrets – deadly secrets. Stifling and muzzling the truth in a myriad of lies. Just to prove that we're just like everyone else. Just to prove we're normal.

I took my cup of hot coffee in my cold hands. It warmed them instantly. Comforting. I drank it by myself, sitting on the stone steps looking out to the bright blue sea. Yes, it was indeed bright today. As always it made me feel better. More able to cope. Alive. Behind me, I could hear Judy bustling and battering about beneath the merry green and white stripey awning. Clattering plastic spoons, heating up sausage rolls and Cornish pasties with flakey pastry. Real life. Real life.

Chapter Thirteen

Paul became immersed in his newly discovered world of financial fiddles. I found myself spending more and more time alone. Becoming increasingly frustrated. Yet still trying so hard to get it right all the time. I wanted my marriage to work. I wanted to be the world's best ever mum. I wanted everything to be perfect. Life never is. People thought they saw perfection when they looked at us shopping together or bowling or choosing plants from the local nursery. But people see what they want to see most of the time. Not what is really happening. People see what makes them feel comfortable. It is as simple as that. I was feeling more and more isolated and disconnected. Paul had not had much time at all for my friends. He and Lucy had never really hit it off. I think he found her too forthright and down to earth. She in turn found him too stuffy and pompous, hard to get through to. I realise, looking back, that it wasn't just Lucy he didn't want in my life, he didn't want anybody in my life – apart from himself. Whereas Lucy spoke her mind on any subject, Paul was more complicated. He couldn't give a straight answer to anything or anyone! The more time he spent working with Allied Investments, the more convoluted and difficult our conversations were becoming. I knew that Paul was hiding things from me, and in the end, I gave up trying to find out what those things were, just to keep the peace. Will was a leveller. He loved us both equally and whenever he sensed storm clouds gathering, he would chuckle his way through to us and encourage us to make up. Flinging his arms around Paul's neck and hugging him so tight. He liked science fiction almost as much as Paul now and it was something else that they could enjoy together. Star

Trek Exhibitions, films and visits to Forbidden Planet in Oxford Street were the places we headed for at weekends and half term.

We spent hours in specialist bookshops in New Oxford Street, making models of the Starship Enterprise, with flashing lights on top. We went to see James Bond movies and to the Motor Show at Earls Court, and the NEC. We ate at Planet Hollywood instead of romantic bistros in Covent Garden. I loved it!

I don't know why I chose the Interior Design Course at the local University. Partly, I suppose, because it fitted in with William's school schedule. Partly because the syllabus seemed fairly straightforward. Mostly because part of me had always yearned to go and create something worthwhile and wonderfully avant-garde. Fresh. That nobody else had ever dreamed of. Something to improve people's lives and make them feel – wow!

Going back to learning felt strange. Half of the students were nearly half my age. But it didn't seem to matter to them… or to me. In the 'olden days' parents were supposed to be seen and not heard, but today's teens and twenties have a much healthier attitude to life. I like it! So I signed up. I felt excited and a warm sense of freedom which permeated my body and sent tingling sensations to my fingertips. I was, at last, doing something for myself. After all this time. Something I had always dreamed of being, once upon a lifetime ago – a designer.

I had put off telling Paul. Did all the usual tacky 'get him in a good mood first' stuff, like cooking his favourite meal, lighting candles, a good bottle of Australian red wine. Listened intently, without falling into a coma, to a long and monotonous monologue all about Allied Investments brand new pension schemes and endowment policies. Then I told him.

"You can't be serious?" he scowled, banging the cut glass wine goblet on the table top. "Going back to College? At your age! It's laughable! Why don't you grow up, Lesley, and act your age for a change? Who do you think you are all of a sudden, anyway? Surely the till at Tescos would be more your style if you wanted to eventually go out to work?" I felt deflated. Humiliated. All the happiness I'd felt brimming up inside me dispersed immediately like someone stuffing the well-known pin right into the very heart of my hopeful little balloon.

I was getting so fed up with constantly being expected to live somebody else's life. Conforming to everybody else's idea of who I should be. Entertaining business colleagues on Saturday evenings, arranging dinner parties. I loved to cook. But we were increasingly spending a fortune on food that I spent half the week buying and the rest of the week preparing and cooking to impress people I didn't even like! I moved saucepans around the top of my Cannon like a wizard, I arranged out-of-season flowers on my dining table and polished crystal till it sparkled, bronze cutlery glowing in the light of a dozen scented candles. Patiently folded pastel-coloured napkins into extraordinary and unnatural shapes, the swans were the final straw. All for what? By the time I staggered in with a tray full of percolated coffee and Elizabeth Shaw mints, I flopped down exhausted into a chair to at least talk to the people who had been enjoying my hospitality and hard work all night long. And now that they had the opportunity to converse with me at last, what did they talk to me about? "Well, that was very nice, Paul. But we must go. Baby sitters – you know how it is?" And they would stand by the door pumping Paul's hand up and down, patting him on the back – "Well done!" making arrangements for their next golf match. Speeding off into the dark street. I hadn't been able to catch more than half a sentence while I was whirling backwards and forwards with arms filled with food, like some kind of mechanical wind-up ballerina doll.

I knew what I needed. A little bit of quality time by myself, to re-charge my worn down batteries. I don't know if it's an 'only child' thing or a 'creative person' thing, but if I am deprived of time and space just to be alone, to think, to dream, just to be, then I feel all wrong inside. Tired out. "I don't understand you, Lesley! Not at all!" He was beginning to fume a little now as outrage crept into his raised voice. Making me feel guilty, as usual. "I would have thought that you would have enough to do here with William and the house to look after!" he said pointedly, running his finger along the table top and inspecting it for dust.

"In fact I would make the suggestion that if you are bored you might spend less time messing around signing up for courses at the local college and wandering round gloomy book shops wasting your time, and take a duster to this house for a change! Our home is becoming a tip and I should like it to resemble something half way decent again. I hate coming home to it. It's a disgrace, Lesley it really is. And so are you. It sickens me to come home to this. Really sickens me."

I could feel my cheeks staring to burn, flushed with anger and embarrassment. I wasn't a cleaner! I had a career when Paul first met me. More highly paid than his. A deadly pattern of verbal abuse was emerging. Denigration and degradation. His words stung. I might not have been the most domesticated of dutiful wives. But our home was exactly that – a home. Since Will had been born it had happily embraced Scalextric cars whirring around the living room, train sets spread around the outside of the dining room. Boots piled in a heap by the door leading to the back garden where muddy games of soccer and cricket took place. I wasn't interested in comparing who had the largest newest TV with the most satellite stations. Or the most massive fridge freezer. I couldn't be bothered. I wasn't prepared to live in a place where friends were afraid to put down a cup and saucer in case it made a ring on the coffee table. Marks can be wiped away in an instant. A little dust never killed anyone. It was our home, it was warm, comfortable and cosy, filled with the aroma of freshly baked cakes and sweet peas and roses. And that's the way I liked it.

Paul was not the tidiest person on the planet. Flinging clothes haphazardly onto the bedroom floor, towels over the bannisters, brief cases, laptop computer and company papers spread all across the shining dining room table. But he didn't have to pick up his own stuff. Not when he had a wife to do it for him. "This isn't the Victorian age, you know, Paul!" I was only half joking. "I'm not your chattel! We should share things." But lately, all he was prepared to share with me was his bad temper.

The going was getting tough again. Time to go shopping. The soothing retail therapy fix, which works like a miracle for most women, of all ages. I needed to cultivate a new image that would compliment the new me. So I started shopping in High Street up to the minute bargain treasure troves like New Look, and trendy boutiques with the latest line in midriff-skimming, floaty-sleeved outfits. "You buy clothes that teenagers would wear!" scoffed Paul. I had just returned, quite elated with my brand new denim designer-inspired jeans sprinkled lavishly with sparkling sequins all down the legs, and a gold top full of stars.

"So what?" I replied, attempting to sound as if his comments didn't hurt me. "I'm still a size ten. The girls at Uni ask me where I buy my clothes, sometimes. That's a nice compliment isn't it?" Disdain dripped down his long nose like icicles hanging from a snow-covered roof.

He sniffed. "You look like a tart, Lesley," he said abruptly. Then he carried on watching an out-of-body experience horror movie on Channel 5.

So I wrapped up my new clothes carefully, in white tissue paper. Put them away. Out of sight. The little silky ivory bodice with embroidered roses that I had impulsively purchased, believing it looked so, *Sleeping Beauty* was a mistake after all. Something Paul had remarked could have come from an Ann Summers Shop. Not exactly the boho-chic I was aiming for. I peered into the mirror. My face looked pale. I pulled back my hair and shoved a tartan patterned scrunchie onto it. At least it kept it out of the way, in a long pony tail. Was it me? Was it him? Perhaps I was merely being unreasonable. Maybe I did look like a ridiculous lump of mutton dressed in lamb's clothes. Who was I kidding anyway? I knew how old I was, didn't I? The proverbial prima gravida. Yet inside I still didn't really feel it. Inside I still felt 18 sometimes. Especially when I tucked my huge white stack of stiff cardboard drawings into my brown leather portfolio. I stuffed paints, brushes of all shapes and sizes, pens and inks, and every colour into my patchwork leather, yellow, blue and orange holdall. I wrapped a ruby red pashmina around my neck, over the top of my black leather jacket. I had a black miniskirt and red tights. I was a walking rainbow! I was a College girl again! Re-training to be someone unique and special. Me.

Chapter Fourteen

Domestic abuse is something we are encouraged to be more openminded about, like racism and sexism. The more tolerant we have become, more accepting. More willing and able to talk about it. Bring it out into the open. Make it a part of everyday life. Yet, like its sneaky accomplice, mental illness, it comes with a stigma attached which reaches a hundred miles long and a thousand miles wide. Still. Divorce, dementia, domestic violence. Three 'D's I grew up entirely unaware of. I must have lived in the clouds of oblivion for there were no signs of any of it in my happy-go-lucky little world filled with pirates and knights in shining armour rescuing distressed damsels. But when you really need a knight – you can't find one. Anywhere.

Divorce was the domain of the wealthy for few others could afford the expense. A small percentage of people were property owners and the unrealistic spiralling house market economy had not even become a pipe dream. Earnings were less. Ordinary men and women didn't even own a fridge, let alone a car of their own. It wasn't worth getting divorced. Legal fees, courts, solicitors, injunctions. Not many had a deep desire to go there. Dementia? Only those locked away inside mental homes were insane and they were out of harm weren't they? As for domestic abuse. Surely that was an unspeakable thing that only happened to a certain sort of person wasn't it? Not Mr and Mrs Average. Not Mr and Mrs Middle Class. Not in the green leafy suburbs, not in a nice red brick house. Not when you came from a good home. A respectable family. Like something out of Dickens it was the poorest and the destitute, despairing and helpless wretches living in squalor who were subjected to drunken brawls and beatings, bruises and broken bones. Or so I thought. So I thought.

Paul could be the charming life and soul of any party. He could be funny. Good company, when he chose to be. A caring father. Good husband. But behind closed doors, I was discovering a different character, just as Dr Jekyll was haunted by Mr Hyde so a more sinister, ugly and unsettling side had begun to emerge. I was fearful. Just like his father, he was becoming increasingly domineering, high handed and dogmatic. Allied Investments and their 'brain washing' techniques added rocket fuel to a fire that would begin to burn just as uncontrollably as any I had seen in the South of France, years ago.

Paul loved power. Paul loved money. Fast cars and fast things. If he bought anything it had to be the most expensive. Christmas was coming and I noticed his watch had broken. "I'll buy you a new one," I told him.

"Unless it's a Rolex, don't bother," he replied. I thought he was joking at first. But he wasn't. "I wouldn't wear anything else." He waved his hand dismissively. So I bought him black jeans from M and S and a silky black shirt to go with them. He returned them all and got the money back. Then he went to Bond Street and bought Yves St Laurent cords.

Allied Investments and their agents were working away like beavers building an indestructible dam. I stood and watched as the man I thought I knew slowly but surely got sucked into their system. Like a huge vacuum cleaner hoovering him up like a tissue. He went quite willingly. I resisted – constantly. And although I realised I only had myself to blame for allowing myself to become increasingly dependent upon Paul, increasingly submissive, I held on tight still to the need deep inside of me. Such a strong belief in the absolute right of everybody to individual freedom and personal liberty.

I found myself having arguments with myself. Trying so hard to justify things that no longer made any sense. Eventually, exhaustion took over and I sat down wearily on my pine wood stool, in front of my drawing board, with a bottle of white wine, my white card, and my design books. My multi-coloured inks, sketching, drafting, styling, modelling, immersing myself in a fantastic fantasy world of luminosity that lit the rainbow of my imagination like a match to a fabulous firework. Till I eventually effectively blotted out all thoughts of Paul and his problems. Disappearing up the paper along with the vivid ink, like a genie released from a magic lamp.

***

Not long after that, I had the accident. I don't know why the lorry driver wasn't looking where he was going. What distracted him? Why his brakes failed to work? All I know is that on my way to take Will to visit his grandmother after school one afternoon we were suddenly, savagely, rammed into from behind, and my white Escort went flying across one of the busiest roundabouts in the South East, like a ping-pong ball.

'Whiplash' is so often misrepresented. So often misused by people intent on obtaining compensation payments. The injuries I received in those first few fleeting seconds were sufficient to adversely affect the rest of my life. Miraculously, William wasn't too badly injured. The doctors explained to me that it was perhaps because he was smaller than I was. The impact of the collision was on a different part of his spine. Also, I had been looking to the right to see the oncoming traffic, my head had been spun around, then thrown violently backwards, and forward. A sharp stabbing pain the like of which I had never encountered completely immobilised me.

I slumped over the wheel feeling sick. Trying so hard not to pass out. The rest is a blur. When my mother called to tell Paul what had happened to us, his office curtly replied that he 'wasn't available'. Too busy to answer the phone. Eventually, he did call back. I tried tearfully to explain what had happened. When he arrived all he wanted to know was one thing. "How badly damaged is the car – and where is it?"

Will and I were prescribed soft neck collars. Will got better sooner than I did. Months, became years, of visits to clinics, and physiotherapy units of the local hospital to see specialists. For nine whole months, I was confined in a hard-neck collar like something you would connect with a Hammer House of Horror villain. I begged my Consultant Surgeon to let me remove the collar so that I could go with Paul to his firm's Christmas party. I didn't want to let him down. It was held at a nearby hotel with its own conservatory and wild fowl reserve. "I can't go looking like this!" I wailed.

Mr Seaman, who everyone referred to as 'God', just looked at me, thick black moustache twitching slightly. "I am sure your husband will make allowances," he said.

"No! No he won't, and all the other wives will be looking so glamorous!" I implored him. I could tell he was not too impressed.

"If it had been a broken ankle, I would have put it in plaster!" he said. "You would not have been able to remove that now, would you?!" Nevertheless, he relented, consenting to let me go, like Cinderella, minus the horrible attachment, for a few hours only. When I got home, I took off the neck collar. Hurled it across the room. Then retrieved it. I went off to Brent Cross to a very expensive beauty salon to have my hair done properly. Tinted blonde. In the 'Christmas rush' the hairdresser put the wrong colour on my hair. I came out with dark brown hair. Shorter. But dark brown.

I got dressed in maroon lace and high heels, for the first time since the accident. I felt terrible. I had a splitting headache. I realised instantly why I was having to put up with the heavy neck collar for support till my body got better. All I wanted, all I needed, was to go home. I felt sick with pain. Giddy from the constant barrage of Insurance-speak. Cold from the draught that was blowing gale force through the crack in the conservatory window looking out over the dim wild fowl feature. Next morning, Paul and his area manager let me have it. And then some. For "not behaving in a way that reflected and appreciated the fact that I had at least been given a free meal. You should have been bloody grateful!" I was angry. A free meal was something I didn't need, or want, from anybody, least of all Allied Investments. A few words of kindness and understanding perhaps.

That would have been a bonus. But a free meal and a barrage of insults? NO.

I let Paul and his Manager know exactly how I felt about their 'free meal'. Paul was livid. "How dare you behave like that!!" he screamed. "How dare you tell him that you don't want or need a free meal! After all they've done!" Indeed. After all they had done, so far.

It was no use me trying to explain that I had only been trying to explain… they just wouldn't get it. Like everything else. And I was in so much pain. I clipped the thick white, unforgiving hard plastic neck collar back around my neck. Took more pain killers. Went dejectedly to bed.

Most jobs have perks of some kind. Prizes were all part and parcel of the game-show mentality of the Allied Investment incentive scheme intended to 'chivvy-up' desperate workers. 'Dream holidays' to faraway destinations, Gala Evenings in expensive West End hotels were becoming Paul's *raison d'etre*. For only the high flyers got the highest awards, unless they were so high up in the Company that they got to go on all the conventions regardless or not of whether they had 'earned the right'. Free holidays, disguised as 'conventions' so that they could fool the tax man. Little wonder that everyone's insurance premiums were going up up and away. No surprise that so many pensions were being mis-sold.

Christmas was coming. I was saving up for William's present. A mammoth box of Lego that would, by the time Will had finished patiently slotting red, white and grey bits of shiny plastic together, magically be transformed into a medieval castle. Complete with turrets, knights, and even a Princess with a white frock, long sleeves – and a pointy hat. "If I reach my targets then I could win a big prize next year!" Paul proclaimed.

I looked up from the heap of sparkling Christmas tree decorations, strewn across the lounge carpet, feeling a sudden chill in the pit of my stomach. "What kind of big prize?" I asked. But I knew already what it was. I had seen the posters on the walls of Paul's office block.

"A Caribbean Cruise!" he proclaimed. Excited. More excited than I had seen him in a very long time. He hadn't even been that thrilled when we went to Disneyland.

"Oh." I didn't know what to say. "Is it for everyone?" I asked. I knew the answer to that already, as well. I don't know why I asked. But I did.

"Well," said Paul importantly. "I am eligible to go of course. Some of the wives will be invited. They haven't decided for sure who yet."

"And William?" I asked.

Suddenly Paul's face was filled with dark shadows of irritation. "No," he replied firmly. "No children! It's not a family thing. They don't want kids around. It's for adults! People don't go on these things to have other people's bloody kids running about all over the place. It's an Insurance Company, Lesley – all the top people will be there. What on earth are you thinking?!"

"We're a family," I replied glumly. Staring down at the box of twinkling trinkets. Thinking of the darling little boy asleep upstairs in his Captain Scarlet pyjamas.

Paul marched out of the room. Slamming the door shut behind him. I didn't want Paul to make the grade. I hated to admit that, even to myself. But I just didn't. I didn't want to be selfish. But I didn't want Paul to be selfish either. I prayed that he would not reach the target. But he did. Two days before Christmas Eve I took out a free-range turkey from Marks and Spencers chill counter to give us all a really lovely feast. Paul took out a life insurance policy on me. Which took his figures for the year just up to target level. Just.

It was the second week of January that the Cruise prize was confirmed. In writing. On Allied Investments memo paper. It was snowing outside. Thick white dollops blobbing onto the window and melting on impact with the warm glass. The garden is an instant carpet of thick white icing sugar perfection. "I've won! I've won! A Caribbean Cruise! The Holiday of a Lifetime! I can't wait!" his voice seemed to boom like cannons exploding from the deck of a ship, echoing round the room, ricocheting off the walls. I suppose it was a lethal combination. I was in pain, my head was throbbing, my back immovable in the cold as if an iron cage had been placed around it and I was being held prisoner inside. My son was still so young. My husband was going far far away from us to the other side of the world without us. I was angry, I was upset. Once more I felt like Cinderella, only this time I wasn't going to the Ball, or anywhere else, it appeared. I truly believed once Paul went on the Cruise without us I would lose him – forever.

I would most certainly lose something that up until that moment had remained so precious to me. Something I thought I would never be in any danger of letting go of. We had never had separate holidays or even days out. I had always thought of us as a complete team. The Three Musketeers. All for one, one for all, no matter what happened around us. But Allied Investments – The Divorce Capital of the World – had set the bulldozers on standby to smash my world to bits. It didn't happen overnight.

"If you go – don't bother to come back – I'll divorce you if you think a free cruise is more important than me and Will!" I heard myself shouting dramatically. The very thing I dreaded. The last thing Will and I wanted – or needed. And I was yelling at Paul, telling him I'd be the one to do it! I thought it would shake some sense into him, and make him change his mind. Had I gone temporarily round the bend?! Maybe it was the pain, combined with the medication, all mixed up together with adoration for my little boy. I couldn't leave him. Paul knew that. Nevertheless, we rowed like never before. I felt as if I had laid out my life carefully like my best bone china plates, cut glass and floral centrepieces on a well-constructed mahogany table, and suddenly I'd whipped off the white damask cloth, like some kind of crazed conjurer. Sending all the contents flying up into oblivion. I went for a walk outside in the snowy park. It was freezing. Even the swans were uncharacteristically skidding across the frozen lake, searching for warmth and security somewhere. A kind of stability. They headed for the island in the centre, filled with trees and shrubby coniferous foliage. Maybe they had even tried their luck at the local pub bordering the park, I wondered. Who knows? Who knew anything any more? I was taking the first tentative and uneasy step towards losing what I had cherished during all the years of our marriage. My wedding day vows seemed to be on as slippery a slope and as out of control as the webbed feet of the sliding swans on the ice-covered lake in front of me.

For weeks we didn't speak to each other. Then hardly at all. Finally, one February morning, the sun came out. Wintry, pale lemon and watery. But such a glad sight. Will was at school. I had the house all to myself. A shrill ring of the telephone cut through the peaceful still and quiet, as I was in the middle of doing something I didn't do every day – dusting the top of the dining room table. I picked up the receiver looking out at the pale lemon and peach and powder blue sky. It was reflecting brilliantly on my newly polished mahogany.

"It's Ainsley!" Just like that. Out of a powder blue and lemon sky. After all this time.

"Ainsley?" I echoed.

"Yes – of course! How many other blokes do you know who ring you up in the middle of the day when they know you are all alone with a mop and bucket? Who did you think it was?!" He started to laugh. The light-hearted chuckle I remembered so well. And all at once, I was twenty-something again. I was me again. And the sudden warmth I felt wasn't just from the rays of the winter sunshine bouncing off of my French windows.

"Ainsley! How are you? Where are you?" So much to say, so much to ask him.

"I've just got back to the UK, Lesley. I've left Images, the company I went to Australia with. I've started up on my own! Look, I've got masses of stuff to tell you Lesley. First of all one of the reasons I'm ringing is because I'm going to be the big four-O in a couple of weeks time. And I'd like to invite you and Paul to a little party I'm having. You're the first person I've asked!" He sounded almost coy.

I was taken aback. "Well, I'm not sure, Ainsley. Paul and I – well, I feel rather like I've blown it at the moment. We haven't been speaking, and I feel like I've thrown everything up in the air!" I could actually feel him smiling down the phone.

"Don't be daft, Lesley. I know you. You'll work things out. You always do. Listen – before you say yes to the party – let's have lunch and a proper chat. Catch up with everything because at the party I might not get the chance to talk to you properly. You know what I mean?" I nodded even though I knew he couldn't see me. "I'd like to have you all to myself for a change. When are you free?"

When was I free? My head was doing the cha-cha. Dear old Ainsley had suddenly, and miraculously as Merlin, sprinkled some desperately needed fairy dust back into my troubled life. Mistakenly assuming my hesitation was because I was searching in my diary for a convenient 'window' to slot him into, Ainsley took control of the situation, deciding for me. "Whatever you were planning to do Thursday – cancel it! Come and have lunch with me at that new place down by the river. I'll pick you up at one. Catch up on all the news then. Bye, Les!" Click! He'd gone.

Wow. Thursday. It shouldn't have, but it actually felt like I had just made a date!

At least I'd discarded the dreaded neck collar. But there was still one pressing question that needed an immediate answer – what to wear?

Chapter Fifteen

I could have told Paul. I should have told Paul, perhaps. For some unexplainable reason, I didn't. I told him about the party, though, because I really wanted to go. I didn't want to risk the usual last minute, "Oh I have work appointments!" excuse from Paul. I wanted Paul to slot in a special space, for me, and him – and Ainsley.

I rang my mum. "Can you look after William on the 28th? We've been invited to a party." Was all I asked, at first.

"Yes, alright," she replied. Always eager for the chance to spend as much time as possible with her only grandson. "Who's party is it?"

My voice wavered just a little as I replied, "Ainsley, Ainsley Logan. You may not remember him." What was I feeling here – guilty? Why? The disapproval in her voice was instantly audible. Already. And I hadn't even met him again yet!

"Oh yes, I do remember him. From your television days. Very good-looking fellow if I remember correctly. You and he were, well – we'll just leave it there shall we?"

Silence.

"I thought he was married?"

There it was again like slices of thickly buttered bread – reproach. I began to feel the back of my neck tightening up, the beginning of a headache working its way up the right-hand side. Tension. I had always tried so hard to please my mum. To make her happy as all little only daughters do. In fact, I was becoming increasingly aware that I was spending my whole life doing my level best to please everyone. Except me. And in attempting to please everyone – I ended up pleasing no one. Least of all myself.

"Yes." I replied. "To Emma. And she's very beautiful, very clever and talented and she's going to be there – OK?"

Silence again.

I put the phone down. I was a grown woman and yet my mother could always manage to do that. How? – I don't know. Some kind of built-in radar with extra sensory antennae attached invisibly. I knew she loved me. That was beyond all question or doubt. Yet she also possessed an overwhelming capacity to try to control me. Maybe in a weird kind of way that was why I had been attracted to Paul. At first, I had found his domineering and controlling attitude some kind of strength. Some kind of bad day I must have been having when I worked that one out!

I thought I would be able to lean on him when my dad died. But I increasingly began to realise that if you love somebody you cannot expect to control them. You have to let them be free. Insecurity drives us to curb, to criticise, crush and challenge the independent spirit of those close to us. To love is to cherish – not to choke.

I put on some music to soothe my spirit. And tipped things from my wardrobe higgledy-piggledy onto the spare bed. "That new restaurant down by the river," Ainsley had said. Probably quite trendy then And he always dressed so perfectly. Effortlessly. So right for whatever occasion. I didn't want him to think I'd turned into some kind of tracksuited frump. I tried on all my things. Then I stuffed them all back into my wardrobe and closed the door. As usual when the going gets tough, the tough have the instant solution – go shopping. I pulled on a bright yellow sweatshirt, and sticking some cash into the pocket of my jeans, headed off to the local undercover shopping mall.

Princess Diana was my source of inspiration for many things. My role model. She had two young boys. She was blonde. She had a difficult marriage. And whenever she appeared in a magazine or on TV looking spectacularly gorgeous I responded in exactly the same way as thousands of others: I wanted a copy of that outfit – whatever it was! I tried on lots of Diana-type things – with frills, bows, polka dots – nothing looked quite right. Not on me anyway. Maybe because she was about five foot ten and I was about five foot two on my tip-toes. I settled for a new pair of light camel-coloured chinos and a cream silk T-shirt with a slashed neck. I already possessed the requisite navy blazer. I would be 'classy and classic' I decided. I splurged on a new pair of pale camel leather pumps, just to be on the safe side. Nothing I had matched the chinos. And, well, since the accident I couldn't wear my high heels any longer. So I really needed them. They were kind of a necessity not a luxury. Anyway – I managed to convince myself.

When I pulled up onto the drive of our house, Paul was already home. "Where have you been?" he asked, looking pointedly at his watch. I told him I'd been out to do some shopping. I showed him the T-shirt and the trousers. Not the shoes though.

"I got some new Lego for William as well. Would you like a cup of tea?" I asked, reaching for the kettle, stuffing the bulging bags behind the pink and beige velvet sofa.

"I've had a terrible day. So I've come home early," Announced Paul. I looked at him. He seemed tired. Distracted. I thought about the Cruise for a moment. Felt a pang of remorse. How all the other wives would be rushing round the shops eagerly buying the new range of brightly coloured designer bikinis flooding into the shops covered with stripes or dazzling floral prints of fuschia and orange and cobalt blue. Sarongs to match. Glittering evening dresses. All guaranteed to show off a glorious Caribbean tan. And I was being made to feel guilty about a new pair of Chinos?

I changed the subject swimming around my head like a rampant mermaid. "You'll never guess who rang up today." To stop feeling miserable. To take away the pain. "Ainsley. Ainsley Logan. He's back in the UK. He's invited us to his 40th Birthday party on the 28th!" I sounded chirpy. Speaking faster than usual as I always do when I get excited or enthusiastic about something. Or someone.

Paul looked up from his cup of tea. "Ainsley? What's he doing back? I thought he had left for good. Didn't you have some kind of a fling with him at the studios? Weren't you two some kind of 'item'?"

I flushed. "No – no we were nothing of the sort!" I replied.

"Well, why has he asked us to this party then? I was never friendly with him. I hope you don't think I'm being dragged along as your escort, just so that you can see him again. Because I'm not!" I couldn't believe my burning ears. First my mum. Now Paul. What on earth was the matter with everyone? Could all the people in the whole wide world have friends – some kind of social life. Except me? Was my life simply to revolve around William, Paul, my mum and domestic dreariness – that was it?

I sighed. "I don't know why you feel that way, Paul. He's back because he has started up his own company. And no we were not an 'item'. We were – and still are – great friends! And I shouldn't be having to explain this to anyone – least of all you!" I felt my face beginning to turn red. Paul knew Ainsley. He knew me. He knew I had nothing to hide. No deep secrets to be ashamed of. "Look, Paul, you are dead set on going on this Cruise aren't you?" I could see defiance immediately in his face. I cut in quickly. "I would like to go to Ainsley's party – with you. He's an old friend. A dear friend. Nothing more and nothing less than that. Emma will be there… So will lots of other people from the studios. It will give us an opportunity to catch up. To see everyone."

Paul instantly banged his cup on the table, spilling tea from the top which splashed over his hand. "You can catch up, you mean! I don't miss any of those creeps from television. It wasn't my scene. I like the people I'm working with now. I much prefer them. They are my kind of people!" He had started to shout once more. Usually, I would have let it go. Walk out of the room. Let him have his own way. To keep the peace. But not this time. I'd had enough of always being the one to give in.

"Well, it's your choice, Paul. We've both been invited. We can do one of two things. We can do a very pleasant evening together, or if you really don't want to go – then I will go by myself!" Paul's face curled with contempt. Then he started to laugh. Short, sharp and brittle.

"You! Go on your own?! You wouldn't go on your own! You wouldn't have the nerve to go anywhere on your own!" he scoffed. I just looked straight back at him. I wasn't going to be drawn into yet another argument. Not this time.

"Please, Paul."

"I'll check my diary," was all he said. Then he switched on the TV.

I ran upstairs to stash my loot in the wardrobe. New clothes. New shoes. At least I had something to wear on Thursday for lunch with Ainsley. I wasn't going to tell Paul, or anyone else, about that!

It took me a long time to get ready. Leisurely. For the first time in what seemed an eternity, I put heated rollers in my hair, letting it swing in loose big floppy curls instead of tugging it back off of my face in an untidy scrunchy bunch. My bath I filled carefully with the expensive Estee Lauder stuff I'd been given for Christmas.

My nails responded with shocking surprise when I lavished 'Ravishing Pink' pearlised polish all over them. I had spent such a long time being a 'mum', it seemed, afraid that chips of nail varnish would drop into William's food when I was chopping up vegetables for dinner, another little 'something else to worry about' tip I picked up from my mother. I'd forgotten the simple pleasure a decent manicure gives a girl – even if it's a homemade one!

Clothes had always been my undying passion. Yet like so many other things in my life I'd allowed the flames of desire to fizzle out and fade. My dress sense had become sense-less – a weird mix of faded jeans, sweatshirts with Mickey Mouse logos on the front, sloppy tops – just like all the other mums with young children. No one needed or wanted to see designer suits at the local Primary School gate. Most of the women went for the unscrubbed, no make-up, natural and windswept hairdo look, which I had perfected quite well myself. Especially the hair. If it was a special occasion, Nativity Play or Sports Day, out would come, a little self-consciously, the floral Laura Ashley frocks. Mid-calf length. With matching tights. And flat sandals.

So it was with a glimmer of elated anticipation that I protectively peeled the plastic covers from my new clothes. Chinos and top. I looked at them, and enjoyed them for a moment. Then

I put them on. They felt soft and yet with the crispness of fabric that hasn't hit the washing line yet. The cut was surprisingly good. I even looked slimmer! Probably because I was actually wearing something that fitted me properly for a change. I put on make-up with the same precise strokes I had used on my grateful fingernails. Using soft brushes with smooth wooden handles, and pastel eye shadows from my make-up box that I hadn't used in ages, I rediscovered a forgotten art. I slicked on glossy lipstick in a nearly natural shade I knew Ainsley would approve of. He had always hated bright red overmade up mouths. I remembered that. There! I pulled on my navy blazer. Squirted perfume with a subtle mix of floral and woody notes behind my ears. I looked and felt like someone I had known once. A very long time ago. Someone I'd completely lost touch with lately. She had suddenly come back into my life like a longlost friend.

My other long-lost friend arrived, unusually for him, ten minutes early. It felt strange looking out of the large bay window in front of the lounge to see an altogether different vehicle parked sideways on my red brick driveway. Big, black and shiny. Ainsley had traded in the zippy little Mini Cooper and replaced it with a 'family man and woman's fashionable mode of transport'— a take you anywhere you wanna go 4 x 4 state-of-the-art Land Rover. Complete with sparkling silver alloy wheels and headlights above the sturdy black bumper.

"Hello, Lesley!" He was here. In my own home. After all the years. In a black leather jacket, black shirt open at the neck, just a little. To my knowledge, Ainsley had never worn a tie. And probably never ever would. And chinos – honey beige. Matching mine like an identical twin. His arms enveloped me as he hugged me tight, kissing me warmly on both cheeks. Grinning widely. His bright white movie star smile. "I've missed you!" he was saying into my right ear. I was blabbering something incomprehensible. All I knew was the minute that he'd reached out to hug me, my legs and my insides had turned to mush.

'Trader Micks' was every bit as stylish as Ainsley had promised it would be. Riverside locations always give a restaurant, indeed anywhere, a head start. And even though it was still too cold to sit outside on the wooden tables and chairs lining the bank, inside was welcoming and cosy. Lots of polished wood. Gold trim. If I had been captured in the Caribbean and put on board a pirate ship I'm sure it would have looked exactly like the inside of 'Trader Micks'. Definitely no parrots though. This place was seriously upmarket with décor as dedicated to exclusivity and excellence as the inspirational choice of food.

"Let's sit in the corner – it's more private," said Ainsley, grabbing hold of a big caramel-coloured menu from the mini-skirted waitress, as she tottered past on very high heels. "What are you drinking?" I couldn't think for a moment.

"Cinzano?" I replied. Half-questioning my own decision. But I'd said it now.

"Oh – very Joan Collins '70s retro!" He laughed. Then seeing my immediate embarrassment he quickly turned to the waitress ordering for me, "Cinzano Bianco – with ice and a slice, please!" He'd remembered. He ordered a pint of special lager for himself. I looked across the table at him, now, allowing my eyes to focus properly on the face I'd thought of so often. Ainsley Logan, it had to be admitted, was still incredibly good-looking! So unfair that women get 'crow's feet' while men get mature with 'laughter lines'. They suited Ainsley. Everything suited Ainsley. Crinkling around the edges of his deep brown smiling eyes. Like a fine red wine, Ainsley had just got better with the years – not old and shrivelled up like a mouldy piece of Brie.

I grabbed my glass. Drank some of the cold liquid. Ice cubes clinking around in the glass. I felt better. "So what have you got to tell me?" he asked.

"You first," I replied. And so we sat, and talked, and talked. And listened to each other. Really listened. I don't know what happened to time itself. As if we had been suspended in one of Jules Verne's time capsules, it seemed irrelevant. I could see it growing darker outside the windows, the lamplights reflecting golden glow that shimmered across the inky blue rippling river. We were still talking. Ainsley's fantastic job in Australia appeared to have been all he could have wished for, and more. A designer's dream come true, with the salary, fame and affluently comfortable lifestyle that kind of wealth afforded.

Knowing how important these things were to Emma I was curious to know what on earth had prompted the decision to come back home. "Well, when Emily started Senior School everything seemed to change," explained Ainsley, pushing his thick fringe back with his hand, the way he always used to. He looked at me from beneath it. "Emma wanted her to come back to England to study here. She wanted her to have the benefit of a private school education, just as she had. And to go on to University – maybe even Oxford or Cambridge." He looked up, looking momentarily a little embarrassed. Self-effacing.

He grabbed his glass of lager like a defence mechanism. "So, we decided to come back. Got an old Victorian house in the middle of London. I've started my own business. Voila!" He laughed, his deep reassuring throaty chuckle. I hadn't heard it in such a long time.

Emptying his glass, he gestured to the waitress. "Top up please?" She went off with it in her hands. Smiling the smile most females did whenever he chose to favour them with one of his 'looks'. Yet he was so laid back I still didn't know whether he was really aware of the effect those looks had! Ainsley was so much the same. Yet so different. Not a young man any longer. All grown up. Self-assured. Confident. But not in a cocky way. "How about you, Lesley? What's all this about you and Paul having some kind of bust-up?"

Maybe it was because I had been sitting there drinking all the time Ainsley had been bringing me up to date with his life story. Talking to me properly for the first time in ages. I was slightly tipsy. Which makes the best of us looser tongued than we would normally be. Maybe it was because at long last I was able to relax and feel safe in the familiar company of someone to whom I could totally relate and freely tell the truth to. To trust. Tell a few secrets of my own. I told Ainsley all about the Cruise. By the time I had finished Ainsley was halfway through his fresh pint of lager. He looked perplexed, mystified even. "I don't understand you, Lesley," he said. His voice was all grown up. Just like he now was. "Why are you so upset about Paul going? I know you don't want to go anyway. You don't want to leave William. Actually, I can understand why you feel that way. But you can't stop Paul, Lesley. How would you feel if you wanted to do something really special? Something that meant a lot to you? Like going to see D'Arcy Bussell performing with the Royal Ballet at Covent Garden – or even meeting Michael Flatley!" I laughed out loud at this because he had always teased me about my fascination with the Irish superstar.

"It's so unlike you, Lesley. You never used to be like this! You were so much more sophisticated when you were younger!" Almost it seemed as if he was scolding me. And I didn't know if I could cope with that. Not from Ainsley. Not when I'd allowed myself specially to confide in him. He was making me feel as if suddenly I was a naughty child threatening to throw all her toys out of the pram. His daughter rather than his grown-up friend. But actually, I also knew that what he was saying made some kind of sense, even though I found it hard to agree with him. I went all quiet. Feeling suddenly foolish. Let down. "Lesley," he took hold of my right hand, holding it firmly in his two hands. "You know Paul, and so do I. We both know that whatever he wants to do – he will do it – with or without your approval. See that brick wall, Lesley?" I stared at it. Tears pricking behind my eyes. "That's Paul. You can keep hitting your head against the wall forever, Lesley. And who's going to end up winning? You? Or the wall? The wall won't even have a dent in it. But you will have a heck of a headache!"

Then he started to laugh, gently. He squeezed my hand. Understanding me still so well, knowing he had said enough. For now. "It'll be alright, Lesley. You just wait and see," he promised.

Chapter Sixteen

Paul went on the Caribbean Cruise with his colleagues, the 'top' people. And girls from his office. I felt as if someone had died. I'd lost him. And as dramatic as that sounded there was no other way to describe the pain and emptiness I felt inside of me.

I also knew without a shadow of a doubt that his triumphal victory would open the floodgates for Paul to do whatever he pleased, go wherever he wished, from now on. Unfettered. Not caring. Abandoning William and me more and more. Like a deadly serpent there was something else in my life I was increasingly unable to control. No matter how hard I grappled. No matter how hard I tried. And believe me – I tried.

Everything.

The terrible temper tantrums were becoming more frequent, and more alarming. William had pleaded with Paul, "Please don't go on the Cruise without us! Daddy – Please don't leave us! Pleeeeeeease!" Holding onto Paul's outstretched leg, which he had wound his tiny arms around. Paul had just told me that 'escorts' would be provided for all the men who were travelling alone. I was upset. To put it mildly. I didn't know whether he was winding me up or whether it was true, either way, it was a pretty cruel thing to say. Paul started to move across the room, with Will hanging on steadfastly, refusing to let go of him. Suddenly, Paul's leg shot straight up into the air like a member of the SS doing the goosestep. Before I knew what was happening, Will had spun off and landed on the floor. Paul grabbed him, and started to shake him relentlessly by the small shoulders. Just as he had become accustomed to violently shaking me when he was angry. Till my teeth chattered. Till my neck was so sore I couldn't move. Now he was kicking him.

William had been playing cricket at school, and had already been smacked in the shins with a bat by one of the boys. "Don't, Paul! Don't! Stop, please stop!!" I cried out hearing hysteria almost in my voice.

Paul looked up at me with menace in his cold blue eyes. "It's correctional behaviour!" he bellowed back at me. "I am William's father. I have a perfect right to do this. I am allowed to do it! It is necessary! How else is he ever going to learn?"

I managed to get hold of Will's little hand. Tiny fingers clasped mine. "Learn what?" I sobbed, the tears streaming down my face. "Learn to be a bully? Learn to pick on the weak and the innocent and be violent towards them – like you do?"

Gathering up Will into my arms I almost ran upstairs with him. To the safety of his blue and white bedroom. He was crying too. Afraid. Confused. Terrified. I put my arm around him. Tried to comfort him. Examining the livid purple bruise and broken skin on his smooth soft little shins. "Daddy didn't mean it," I told him. I didn't know what to do. I phoned my mother. I didn't phone the Police. I didn't want to get Paul into trouble. Surely this would never ever happen again? But I was also sure that this wild and out-of-control streak that ran through Paul's personality like an incurable virus had to be addressed, dealt with – but how?

My mother was frantic. She rang Paul's father, who flatly refused to get involved. "My son is a bastard," he told me with no expression in his voice. "But you must learn something from all this too, Lesley." His voice was coming down the phone from far away. "Never ever go up against Paul. You should have realised by now that you always have to let him have his own way – always! It's always been like that. Even when he was a boy. We took him to see a psychologist. He'll pull the carpet out from under yours and William's feet when it suits him to do so," he said bluntly.

"No – Paul would never do that," I replied.

"Well, it's up to you, Lesley. I'm merely warning you – for your own sake. It will be worse for you and William. You will end up bringing trouble on yourself if you don't make any attempt to sort yourself out!" I couldn't believe what I was hearing. It should have been Paul who needed sorting out – not me. Was I some kind of worthless being, a possession to be booted about, ordered about, battered about along with my son, and just be expected to be grateful because my bills were being paid? Some kind of nightmare I was living. My despair was only beginning to make itself transparently apparent. I had a long way to go yet before I would find the courage to speak out. Like so many women of my generation I had been brought up to believe that a certain amount of 'female compliance' was necessary when dealing with men. Acquiescence almost. Turning a blind eye. But fortunately for me, I had a dad who treated me like a person – not just a girl. Certainly, he had never treated me as a second-class citizen. Paul, it seemed, had no respect for women, or children. Or anyone. And I'm not sure he even respected himself. When we had been dating he had been charming. Now when we dined in restaurants he didn't open the door for me as Ainsley had done. Instead, he marched straight ahead. When waiters hovered offering a chair for me, menus discreetly tucked under their arms, Paul would immediately sit down in it, leaving me and the embarrassed waiter staring at each other. My fairy tale was going all wrong. This wasn't the script I had been given.

The social faux pas and clumsiness I could overlook. The physical attacks, verbal violence and abuse, I couldn't. It was eating right into me, to the very core of an apple that was going mouldy. I didn't recognise my life or myself any longer.

I made Will some Cadbury's Hot Chocolate with warm milk. And read him to sleep. His favourite book. *Treasure Island*.

***

I left William with my mum when we went to Ainsley's 40th Birthday Party. Held in an Italian wine bar, in a very discreet but trendy part of the West End. There was a terrace out the back, festooned with twinkling white lights that draped like a necklace and orange paper lanterns that fluttered in the breeze. Food had been generously supplied by a friend of Ainsley's who ran a Portuguese restaurant near Charlotte Street. Lots of seafood, shellfish, and intriguing salads with unexpected dressings.

Chunks of thick white French bread. Bowls of fresh out of season Strawberries. Small pastries smothered in syrup like baklava. "This is lovely, Ainsley!" I told him, smiling up from my red Venetian glass of finest Moet et Chandon with frosted rim.

"Yes." He smiled at me. "It is…" he murmured. And for just an instant the way he was looking at me, made me wonder if what he was really thinking was – "Yes – she is."

My party frock was a black chiffon confection with shoestring straps. I had bought a ravishing pair of very, very high heels. Black patent leather, with diamante bows. For once my way-ward fringe had stayed put, and so, amazingly, had the Carmen curls I'd carefully coaxed into place just before leaving home. The main man, Ainsley, of course, looked great. Also wearing black. Gleaming satin shirt, open neck with a cinnamon and turquoise coloured beaded choker that looked suspiciously like it could have, and in fact, probably would have, been carved by an elderly and wise Aborigine.

Black Levi's wrapped themselves around his tiny behind. Taking me by the elbows, ever so gently, I could feel Ainsley steering me slowly through the noisy crowd onto the moonlit terrace. "So how are you then?" he asked. Looking straight at me. Directly in the eyes, as he always did.

"Great!" I heard myself reply.

"And the Cruise, and everything else?"

"Yep! No problem. Paul enjoyed it and he's back home and things are fine! Absolutely fine!" I lied to my best friend. Longing to tell him the truth. How could I?

"Good!" He smiled. "See, I told you everything would work out alright in the end, didn't I? You were worried about noth-ing!" He put his empty lager glass back down onto the red and white checked tablecloth. "I'm off for a top up!" He weaved his way back to the bar. I had to admit, I had never really seen Ainsley drunk before. It was a very funny sight. He was singing mostly old Beatles songs, and a little bit of Elvis. Out of tune. But loudly. He had his arms around half a dozen people at the same time. And he laughed. A lot. But he never ever got vulgar or offensive. He did get hold of an old wooden acoustic guitar though and played that with the same passionate tone-deaf intensity he lavished on his singing.

Ainsley may have hit the big four-O but he didn't have a nice big birthday cake to help him to celebrate the fact. I had baked Paul's and iced it in swirling shades of cream and chocolate. "Emma doesn't do cakes!" he grinned at me, and then put his hand up to his mouth, giggling like a little boy. A little lop-sided but daftly endearing. Emma did not comment on the cake. Or the lack of one. No excuses. She never made excuses or took the blame – not for anything. In fact her attitude was simply, why should anyone expect a cake from her of all people on their birthday anyway? She looked very official and serious, amongst the cavorting chaos of the increasingly inebriated and dishevelled party guests all around her. In deep green velvet. Black hair, short, shiny and immaculate. No hair would dare to stray out of place! Not on Emma's perfectly groomed head. Emma was the sort of woman you would never catch out without her make-up or in curlers, or in a tracksuit when she should be wearing a suit. She simply never allowed herself to be seen to get it wrong. Bad hair days just didn't happen to women like Emma. Or runny mascara. Or real life, really. She had been born into a quite wealthy family. All her life she had wanted for nothing. She had been to private school with loads of girls with double-barrelled surnames, always had her own horse and had a Harrods and Harvey Nichols special credit card. Ainsley quite obviously adored her. Would strive to keep her happy and give her anything and everything she desired. Even if he worked himself to a standstill in order to keep up with her relentless demands.

"Nice to see you, Emma!" I trilled. I'd lost count of the number of glasses of bubbly I'd consumed, by now. It didn't usually take more than a couple though! Then, as Ainsley had, I giggled, just a bit. It was enough to make Emma's face drift off into one of her vague kind of smiles. As if I wasn't really there at all. Managing to look at me, but straight through me and past me all at the same time.

"Hello Duncan!" she called, turning away swiftly and burying herself in conversation with a cameraman I'd once dated.

Paul was impatiently looking at his watch for the umpteenth time. "We should have gone ages ago – I'm bored stiff. Let's go!" he demanded.

"We're off now," I told Ainsley. A little reluctantly.

"Oh." He turned. Hugged me tight. Embarrassed suddenly as I felt Paul come up behind us. Reaching out past me Ainsley grabbed hold of Paul's hand. Shook it firmly. "Bye, Paul – thanks for coming! Thanks for bringing Lesley along!" Then he gently brushed the back of his hand against my cheek, for just a second or two. Took my hand, lifted it to his lips – and kissed it, contemplating me through his luxuriant floppy fringe. "Bye precious – see you soon!"

Emma appeared out of nowhere. Like the jolly green giant, the singing princess in the *Lord of the Dance* in her long emerald dress. "They've run out of strawberries – we need some more! Now!" she instructed Ainsley, ignoring me completely.

"OK, OK!" Ainsley let go of my hand, looking about six years old, as if he'd been caught stealing lollypops. "I'll go and pick some more! 'Strawberry Fields – forever!" he was singing at the top of his voice. "Strawberry Fields – for-e-ver!" I could still hear his merry off-key notes ringing through the air like jesters as he disappeared out of sight. Into the crowd. Vanished.

Leaving behind him an unmistakable Armani haze.

In the car, Paul was already cross. "What was all that about with Ainsley?" he yelled.

"What?" I replied, a little slurred perhaps. But I did reply.

"I saw you go out onto the terrace together. What did you tell him?"

"Nothing," I replied. Truthfully.

"What were you talking about then? The pair of you must have been talking about something. If not – what were you doing?" And so he went on, and on. Twenty thousand questions as usual, until I ended up being forced into telling him every tiny detail of the innocent conversation with Ainsley. He still didn't appear to believe me. "Why did he put his arms around you?" he demanded.

"He was drunk! It was nothing!" I laughed.

"I don't see anything remotely funny about it! You let him do it!"

I just wanted Paul to be quiet so I could sit and savour the memories of the evening. "He was just being friendly – that's all!" I said. Trying to find a calming CD to stick into the player to drown out Paul's rage.

"You're not to have anything more to do with him, Lesley. Nothing at all. Do you understand?" Yes. I understood alright. Then Paul put his foot down firmly on the accelerator. Pressing it hard down to the floor. Speeding home down the fast lane of the Ml I closed my eyes pretending to be asleep. Hearing the music softly singing.

Feeling sick with fear. It wouldn't be the last time I would suffer that sensation as a direct result of Paul's actions.

Chapter Seventeen

We didn't see eye to eye on absolutely everything, but one thing that Ainsley and I were in total agreement with was our attitude to education. And only the best that was available was good enough for our offspring. So when Ainsley and Emma despatched 12 year old Emily to a very smart and well-established private school for girls on the rolling cliffs of the South Downs, Paul and I decided that the best bet for William would be the local private boys' school. It didn't just cater for the needs of the super-bright, intellectually gifted 'exam-orientated', life in the fast lane out and out winners, it also was happy to take under its caring wing the normal boys who seemed to flourish in the Catholic philosophy of a school which believed emphatically in educating what they referred to as 'the whole person'. I was not a Catholic. But I was a believer and felt very comfortable knowing that William was getting the best academic training from caring teachers and a nurturing community which believed that spiritual guidance and support was every bit as important as exam results.

William was happy at school, at last. His reading, writing and maths ability was steadily brought up to comprehensible levels which the local Primary School had done their level best to destroy. Right from the very moment, he set foot inside his new school – St Matthews – William was absolutely determined to work hard and pay back Paul for the money he had invested in his education. Superman could not have made a more superhuman effort. And the rewards were plentiful. High grades, school commendations and prizes. And good exam results on top of all that. William, it seemed, was a 'model pupil' who everyone responded to and respected, teachers and boys alike. Whenever

I went to a parent's evening we were told what a pleasure it was to teach him. I couldn't have been more delighted with Will, who seemed to have inherited the easy-going sense of humour and good nature of his grandfather – my dad.

Since Paul's outburst in the car, I hadn't seen or heard from Ainsley. Or Lucy. Whenever she did phone to make arrangements to go to the local multiplex cinema or her health club, Paul would immediately find a reason to stop me from going with her. Usually right at the very last minute when it was simply too late to get someone else to keep an eye on William. So many times the phone would ring, at about 5.30 in the evening. "Lesley, it's Paul. I'm working late tonight. I have clients to see. Appointments." Protestation fell on ears that remained steadfastly unhearing. "But I've made arrangements. It's my job, Lesley. May I remind you that it is my money that is paying the bills?!" Oh, how I was learning to hate that phrase.

So I would ring Lucy. Apologetic. "Sorry, Lucy. I'm sorry it's such short notice. I can't come after all…" I would stammer half-heartedly. Regret in her voice seemed to turn increasingly to mistrust, I felt. Eventually. Was I just putting her off on purpose because I didn't want to see her any longer? In the end, I just stopped making arrangements to see her – or anyone else for that matter. It was simpler. Saved me the embarrassment and upset of continually letting them down. No one felt disappointed then after all – did they?

I was becoming increasingly isolated. Lonely and desperately in need of something to return to me some sense of self-worth. I picked up the Design folders I'd discarded in a heap behind the desk in my work room. The ones I'd once worked on with such enthusiasm and spirit. As I sipped a glass of Highland Spring mineral water from a fat tumbler, I realised with a tinge of surprise that my drawings, my sense of colour and my perspective work – were really not too bad! It wasn't excitement that seeped right through to the tips of my fingers. But something close! "Always use your talents!" my dad had repeatedly urged me. "You've been given a brain! Use it!" But I hadn't been using it lately had I? Not at all. I'd let it lay about being useless. My dubious talents were overlooked and passed by. Forgotten. I felt a stab of remorse. I felt I'd let him down. And me.

Not long after that I saw the advertisement in a little local design studio. A and B Design. "Part-time staff wanted. No experience necessary. Please enquire within." I went into the Italian coffee shop on the corner. Sat down by the ornamental fountain with the serene lady holding a pitcher with water tumbling from it in a slow, steady rush. I knew if I went home and thought about it for much longer I would change my mind. Or Paul would manage to change it for me!

The cappuccino was hot and piquant and burned my tongue. It perked up my spirits. Gave my energy level a much-needed adrenaline boost. I walked back down the street, smoothing the creases in my trousers as I determinedly approached the shining newly painted glossy red door. "Enquire Within". There were a list of names, and a round white doorbell. I pressed it. "Yes?" A friendly female voice over the intercom. Audible through a metal grille above the bell.

I cleared my throat. "Em – hello. I've come about the vacancy." Before I could finish what I was saying there was a loud buzzing. A 'click'.

"Come up!" she said brightly. Gingerly I pushed open the door. Felt my heart start to beat a little fast. Then walked smartly upstairs.

Alana Bentley's face was round with large tortoiseshell framed glasses halfway down her nose, a bright pink pashmina draped casually across her shoulder and the warmest smile I'd encountered in a very long time. "Hello!" She started to get up from her chair. Reaching out to shake my hand. Hers was chubby, with a ring on every finger – and her thumb. "Sit down. Coffee? Tea?"

"No thanks, I've just had one," I replied, sliding back onto a cream leather swivel chair. Alana got up. Walked over to the kettle. Switched it on and filled a yellow cup with instant coffee. Her dress was cream wool, calf length. With suede boots.

"So you're interested in the job?" she asked in a matter-of-fact way.

"Yes," I mumbled. "I have to tell you, I haven't been working for a long time. I've been bringing up my son, and…" I stopped talking at rapid speed. I felt foolish. What was I doing here anyway? Wasting her time?

But Alana wasn't looking vaguely into space as if I was wasting her time. Not at all. She was looking straight at me with a warm smile. Stirring her coffee. "Do you have a portfolio?" she asked.

Stupid – stupid me! Of course, I did! But not here! Not now! I screwed up my face a bit. "At home…" I replied in a feeble-sounding voice. She must have thought I was some kind of dipstick.

"When can you let me see it?" I was startled by her response. I couldn't believe she hadn't immediately shown me the door. Thrown me back out onto the sunny pavement, for wasting her time.

But Alana was still smiling. Like a long lost benevolent and kind auntie. I more or less bounced my way back home on a sort of 'high'. I didn't know what exactly she would want me to do at A and B Designs. And it really did not seem to matter. I only knew that when Alana had calmly asked me, "Can you drop it round tomorrow?" I was instantly alive, alert, and more in tune than I had been for a long, long time. She was actually prepared to look at my work! My work! Well, even that was a start!

That night I sat down and sifted all the rubbish stuff from the pile of papers in my brown leather portfolio. Carefully placing the coloured drawings and designs in order of impressiveness. Or so I thought! Then I re-arranged them. Then I did it again. Then I went to bed. Paul was still out.

The next morning I got up early. Showered all over in aromatherapy 'Lemon Zester' which was supposed to bring you 'vibrantly alive at the beginning of the day'. I dressed carefully in camel chinos and short chocolate-coloured wool jacket. It was a bright early spring morning. One of those mornings where you feel anything is possible. The first shift of the seasons and the smell of incoming warmth on the breezes. Eager daffodils were forming a tidal wave of sumptuous dazzling yellow. For the first time in a very long time, I felt optimistic. No, it was more than that. I actually felt happy!

Alana looked enthusiastically at my pictures. She liked my work. Resting her fingers on the edge of her oversized glasses she held my precious papers in her left hand. She stood casually flicking through them, for what seemed like forever. Then she slowly looked up. "I really like your style, Lesley. You have a special talent it would appear! You're what I would describe as a 'natural designer'!"

Wow. Compliments. I couldn't believe it. I grabbed for them like a starving rabbit fortuitously coming across a bunch of hidden carrots. "I'd like to take you on, Lesley. Are you interested in the job?" O – sweet music! "But, I have to tell you, it's my own business and I've not been up and running for very long. I was made redundant recently, from a large design company in London, after twenty years of service, so at the moment I am still in the early stages of getting – and keeping – clients! But we are moving forward – slowly! I need help desperately because as the work's started to come in I realise I cannot manage all by myself. But the bottom line is – I can't afford to pay much." She gave me the figure. She was right – it wasn't much! But I didn't care. "And part-time would be perfect if that's alright with you because – well, to be honest, it won't cost me so much!" She laughed. Honest and down to earth, I liked her enormously already.

"I'll take it! I mean – I'd like to do it – if you want me!" I could feel myself grinning. Feeling absurdly and ridiculously pleased and chuffed with a promised salary that wasn't even close to what I'd been earning in television all those years ago, never mind what that rate with its annual Union increases, incremental payments and London Weighting Allowance would amount to now!

"When can you start?"

"When do you need me?"

"Now!"

"I'll put the kettle on!" I replied cheerfully, taking off my jacket and flinging it loosely over the back of the swivel chair.

Naturally, there were people I just had to tell. As soon as I could. Bubbling over like a bottle of fizzy lemonade, I phoned Paul during what I assumed would be his lunchtime. "I've something to tell you – tonight!" I said. I couldn't wait to tell him. I thought he would be so proud of me.

"What do you need a job for? And what on earth makes you think you'll be any good at it? After all, you've never ever done this type of thing before have you, Lesley? You'll fall flat on your face. I can see it happening I'll give it a couple of weeks – at best! Then this Lana person will realise how clueless and hopeless you are A couple of weeks!" Then he flounced off to pour himself a large gin and tonic.

I phoned my mum. "What about Will?"

"It's part-time!" I wailed back at her. I could hear it, feel it, right down the phone. The wavering. Questioning. The guilt thing.

"Well, I suppose if you want to try it. It's up to you. If you need me to sit with Wiliam and look after him, you must say and I will come over." I assured her it was not necessary. "Well, as I said, it's up to you, Lesley. You do what you feel you want to do," she conceded.

"Only I don't do I, Mum?!" I wanted almost to scream back at her in exasperation. The one thing I hadn't done over the years was what I really wanted to do! Continually putting everyone else's feelings and well-being before mine. Everyone else's lives first. Folding up my precious dreams and putting them away like my special satin underwear edged with pretty French lace. On the back burner. Twirling up the chimney like a puff of disappearing smoke.

I stared at the Nokia mobile sitting in the palm of my hand. 'Phone Numbers – Search?' was the illuminated request shining up at me from the little grey screen. So I let it search. 'Ainsley Logan' – in black letters. I pressed his number – quickly before I had a chance to change my mind. "Hello?" his voice sounded unusually distant and far away. Distracted almost.

"Ainsley? It's Lesley!"

"Hello, Lesley." Silence. "How are you?"

"Fine thanks! Ainsley, do you fancy having lunch sometime – or a drink?" At this stage, I felt bold even suggesting it, but what the heck? I was a fledgling little duck emerging, and with a bit of luck I would turn out to be a very fine swan! "I've got something exciting to tell you! Some good news!" There! If I said it out loud then Ainsley would come. Curiosity would almost certainly get the better of him. He wouldn't be able to resist that

"Alright – Wednesday – is that OK?" he still sounded a bit vacant. Hesitant almost. I'd done the wrong thing. Contacting him. What was I thinking? Maybe he just didn't want to meet me again after all. He was happily married, wasn't he? So for all intents and purposes was I. But it was only lunch.

"Yes," I replied. I couldn't really backtrack now, I'd already asked him to come.

His voice came back through the mobile. "I'll meet you at Zizzi's down by the river." Another pause. "I've got some news to tell you too," was all he said. And I got up to shut the French windows as the chill evening breeze blew across the room, cooling my burning cheeks.

Chapter Eighteen

I got to Zizzi's ahead of time. Waiting for Ainsley in the car park, as I always did. Still not comfortable or confident enough to walk into a pub or restaurant all by myself. Why? Heaven only knows, but I felt more relaxed walking in with Ainsley by my side. His black 4 x 4 drew up sharply on the shingle, spitting small stones here and there. He looked unusually serious for just a moment. Then he smiled and tucked my arm in his. "Come on then, let's get a table. Let's open a bottle or two of wine. And let's tell each other our secrets!"

I hadn't ever let myself believe that I could share my deepest secrets with anyone. Not even Ainsley. But sometimes we surprise ourselves. Ainsley ordered a bottle of Pinot Grigio. Asking for, "Two large glasses – please!" We tucked ourselves into a cosy window seat, beside a roaring log fire, which glowed amber and warmed our chilled faces. We selected food from the special menu. It was one of my days off from Alana's so I had no need to hurry back, for which I was thankful. Ainsley seemed to be in no particular hurry either. But I noticed he was drinking more speedily than usual. "Another bottle, please!" he asked the waitress, who scurried off to the bar to fetch one. Leaning across the oak table with his elbows on it, he gazed straight into my eyes. I told him all about the job. He seemed absolutely delighted.

"Best thing you've done for a long time, Lesley! It's about time you started doing something for you for a change. For once in your life – follow your dreams!" Suddenly I didn't feel guilty anymore. I felt that what I was doing was being true to myself – at long last. And it just felt right. Ainsley had single-handedly given me permission to feel that way! He picked up the bottle, carefully wiping the side of it where the condensation had gathered and poured out more wine. I was feeling warm. I felt safe. "Are you happy, Lesley?"

He'd asked me that question once before. Such a long, long time ago it seemed now. In another lifetime. And I had told him, "Yes of course!" Why then didn't I do that now? Why couldn't I do that now?

"Sometimes what you see isn't real," I heard myself reply quietly. "Sometimes what you want to believe is true – isn't." I was talking rubbish, wasn't I? Or being very profound. Either way, the fine white wine was having a strange effect on my senses and my in-built ability to keep secrets. Hold on tight to them. That's when he reached out across the table and took hold of my hands which were clasped together tightly. That's when he stroked them tenderly with his sensitive fingers That's when he pulled me across the wooden table towards him – and kissed me. That's when I started to cry. That's when I knew I couldn't lie to him any longer. That's when I began to tell him the truth, the whole truth... and nothing but.

Ainsley was blessed with a very mobile face. Every expression was almost exaggerated as if sometimes it was made of rubber. It had always been like that. But as I started to confess to him the reality behind the closely guarded façade of my marriage to Paul, I could see so many emotions flicker across his features, linger, and die back. Anger, frustration, sadness, incomprehension, compassion, and finally – shock. "I can't believe what you're telling me, Lesley," he said slowly. "I just can't believe Paul could treat you and Will like this. I had no idea. If only – twenty years ago..." He stopped speaking for a moment. "I'm going to the Gents, Les. Get some more wine." He stuffed twenty pounds into my hand.

I felt strange. Lightheaded, liberated as if someone had just removed a huge bundle of rags from a sack of steel on my back. Yet instantly guilty for betraying Paul's trust. What trust? I couldn't explain it. I had never told anyone deeply personal secrets before. I didn't know whether I had done wrong.

Maybe Ainsley wouldn't want to know me anymore. I felt dirty. Ashamed to confess what my life truly was. I wasn't the person Ainsley thought I was. I had changed all that in the split second I chose to be honest with him. I felt as if I was being somehow unfaithful to Paul. Yet I realised that I had needed so desperately to confide in someone I could depend upon to protect my sensitive suffocating privacy.

Maybe I needed to prove to myself that other men didn't behave that way. If he had turned round to me and said well – it was a bloke thing and some of them did those things, perhaps I would have felt differently. Only he didn't say that. He didn't say that at all.

Ainsley came back, smiling ruefully. "I don't know what to say to you, Lesley," he said as he slid back across into his bench seat.

"There's nothing you can say," I told him, sipping some wine, looking at the table. I felt his hand beneath my chin, tilting it up so that I could look at him properly.

"Why on earth do you stay with a man like him, Lesley? How can you let him do it to you both? I just don't understand you!" I felt myself begin to flush, red creeping like a stain across the open neck of my cream V-neck sweater. I put my hand up to cover it. My wedding ring glinted gold in the gleam from the fire.

"We're married, Ainsley," I heard myself say. Hollow. Shallow. Lame. Unconvincing. "He's been good to us too! He's not like it all the time – when he's nice – he's wonderful!" And so I carried on, defending the indefensible, the years we'd shared. Defending my abusive husband to my best friend to who I had just poured out my heart to. As if Paul were actually sitting in the corner of the pub and could hear us As if!

But I was also desperate to hold on tight to all the joy we had shared. Not the pain. Not the tragedy. "Good!" Ainsley half-scoffed. Pulling back from the table. Instantly letting go of my hands. Dropping them like loose unwanted pebbles back onto the beach. Could it actually be disgust that was creeping over his handsome, usually magnanimous face? "I could never hurt anyone. Not anyone – especially not Emma or Emily! How can you let him demean you so? How can you let him get away with being so bloody, chillingly cruel?" So suddenly it seemed it was all my fault? Not Paul's at all from what Ainsley was saying to me. OK, so he had a perfect wife and a perfect life. Well lucky old him. Was it just the effect of too much white wine that was making Ainsley so uncharacteristically belligerent? I guess looking back, he was just being dependably forthright. But I couldn't see it that way then. I was too much on the defensive to realise that.

"I didn't realise you disliked me so much!" I said.

He pulled a face. "I don't dislike you, Lesley. Heaven knows you of all people should realise that. I wouldn't be sitting with you now, after all these years, if I disliked you, now would I? But I do dislike what Paul has managed to do to you. He's completely destroyed the person you once were. What's happened to the happy, confident young woman from your television days? So in control of her life – so attractive?"

I felt awful. "Attractive?" I mumbled back.

There was a short burst of laughter. "Well, in a weird sort of way! You know what they've always said about beauty being in the eye of the beholder and all that!"

I swiped him with a maroon paper serviette. "I've always been able to talk to you, Ainsley," I told him. "About absolutely everything. You're like my best girlfriend."

That's when he got really exasperated. Sighed. A long deep humming sound. "But I'm not am I, Lesley?"

"What?"

"Your girlfriend! I'm not anybody's girlfriend. I'm a man for God's sake! Maybe you should start treating me like one for a change!"

I was taken aback. Now it was my turn to be speechless. "But, I thought... I thought you didn't..."

"You thought! You thought! But you never ever bothered to ask me what I thought, did you?" His face was turning a deep shade of pink under his pale winter tan. He almost looked angry. Well, as angry as Ainsley ever allowed himself to get. I didn't want to fall out with Ainsley. Not now. Not ever.

I called the waitress over and asked for a large cafetiere of fresh black coffee, with pots of Devon cream for me to tip into mine. "You never told me your news," I said softly.

"News?"

"Yes, on the phone you said that you had some news of your own that you wanted to tell me."

The lighthearted chin wag I had thought we would have about my new job had steered itself dramatically off course, into deep and uncharted waters. I needed to steer it back firmly into calm, safe and familiar seas. Not only that the people at the next table had been looking over at us with increasingly enquiring eyes. I didn't want them listening to any more intimate details of my personal life. Or Ainsley's for that matter. Ainsley stirred his coffee thoughtfully, looking down into the white china cup filled with chestnut-coloured liquid as if it were some kind of mirror. He didn't even look up when he dropped his unexploded bomb right into the middle of our revealing conversation. I could just about make out his deep brown eyes beneath the familiar fringe flopping down over them, partly concealing, partly revealing. Partly.

"Emma and I are splitting up. She's asked me for a divorce. And I've agreed." His words rained down into the air like breaking glass.

"What?" I could hardly take in what he had just said. He adored Emma. And I could simply not believe that any woman in the world would carelessly toss away a man like Ainsley.

"She thinks I've been having a fling," he said in a flat, resigned voice.

"Fling?"

"Yes, with a guy from work called Chris Toomey! He's a graphic designer."

"Is he gay?" I asked.

"He is, yes," replied Ainsley.

"And – you?" There it was at last. The question. Out in the open. A question I had kept in the back of my mind all these years. Resisted asking him. And now I had. Outright. I was almost afraid now to hear his answer. But I had to know. He smiled. Then he began to shake his head. Very slowly. Looked up.

"Apparently not, Lesley, so it would seem! I've had my moments. I've had friends of both sexes, male and female. Very deep relationships. But I have to tell you, Lesley, sincerely – it's not men who continue to make my pulse race!" I was relieved. Also, stunned. For once, unusually for me, I didn't know what to say to him. So I just sat there, probably looking as stupid as I felt. "I just couldn't take Emma's controlling ways any longer. Her continued distrust of me. Her demands. She's even jealous of you!" He swigged back his coffee and gave an ironic half-stifled laugh. "Imagine that!" Yes – how absolutely ridiculous, I thought. Who in their right mind could ever be jealous of me?

"I work so hard, but it's never enough for her. She wants more and more. It's just stifling me, Lesley. I feel like I can't breathe anymore." He smiled and pulled a comical face. "No good for the old creative streak – you know! I need to be free now. Emma has decided to move to the South Coast to be near to Emily, till she finishes school."

I hardly dared ask the next question. But I did. "And what about you? Do you have someone else? Do you have somewhere to go?"

He paused for a moment, drained his coffee cup and firmly replaced it on its saucer. "Yes, I do. I wasn't quite sure what to do but now I've had this long conversation with you this afternoon, it's helped me to make up my mind once and for all. I'm quitting my job, Lesley. No one gets to live their life backwards, do they? Look ahead – that's where the future lies – you told me that once!" Did I? He'd remembered. "I'm going to Australia – for good!"

It was surprisingly lonely after Ainsley left. I sent him a 'Good Luck – Bon Voyage' card. I thought about him every second until his plane took off from Heathrow to Sydney. But I didn't go and wave him goodbye. Or see him for a farewell drink. I just couldn't do that.

Alana and her little design business became my lifeline. Work saving me once more, as I poured my energy into running errands, searching for reference books, swatches of curious or obsolete special fabrics, bits of rare imaginatively grained wood and loads of pots of brightly rainbow coloured paints and handmade squirrel hair brushes. I just immersed myself in fantasy, for a while at least. Alana was a comforting person to be around. No airs or graces, she spoke with a slight north London accent. She always looked quirkily original, fashionable yet with a classic twist.

She tried awfully hard not to conform, by flirting with brilliant flashes and clashes of brilliant chunky jewellery in pewter and gold, surprising splashes of topaz beads or dangling earrings with intricate lacy silver filigree, with artificial cherries or tiny bananas stuck on the tips. Scarves, pashminas and cashmere wraps in every colour of the spectrum were Alana's fashion signature. I never came across another woman who could invent so many clever ways of tying, draping or pleating a small piece of fabric.

I had told Ainsley I loved Paul. And I truly believed that I still did. He was the father of my only son. We had endured so much together. Shared so many things. Will thought the world of him. But there was something I hadn't confessed to Ainsley, or even admitted fully to myself up until now. I desperately wanted Paul to love me again, as I knew he once had.

"Let's go to the pictures, and maybe have a meal afterwards – my treat!" I suggested. We were all sitting in the conservatory, eating strips of tagliatelle smothered in creamy smoked salmon and courgette sauce for supper. I'd put chunky vanilla scented candles in the middle of the table and lit the lamps in the garden, dusk was wrapping it in warm russet and gold twilight. A full moon was hovering about in the distance, ready to land, like some kind of spaceship.

"To see what?" asked Paul.

"Well – I'd like to see that new Tom Cruise film!" chirped Will.

"OK. We'll go on Saturday. I'll book it! And how about having a meal in Chiquitas, the Mexican restaurant, afterwards?" Paul and Will adored hot and spicy food from south of the border.

"Alright," agreed Paul.

We got ready together, sharing the bathroom and the dressing table mirror. Went to the pictures, sitting surrounded on all sides by all the other Saturday night treat everyday families. We ate popcorn from wide red and white tubs. Drank Coca-Cola.

Chiquitas was packed. I was glad that I'd prebooked. We were led to the table in a booth beneath a vibrantly coloured painting of cacti and bandits. Adorning the wall was a huge Mexican hat with gold tassels and a blue and brown poncho. Golden lanterns hung provocatively from the ceiling. And the edges of the booths. The ambience reminded me so much of carefree and silly days in Disneyland when Will was small. When we all wore dopey hats and stood watching in enchantment as the electrical parade passed by with Snow White and the seven dwarfs waving to us and Aladdin and Cinderella herself in a sparkling silver coach. It felt right. Safe. "This is how life should be," I convinced myself. "We are a happy little family. And nothing. No one is going to come between us and spoil it. Not ever. We've too much to lose. I won't let that happen."

Will and Paul were laughing their heads off at some shared daft joke, which only teenage boys and grown-up men could fully appreciate the not-so-subtle subtext of. Will playfully nudged Paul on the arm, and he tousled back. They both roared with laughter. Will took another slug of non-alcoholic Pina Colada from a massive glass filled with more plastic toys than a Christmas stocking. Then he threw his arms around Paul, hugging him tight. We walked back across the car park arm in arm. Still laughing. I've done the right thing, I told myself. Blow Ainsley and his stupid opinions. What did he know about anything anyway? What did he care? His own marriage was a mess. His life in disarray. He'd obviously found someone else, even though he hadn't told me their name – on the other side of the world. Ainsley had chosen to fly far away to lose track of reality. Erase it. I wasn't like that. I lived in the real world these days. Not a world of day dreams. This was how real life should be, forever – Paul, Will and me – just the three of us. A family.

Chapter Nineteen

Winter set in early again that year. I remember. Because that's when Denise joined Paul's company. And when the first sparkling white frosts started to stick to the pavements covered in black ice, Denise donned her fake fur jacket, the colour of caterpillar fungus and smelling of dead rat and marched into Paul's office demanding that he provide her with a brand new state of the art computer, increase her salary, buy her a luxurious brand new red leather chair. A woman like her deserved no less, she told him firmly. And for the very first time in his life – Paul did as he was told.

***

"You know, I think the decoration in my bedroom is getting a bit juvenile for me now don't you?" said Will. His mates had just been round for an impromptu 'jam' session with guitars and a drum kit made of cushions. Even I had to agree that the rainbow-covered wallpaper and matching duvet that looked just dinky when he was six, looked plain idiotic when his friends were armed with Yamaha's latest line in electrics and brand new Playstation games to put on his TV. The compact pine wardrobes that had uncomplainingly held armloads of little boys' outfits just couldn't cope any longer with suits, rugby shirts, jogging top and bottoms. Not to mention working *Star Trek* models, cars and a mountain of chart CD's that grew daily.

Paul and I agreed to let him re-design his bedroom. In shades of deepest blue, silver and wood. Will had always had surprisingly good taste even when he was little so I had no problem letting him loose to choose what he wanted for his own 'space'. I knew it would look fantastic. We went to the Ideal Home Exhibition at Earls Court, trailing round crowded stands and show houses with dozens of catalogues. Getting ideas, grabbing exotic snacks and having lunch in the first-floor restaurant.

We went to every fitted wardrobe specialist retailer we could see. And then we found Ikea. And we knew we had found Utopia!

William's wardrobes were made of wood with blue bits and smokey glass with concealed lights. As far as he was concerned they were 'the business'. He was seriously pleased. The new light fitting swinging down from the ceiling like something that had escaped from Cirque du Soleil on silver chains in cobalt blue glass completed the fascinating structure. "Oh wow! This is great, Mum! Now I can ask the lads back and it won't be embarrassing anymore! All my own things around me!" I was just glad that he was so happy. Glad we had started to do normal things once again. Glad we were so completely secure.

Paul had always enjoyed decorating our first homes. But since working with Allied Investments he seemed to be increasingly reluctant to pick up a paintbrush or do many of the little things he used to. I could understand if he was simply too tired or just didn't feel like doing it. After all, he was out most evenings now, till late. "Get someone else to do it!" I said. "A decorator, of some kind."

"No." Paul was insistent. "I'll do it when I have the time. You'll just have to wait. I won't have strangers tramping in and out of the house. Or cleaners either!" So I accepted that was Paul's attitude and I went along with it. To keep the peace. I was quite content to do all the cooking because I simply loved to cook, the garden was 'my territory' which I could fill up with terracotta pots spilling over with dazzling crimson geraniums in the summertime, daffodils in spring. Hanging baskets with pale pink petunias, impatiens and trailing lobelia. Clusters of peach verbena, richly scented sweet peas, and roses. So if it was a choice between housework or the garden there was simply no choice at all. It just wasn't number one on my list of things to do! There was always something more worthwhile to get involved with. Rather than drifting about with a duster glued to one hand and a vacuum cleaner stuck to the other, I would much rather create things. In the kitchen, in the garden, in my studio. Food was seductive and sensuous even. The feel of the fresh ingredients, the colours and the aromas. Flowers are blindingly beautiful. But an aerosol spray can filled with polish and a horrid artificial smell that was supposed to resemble 'spring bouquet'? Not even close!

Re-fitting Will's bedroom turned out to be a mammoth task. The wardrobes had to be carefully built-in and measured to the finest degree of accuracy. Eventually, Paul consented to allow a qualified electrician to install the complicated concealed lighting properly. Wallpapering, I had learned to leave to Paul. He always seemed to get so grumpy when he was doing it; I felt these days that I was constantly in his way. I provided tea, coffee, and sat cross-legged on the floor telling him how wonderful it was beginning to look, making encouraging 'ooh' and 'aah that's lovely!' noises.

"Eurgh!" I heard Paul cursing through the half-open door. I peeped round it.

"What?" He was pulling off a large piece of blue paper with glue all down one side. The wrong side. "Do you want any help?"

"No!" he bellowed back.

"Alright, listen, I'll do what my dad used to ask me to do at times like this shall I?" I reasoned with him. "I'll take Will out shopping for the day. Out of your hair. You'll be able to have some peace and quiet!"

We went off to the undercover shopping centre, raiding every sports shop and sitting in coffee shops. Spending precious time together, giggling at the antics of some of the passers-by as we sat people-watching and imagining how fantastic Will's new room would be when it was all finished.

Paul was still papering when we got back. I made fresh spaghetti bolognaise, which Paul loved. Then Will and I sat down and watched a Sylvester Stallone movie on TV. I couldn't hear any noise as I went upstairs with Will at about 10.30, with a glass of orange squash in one hand. Will's door was ajar. But no lights were on anywhere.

Paul had left the windows wide open. It was freezing cold. Our bedroom door was uncharacteristically firmly closed. Shut tight.

"Paul?" I called out to him. I opened the door. He was lying on the bed in his dressing gown and pyjamas. "What's happened?" I asked. That's when he started to bellow. Shouting, shouting at the top of his voice. I ran out of the room into Will's. It looked like a rubbish tip. Pots of paint discarded everywhere, bits of wallpaper strewn across the floor, a chaotic collection of Will's cars in boxes, clothes, CD's – all piled up in a massive heap on top of his bed. With a chair balancing precariously at the summit.

I went back to our room. "You can't leave it like that!" I protested. "You can't expect William to sleep in there!"

"Oh, yes he can!" Paul yelled back at me defiantly. "You've been out all day long and watching a film on TV tonight! While I've been by myself all day – slaving away for the pair of you! If he doesn't like it then he can damn well tidy it up – by himself!" Paul was almost screaming by now, his face contorted by an ugly coal-black thundercloud of sheer rage.

"But, Paul, Will didn't make all that mess – you did! He shouldn't be expected to clear it all up just so he can go to bed! And it's freezing cold in there – what's the matter with you?!"

"He's got to tidy it up! He's just being a lazy little bastard!" screeched Paul. The torrent of foul words fell out of his mouth like vomit. It shocked me. But not as much as what happened next. In an instant, Will had somehow ended up on the bed with Paul. And they were actually fighting. I still had the glass of orange squash in my right hand. I don't know what made me do it. I just had to make Paul stop. I tossed it up into the air, and straight over the top of Paul's upturned face. I just wanted him to stop. He did so, momentarily startled. Then he started shouting again, saying "You're a fucking bitch! You're a whore!" Menacing. Macabre.

"Stop it, Dad! Just stop being so foolish and grow up! Help me to tidy up my bedroom!" Will's teenage voice was wobbly, and not because his voice was breaking. Something else was breaking – with the awful and unexpected speed of a terrorist attack.

That's when Paul did it. I watched as Paul grabbed hold of William with his massive hands and placed them on either side of our son's small neck – and Will began to choke. And Paul would not stop shaking him. At first, my strangled screams couldn't even come out, and then I heard my terrified voice – "Stop!!!" I tried to pull them apart. Father and son. Then I grabbed hold of the telephone on the bedside table. "I'm calling the Police – you're a maniac!" I shouted.

As Paul let go of Will with one hand he pulled back the duvet with the other. Hidden beneath the bedclothes was a tiny black tape recorder. "Go ahead! There! I've recorded everything!" he exclaimed triumphantly.

"What?" I couldn't comprehend. Couldn't take it all in. "Everything! It's all on tape!"

"Why?"

"For evidence!" he replied with a self-satisfied smirk, like some kind of madman.

"Evidence of what – exactly?" I asked. This was bizarre. I was shaking with fear. The palms of my hands felt sweaty and cold. But I knew I had to appear to be calm and in control.

"To take to Court – the Police – anyone! To prove to everybody what you and William are really like! Everyone thinks you're both so nice! Well now they'll see what you're all about! And that it's all your fault!" I didn't know whether he was going round the bend or if I'd woken up in the middle of a terrible nightmare and any minute someone would click their fingers and I was still watching Sylvester Stallone on TV. Only I wasn't. Will was standing by the door – trembling.

I reached out and put my arm around him, holding him tight. I picked up the phone. "You have two choices, Paul. Either you go to the spare room now and leave us both alone, or I call the Police. I mean it!" Paul went to the spare room. Not another word was spoken.

***

On Sunday morning I got up early. Dressed hurriedly and left Paul lying in the Jacuzzi that we had purchased, what now seemed a lifetime ago, at the Ideal Home Exhibition in springtime. Will had arranged to play football with the local junior team. I wrapped a scarf around my head and pulled on old clothes. I must have looked a very sorry and dishevelled sight. But I just had to get outside into the fresh air. Which was cold. I didn't mind.

I left Will at the football pitch with the rest of the team and then walked slowly over to sit down on a wooden bench. On the edge of the lake, on the edge of the seat, with the words, 'In Loving memory of Elsie Warren – she loved this spot', engraved on a bronze plaque stuck to the top of it.

The ducks were ravenous and so were the white swans and greedy geese. They were out of luck though as they pecked around the tips of my frozen, empty fingers. Eventually they got fed up and waddled away, sticking their orange beaks haughtily skyward.

Water calms my thoughts and settles the emotions running through me. Maybe it's got something to do with being an astrological water sign. Rivers, the sea or a tranquil lake balance the senses in a way that other places cannot. The oneness with nature itself, I guess. And no matter how many times I went over and over it inside my head, only one thing was as clear as the crystal water in front of me. "This is not right! This just cannot go on any longer!" I felt so alone. My life was turning upside down from the happiness we should be feeling at decorating William's bedroom and making things nice and secure – a home for him. I wondered what Ainsley would say if he was perched on the other end of the bench next to me. But I knew already.

Anyway, it wasn't Ainsley's problem, was it? It wasn't his life that was wrecked. He had a life of his own to get on with, and problems of his own to sort out. I had to take control of my own life. Take responsibility. It was, after all, my husband, my son – me. And I couldn't keep papering over the cracks any longer to pretend, to hide the filthy mess beneath. I walked over to the kiosk by the empty tennis courts and bought myself a cardboard beaker of steaming hot chocolate, which was surprisingly good, warming and welcome. And as I sat in the fresh air I knew exactly what I had to do.

Chapter Twenty

Authorities, governing bodies and agencies, rules, regulations and red tape, like hospitals, scare me silly. I hate them. Nevertheless, realising as we all do that sometimes there is just no avoiding coming into contact with them, I took courage in both hands and made an appointment to see my family doctor. I sat in the pale green waiting room, still uncertain whether I was doing the right thing. I glanced down at the headlines on one of the woman's magazines carelessly discarded on the coffee table. "Are you guilty of having a secret affair?" screamed the headline. Well, chance would be a fine thing! I thought ruefully. I quickly looked away in case someone was watching me and actually thought I was having a secret affair! But I could not have done that to Paul, or to me or to William. I don't know why I inherited the deep-rooted 'loyal and faithful' genes, but they are as much a part of me as my green eyes, and just as unchangeable.

Dr McKenzie had big black-rimmed glasses which seemed to sit halfway down his face, and a Doctor's kind of wonky half-smile no doubt acquired after years of not being able to know whether the stranger stepping into your surgery was suffering from Athlete's Foot or terminal Cancer. "What can I do for you?" he asked.

"Well, it's not me really. It's my husband. I've come here about Paul. I don't know if he's showing the first signs of Alzheimer's Disease, or whatever," I blurted out the words and then began to sob. And suddenly I couldn't stop what had been bottled up inside of me from pouring out. Dr McKenzie didn't say anything. Just handed me a bunch of tissues from a box on top of his desk.

"Take your time," he said. And so I told him. Everything. Even admitted for the first time how Paul had hit me in the past, twisting my arm up behind my back and shoving me backwards so that it ended up being put in a sling on two separate occasions, giving me a karate-learned version of 'Chinese Burns' up my arm and into my elbow making a vicious pain shoot up and immobilise me so that I couldn't lift anything heavy for weeks afterwards. How he had violently shaken me.

Holding onto my shoulders till my teeth chattered and I thought my head would tumble from my neck. How the injuries I sustained were not black eyes – because they would have been visible to anyone who saw me and people would know what he was doing. The injuries Paul inflicted on me could only be seen by a doctor, physiotherapists and medical experts in confidence, in white-walled rooms in hospital wards dealing with bones and ribs and soft tissue injuries. There was no visible 'proof'. The verbal violence was an altogether different matter. How on earth could you prove that? I felt tired. And so guilty. Filled with remorse. Everything was so confused inside my head. I felt I had somehow betrayed Paul's confidence again by telling somebody else, even though he was my doctor, and here to help me. I felt I had betrayed my own confidence. That I shouldn't really be talking about such things. Not to anybody. I should be protecting Paul. Because when he behaved in a 'normal' way he was lovely. Fun loving. One of the good guys. Where had Paul gone?

Dr McKenzie spoke to me quietly, but firmly. "It sounds rather like Jekyll and Hyde," he said. "Only you just want the nice Dr Jekyll to be there all the time don't you?"

I agreed with him, nodding my head silently. "Yes." I asked if there was anything that Paul could take to control his violent temper. Tablets or something. Or maybe someone could have a quiet word with him. To steady him up. Make him realise what he was doing and the seriousness of his actions.

"I'll ask you a straightforward question," said Dr McKenzie, putting down his fountain pen. "Do you want a divorce?"

"No!" my reply was emphatic. "No! If I wanted that I wouldn't be sitting here with you now. I would have gone to a solicitor for legal advice. I want to save my marriage. All I want is a normal life." He was writing something on his notepad.

"William is under 16," he was saying. "So I have no choice but to report what has happened to him to Social Services and to William's school." I felt a wave of nausea sweep over me. I'd made totally the wrong decision in coming here. I'd well and truly screwed things up.

"You can't!" I cried. "Please, please don't do that. Paul will be absolutely furious, and so angry. He'll take it out on me and William and then things will never ever be right again. He will never forgive me for this."

Dr McKenzie put down his pen, looking at me levelly across his doctors' desk. "Lesley, do you realise that when Paul was gripping William round the throat and violently shaking him – if his fingers had slipped just a fraction, there is a point on the neck that if pressure is applied it would have killed William – instantly." I went stone cold. I agreed to take Will to my mother's home for a week so he would stay safe until things settled down. I agreed to see Dr McKenzie with Paul if he would agree to come and I very reluctantly agreed to be interviewed by Social Services.

Walking home two things kept echoing through my head. Dr McKenzie told me, "If Paul isn't made to realise now exactly what he is doing, or is capable of doing, one day in the future he will do something he will regret. With tragic repercussions." Then he had written something in thick black ink in the margin by the notes about Paul's behaviour. Paranoia?! My dreams were spiralling up in flames more deadly than those I had witnessed in the South of France. Paul's brutality was crushing them to pieces. He had left me with no alternative, no other choice. William was my son. And Dr McKenzie had made me realise that I had to protect him. At any cost. Even if it meant I would have to sacrifice my dream of happy ever after with Paul. William was more precious than any living thing on the planet. And like a lioness protecting her little cub from the wildest fiercest beasts in the jungle, I was prepared to do the same.

Mother Nature was unequivocally right. But I still dreaded doing it.

***

'Bleak House' was aptly named. A freezing, foreboding, decaying Victorian building with crumbling walls papered over with posters depicting horrible scenes of domestic violence and abuse. Pictures of women with black eyes, children with terrible bruises. "I always covered up for him," said a bubble coming out of the mouth of a well-dressed, swollen-lipped wife, with a shadowy picture of a man in a suit carrying a briefcase, standing behind her. I shuddered.

The social worker was young, with open-toed sandals over bare legs, and a long cotton hippy style '70s murky coloured patchwork skirt. She listened to what we said. Asked pointed questions about what had occurred that night. William and I went along together and my mum insisted on coming too. Paul had a separate appointment. "My doctor is sending Paul a letter to make him aware of how serious this is, and that his behaviour towards Will was not right or acceptable," I said. "And I'm sure that he will make very sure that nothing like this ever happens again."

"They've always been such a close and happy little family, until now," ventured my mother. "It's such a pity that all this has happened. All so unnecessary."

The social worker just smiled politely. Then she turned back to me and said something I never forgot from then on. "It's fear that makes people behave in this way. Like a frightened animal." Fear? Surely that couldn't be right, could it? Paul had never been afraid of anyone or anything in his life as far as I could tell. And yet I instinctively knew she was telling me the truth. All bullies are afraid. Whether it's in the playground or in the workplace or in a family situation it is the bully's own insecurity that makes them boil over with frustration and temper – not the person they are abusing. "So when he flares up like this, don't look him straight in the eyes. Just talk slowly and calmly. Don't antagonise him in any way, any more than you would a tiger hell-bent on attacking you. Just treat him and speak to him in the way you would an animal that is scared. Then walk away."

When Dr McKenzie asked if I wanted to attend counselling sessions with Paul, I declined. There seemed little point. I knew very well that Paul would only try to twist everything around to make it all seem as if it were my fault, just as he had always done, from the time we were told we would never be able to have a child of our own. Also, I had already endured an almighty humdinger of an argument with him about the whole episode. I didn't want William to be taken from us 'into care'. I was terrified that our family would be exposed and split up, fractured and tortured and no longer be 'normal and acceptable'. I just wanted a curtain pulled down over the whole thing. Closed. Hidden. Swept away as if it hadn't happened. And my mother was the one persuading me most of all to do this –

"For Will's sake, Lesley – you must think of William at a time like this – not yourself!" Only deep inside me, I knew that what happened that night could never be allowed to be repeated. It had taken all my courage to bring things out into the open in an attempt to confront Paul's demons. And instead of affording me peace of mind, my constant fear now was that if I antagonise Paul, disagree with him, don't put the right kind of mustard on his Sunday roast, just how long will it take until it all flares up again?

I didn't tell Alana what had gone on. In fact I did a pretty thorough job of hiding it from everybody I knew. Except for my mother. And she seemed to draw a veil over the whole affair, like a shroud. I threw myself into my work, whirling around in a mind-numbing amount of activities. I never had a minute to spare to give myself a chance to think. Of anything. Spinning a web of stifling stupidity in order to smother and extinguish the stigma and shame of oppression, physical mistreatment and emotional abuse. All I was doing was aborting my attempts at seeking ablution, handing to Paul on a smashed plate, my complete complicity in his subterfuge.

***

I pulled the jacket collar tighter around my neck. Early spring breezes were beginning to get chilly as they blew in across the choppy dancing blue and white waves. I threw the empty coffee cup in the bin. "I'm off now, Judy – for a bit of retail therapy and a wander round the harbour!"

She smiled back, wincing slightly as she leaned across the counter on her bruised arm. "Why do we put up with it?" she asked, then before I could reply she began to answer her own question. "It's because when they're nice to us – they are really so nice! Compliments, extravagant gestures, making us laugh and buying us expensive and beautiful things. And we don't see why they can't be like that all the time!" she sighed, then softly admitted, like a guilty transgressor in a confessional box talking to a priest behind a wall of silence and deceit – "I don't want to be on my own, Lesley. Despite everything. I don't want to lose my lovely home and everything else and end up living in some tiny little flat somewhere. I couldn't handle that. And I'd miss the sex too much as well. I don't think I could live like that – could you?" I patted her hand. "See you tomorrow!" I assured her. Then I walked slowly away, back up to the top of the hill.

Chapter Twenty-One

Denise Marriott wanted to be my new 'best friend' it appeared. Every time I rang Paul's office to speak to him, it was she and not him who picked up the receiver. Her shrill mendacious tones brimming with artifice. Denise always answered the phone using her own name, never Paul's, even though it was his office, his business.

"What do you want?"

"Well, to speak to Paul."

"What about?"

"Well, it's between me and Paul. I need to talk to him. Please put me through."

"But what is it all about? I can help!"

"No, honestly, I'd really rather speak to Paul."

"Is it about your job – how's that going, and William and his school – are things OK there – anything you'd like to tell me?"

"It's going well, and William's school is fine."

"You know, Lesley, if ever you feel that you want someone to come round to your little design place and give you some help with improving your ideas, some tips that might make things, well, I don't mean to sound impolite, but maybe you and Alana could do with a few attempts at raising the level, so to speak. From what I've seen your designs do appear to be rather ordinary – even mundane wouldn't you agree? More 'Homebase' than 'Harrods' I think is what I'm getting at – do you see?"

Yes, I did see. I was beginning to get seriously irritated by Denise and her uninvited swipes at me. But what was even more distressing was the way Paul reacted whenever she was around, or whenever her name was mentioned.

"I'm fed up with this, Paul," I told him. It was early evening. The day had been long and exhausting. I'd been working on some budgets for Alana and concentrating on columns of figures always made me feel tired.

"She's only being polite – showing courtesy. She's being friendly!" his reply was instant.

"Well, I don't agree," I countered. Feeling slighted. "Every time I speak to her she manages to get about twenty questions in before I even get a chance to speak to you. She seems to want to know everything about me, from what I eat for breakfast, where I shop, what perfume I use to where I buy my knickers!" I felt like our whole life was eerily being inspected by Denise through a long-range telescope clutched in her blood-red painted talons. "Why doesn't she look after her own husband instead of constantly interfering in our life so much?" I said angrily. "She should be working for you not wasting time chatting on the phone." He looked annoyed.

"It wouldn't do you any harm to take a leaf out of her book, Lesley," he retorted. "At least she is well-bred, speaks perfectly and is very courteous – Denise is a very caring person – not rude like you!"

I guess if I'm honest that's when the alarm bells started ringing like they were coming out of the top of Notre Dame itself. At full blast. Paul ringing them like a Quasimodo wannabee. It was only the beginning. Everything I had cherished up until that moment was about to come tumbling down around me like a demolished skyscraper.

I carried on trying to convince myself that the dreadful things Paul kept telling me about myself just were not true. "You have a problem! You need therapy or counselling!" he would roar at the top of his voice coming right up to my face and staring into my eyes like a crazy person. Or somebody high on drugs. It wasn't me that needed the help, I could hear myself silently screaming inside. Or maybe I did?

Perhaps it was me that was making Paul behave in this way. Something I was saying or doing, or not doing or saying, that seemed to make him despise me so. Lately, it seemed as if absolutely nothing I did was right. My friends were 'losers' my interests were 'childish and boring', my clothes were 'too young' my designs were 'insignificant and ordinary – anyone could draw them'. My personality was 'immature'. An endless and pointless stream of criticism about every aspect of my life that I could not breach. Each time it became harder to pull myself back together; like sticking your legs into tights that refuse to stop laddering. I couldn't comprehend. Had no experience to cling to which would stop me from falling right into the bottom of the pit of what was about to become a devastating depth of utter despair. I had a long way to travel downwards yet before I would be able to find the strength to straighten up and fly right once more.

I had begun to confide in Alana, just a little. But to me, it seemed an enormous amount for such a dedicated keeper of secrets. We'd shared mugs of brimming Nescafe Carte Noir and home-cooked gingerbread biscuits. "You'll have to do something about this woman!" she declared, dipping her gingerbread into her coffee and looking at me directly through thick black mascara. "You must find out what's going on, Lesley – you just have to! For your own peace of mind if nothing else!"

I thought about what she had said to me, as I strolled back home through the park. It was a warm evening, pale pink blossom was sprigging on the ornamental cherry trees. Sweetly scenting the early evening air. I felt optimism sweep through me like thesudden surge of sap up the trees that is nature's renewal.

Spring fever had struck. Yes, I could do this. No problem. Instead of returning home straight away, I headed up towards the cathedral, weaving through the back streets and cobbled alleys leading to the centre of town. To the centre of Paul's office at Allied Investments. I would surprise him. We could maybe go for a drink or a pizza.

I rarely visited Paul at work these days even though when we had worked at the television studios together we were never apart. Most of the office staff had skipped off early. Determined to savour the first whispers of spring sunshine. Mitch Ryan, big,

Irish and always in half rolled up shirt sleeves with his tie hanging halfway down the neck of his unbuttoned shirt collar, greeted me with a wide smile. "And don't you look lovely tonight, Lesley? What a picture!" A touch of the much-needed fully appreciated blarney, cheered my spirits even more. I grinned, as I took the stairs two at a time. "He's still up there – second floor!" Mitch's voice echoed behind me following me as I hurtled skywards.

I pushed open the heavy glass door and looked around. Most of the lights were out; I couldn't see Paul or anyone else for that matter. I made my way over to his office door and looked through the window, papers were on the desk, coat on hanger. No sign of Paul. "Hello, are you looking for Paul?" A sharp young female voice. I turned round. "I'm Sara!" A red-headed twenty-something in a long black skirt and indistinct blouse with puffy sleeves was standing in front of me. "Paul's not here at the moment. He's gone, em…" She looked to one side.

"Where?" I asked.

"Well, maybe I shouldn't say this but earlier he went over to the wine bar across the Square?" she spoke what she thought was 'trash trendy' , raising the tone of the end of each sentence in an attempt to sound mildly mid-Atlantic, mildly irritating and turning a simple statement into a question, that needed no answer. "With Denise."

"Denise?" I could feel my neck beginning to go red.

"Yes, that's where they always go."

"Always?" I repeated.

"Oh, well surely you've heard all the office gossip already?"

"No." I replied flatly. How could I – I wasn't even in Paul's office was I?

"Well, he and Denise are constantly with each other. Everywhere he goes – she goes with him. Lunch, meetings, conferences. They go out in the evenings too? A lot. They've been bowling, and dancing." My brain was racing to catch up with my trembling emotions. They'd both gone into rapid overdrive. "The talk is." She was still offering her version of 'confidences'. But no friend of mine would stand there like a worm writhing its miserable way into what little self-respect I was still cling-ing to. "It's been common knowledge for ages, everyone here knows all about them. Talks about them. What she doesn't get from her husband – who is a lot older than her, and very ill – she is getting from Paul!" She was triumphant. "Or so they say anyway!" I felt sick.

"I see," I managed to reply. "Well, thanks for the update, it's been – enlightening – I'll see myself out." I more or less fell down the stairs that I'd sprinted up happily only moments beforehand. I needed to get out of and away from this place so that I could think properly.

I ran out of the front door, past a bemused Mitch Ryan, into the warm evening air, right into Paul and Denise sitting side by side with their heads together in the middle of a wooden bench in the secluded part of the gardens in front of Paul's office build-ing. Surrounded by thick-leaved laurel bushes. I found myself drifting toward them as if I was in some kind of self-imposed trance. "Hello Paul!" my voice came out surprisingly bright, alert, only trembling slightly despite everything. Cheery almost. He looked up at me with ill-concealed impatience.

Denise just moved her head languorously leaning it down on her left shoulder as if to relieve a crick in the neck. She seemed bored, glancing down to inspect her perfectly manicured blood-red nails. "What are you doing here?" snapped Paul.

"I came to see you. To see if you fancied a drink or a pizza, or something. It's such a lovely evening." I felt so foolish. Redundant.

"I'm busy – surely you can see that?" he retorted. Anxious to be rid of me. Anxious to return to whatever it was he was doing with Denise, who was now looking vexed. She nodded silent agreement and they both dismissed me. "I'll see you later, Lesley. Goodbye!" He raised his right hand into the air and flicked it towards me, beckoning me away. In a way, an ill-bred Lord would treat a servant. Someone inferior. I was standing bolt upright still clutching my precious portfolio of dream designs and my over-stuffed canvas handbag in my arm, feeling stupidly upset. Denise should have been 'sent home' – not me!

There it was then, in black and white. It could not be clearer if it was written in black banner headlines on the front page of the *Daily Mail*. "Find out for yourself," Alana had urged. And I had. And how I wished I hadn't.

Of course, Paul denied what Sara had said. Rubbish! Office gossip is not to be taken the slightest notice of. I was totally unconvinced. And then it started all over again. I had done the one thing I had been warned by all the experts not to do. I had gone up against Paul. Tackled him again about his misbehaviour and mistreatment. Now it was to be my turn to face Paul's vengeance. And I knew that he would get his own back. One way or another. "When did you last see Ainsley Logan?" he demanded.

"I haven't see him," I replied truthfully. But still questions and accusations poured out rat-tat-tat! Like bullets being fired from a fully loaded shotgun.

His hand was outstretched for a moment, I could see something stuck to the massive palm. "What do you have there?" I asked him. Instantly he let go of the package and threw it across the dining room table. As they skidded to a standstill I could see some glossy photographs.

"I think you need to explain yourself! I'm waiting for an apology!" he exclaimed triumphantly. I picked them up and turned them over slowly so that I could see exactly what they were. It was me, and Ainsley. Together in the pub by the river and the restaurant we had visited where we had shared our secrets. Holding hands across the wooden table. Ainsley and me. I felt my face flush hot with embarrassment, humiliation and outrage. Paul had been treating me badly, getting up to goodness knows what behind my back with Denise, and he had been spying – on me?

"Where did you get these?" I managed to ask him.

"I don't have to answer that!" he shot back at me. "More to the point – what the hell is going on? What do you think you are doing carrying on like that with Ainsley Logan? It's shameful, Lesley – that's what it is – shameful! It's blatantly obvious that you and Ainsley Logan are not just good friends. No! Not at all! You are far more than that! And I demand to know the reason for your behaviour!"

I was furious suddenly. How dare he violate my privacy and my liberty like this. Accusing me, of something I hadn't even done. "You've got it all wrong!" I stammered, trying half-heartedly to explain. But now I felt weary. What on earth was the point? Paul had concocted a story of his own in order to squirm off the slimy hook he and Denise had landed themselves on. "Ainsley and I are friends, Paul. Good friends! And nothing more than that. You know that. Why won't you believe me?" Only I knew that Paul did believe me. He knew the truth.

He knew there was nothing physical going on between me and Ainsley that shouldn't, because Paul knew me – his wife, very well indeed. Paul went back to the table, deliberately picking up pieces of paper. I recognised my designs. Rough drawings with scribbled notes and private and special thoughts that I had written in my diary. For my eyes only. To help me to sort out my feelings, try to make sense of the confusion. My Reiki teacher had told me to "Write things down, Lesley. Everything. It will help to clear your mind. Make you feel better." They were my most private thoughts – all photocopied by Denise on Allied Investments' Xerox machine.

"Where did you get this stuff?" I cried out. Horrified. I'd been raided. Invaded.

"I've got these as well!" He was rattling dozens of tiny tapes in his hands like crazed castanets clutched by a fiendish flamenco dancer. "They are tape recordings!" he cried exuberantly. "Of you, Lesley! Of you! Every time you argued with me, shouted at me, conversations – loads of things! It's all here! All of it! I had a tape recorder hidden in the bedside cabinet – all the time!" He was triumphant.

I was mortified. Sickened. Disgusted. Why had he not kept all the birthday, Christmas and Valentine cards of love that I had sent him every year? Why had he done this? Destroyed everything. "Paul – this is perverted! I can explain all about Ainsley." I struggled lamely on, still attempting to pull things back and repair something precious that I knew was now irretrievably smashed to bits. Desperate. "Paul there is nothing going on, there never has been.

He's mar…" I stopped myself just in time. I couldn't say he was married now could I? Even though that had nothing to do with it. So I didn't say anything. Apart from, "Ainsley Logan has gone back to Australia, Paul. To the other side of the world. He cannot go any further away from me than that can he? We're not having an affair. Surely Australia is far enough away Paul – even for you?"

***

The landslide was unstoppable. "It's my money that pays all the bills – not yours! I am keeping things going, so don't question me about how I manage to do so!" He stopped even telling me where he was going or who he was seeing. I watched him as he smacked aftershave onto his wide cheeks and pulled on a recently acquired leather jacket.

"Where are you off to? You're very dressed up for a Saturday!" I was half joking. Only half. Maybe he just wanted to wear nice things to make him feel better, as we all do sometimes.

"Out!" was all he said. He slammed the street door behind him. So – Paul had been spying on me, had he? Well, much as it was totally at variance to my liberal-minded belief in absolute and complete freedom for each individual and their total right to privacy – I followed him in my car. Paul had always driven much faster than me. I had to keep my distance so he didn't spot me in his rearview mirror. I lost him at the roundabout. Leaving him speeding off in a southerly direction towards the little town that Allied Investments had recently moved to.

What a weird thing to be doing on a Saturday morning when I would much rather have been wandering around Brent Cross searching for shoes. But I kept going, as dappled sunshine burst through the leaves on the tree-lined country road, making strange dancing patterns across the steering wheel. The heat through the windows was warm, my hands felt clammy. I opened the sunroof to let in the fresh air.

Few vehicles were in the car park when I arrived. I couldn't see Denise's purple Peugeot. Paul's Mercedes was parked right in front of the building. I started to feel nervous for no reason I could explain. Unsettled. This is stupid, I reminded myself. I wasn't doing anything wrong. I wasn't a thief or anything. I had dropped by to see how Paul's new office move was coming along. He had complained that I wasn't showing any interest in his work often enough. Well, I would show some. And remind him and Allied Investments that he still had a wife of his own – me. The reception was empty. But a smiling security guard in a pale grey uniform arrived with a huge bunch of keys dangling from a chain on his belt. "Would you like a cup of tea?" he asked pleasantly.

I said not now thanks. He showed me up to Paul's new office. It was open plan. Desks in rows like kids in Primary School. It was complete and utter chaos. Paul was standing by his desk, surrounded by boxes, crates filled with papers that spewed from the top and down the sides. He was distractedly scratching the top of his head. And I felt sorry for him. He had lost his lovely office with the view over the park. He had lost his great big mahogany desk. As far as I could tell from looking at the mess in front of me, he had lost his status.

"Hiya!" I called out to him. Surprise flickered momentarily across the face I knew so well.

"What are you doing here? Have you come to help me move?" Unconcealed sarcasm laced the question like arsenic added to lemonade.

"Yes, if you want me to," I replied. Aware that the security guard was hovering still by the doorway. He waved and went back down the pale grey carpeted stairs. I hadn't intended to help Paul with his office move. I hadn't really thought of anything when I had thrown on my beige skirt and jacket and headed off like Inspector Gadget to follow Paul in my car.

But if he needed my help then I was glad to provide it. I discarded the jacket onto the nearest chair, went to the Shell garage next door to get some sandwiches for our lunch, and drinks, and packets of salt and vinegar crisps. We talked. We laughed. Paul made sure that he connected Denise's phone first. It started to ring, intermittently. "Shall I answer it?" I asked him.

"No!" he bellowed. So I continued to leave it alone, while it continued to spasmodically make shrill shrieks into the air.

I was telling Paul a stupid joke that someone had sent to me on the internet, making him laugh out loud, when suddenly Denise came swooping across the office floorboards like Dracula's mother in tight Fiorocci designer jeans and wearing no bra, a maroon cloak draped across her shoulders. "What are you doing here?!" she demanded.

"I've come to see Paul, and to help," I replied, as calmly as I could. Denise was quite evidently furious. Throwing a large bundle of keys attached to a silver fob with the letter 'D' embossed across them she began marching backwards and forwards. "You know, you could put all those files up here out of the way to give you more space," I ventured. "And some of this stuff could be stored at Head Office, perhaps on microfiche, to give you more room here."

Denise's loud, piercing whine shot right through me like a dagger. "How dare you!" she cried. "Coming in here – interfering! Don't you tell me what to do! This is none of your business!"

I reminded her politely that it was indeed very much my business. Paul was my husband. As he had told me so many times, especially recently. It was his job that kept a roof over our heads. Also, I was strangely, actually concerned for him. For he was looking strained and drained and grey these days. Rage ignited her like a firework on bonfire night. Banging her fist down on the table she yelled at me accusingly. "Whose name is it on the Partnership papers? And whose name is it on everything else? On the Accounts? Cheque books? Diplomas on the wall? Absolutely everything? Lesley Pearson? I think not! Denise Marriott – that's whose name is on them! I am Paul's new partner! And have been since the beginning of this year! So – don't you ever forget that!" I gazed at Paul in disbelief.

"Is this true?" I asked him, trying to stop my voice from wobbling like a violin with slack strings.

"Get out!" he fumed. "Leave immediately! You shouldn't even be here! You must leave – now!" Why he hadn't asked me to go home three hours ago when I'd first arrived, I didn't know, before we'd tidied up the office, had lunch, laughed together for the first time in ages. Denise tossed her newly blow-dried head and flounced away towards the door, diamante trim on her Fiorroci's glinting as she wiggled her bottom making a great show of pretending to retreat.

"That's it!" she cried out dramatically. "You can find yourself a new partner Paul!" Now he was yelling at the top of his voice.

"No! Come back! Don't go! Please!" She spun around on her high heels to face me. Triumphant. Cat with cream glint in steely biting cold colourless eyes. "You go – now!" Paul demanded, once again.

"No," I heard myself reply. Surprising. "I want some answers first." I looked right at Denise. Slicing for a moment through the lofty façade that she hid behind. Standing up for myself, at last. Yet beneath the desk, my legs were trembling. It was such a noodle of a cliché I almost couldn't quite keep a straight face as I asked her the ludicrous question. I'd seen it so often on TV now it was my turn to play a part I hadn't asked for. Lines that didn't belong to me. "I want to know just exactly what is going on between you and my husband?" And I half giggled, as I realised how absurd this all sounded. Like a reluctant Sue Ellen in Dallas or something.

But Denise didn't see any funny side – at all. She spat words back at me like some kind of wild deranged alley cat. Not a lady at all. Leaning right across Paul's desk she looked me right in the eyes and in a voice brimmed full of malice said, "Oh – when will you ever get the message? You are a sad old cow! Why don't you fuck off?!" She then flicked her fingers from the limpness of her Cartier-encrusted wrist and waved me away scornfully. "Look at the state of you! Do you work? In that little design shop? Hah! What you produce is nothing but cheap rubbish. Look at the state of you – the way you dress – everything! I even know all about your sex life! No wonder Paul wants to get rid of you!"

I felt like I was being stripped of my skin, leaving me standing there naked and alone in Paul's office. A terrible tirade of deadly poisonous venom tumbled from her Elizabeth Arden painted red lips as if the Chamber of Horrors had just exploded all around me. Deeply personal insults, things that were not true, but things that only one person could have told her. Paul. Then she crossed the office in swift strides, grabbing him by the arm. It was a tiny but absolutely complete act of ownership. Paul immediately put his hand on top of her arm. He was now her protector. Not mine. Humiliation hurled through me like a runaway train about to fall right off the track. Questioning my very reason. Was it true, all that she was shouting at me? Was I really a sad old cow? I wasn't young any longer, that was a fact of life. But sad, and old, and shabbily dressed – me? And although I could feel it all welling up inside of me threatening to overwhelm me like an avalanche, I wasn't going to let them see me cry. Not that. Not now. I made my way carefully to the Ladies, hardly able to see where I was walking. Then I couldn't stop the tears that consumed me.

I went home with my head in a state of shock, my heart in tatters. I went to bed with a throbbing headache. The next morning, Paul suggested a walk in the park. "I think we should get things sorted out." I nodded in silent agreement. "We should get a divorce, Lesley. It's the only answer." He carried on looking straight ahead, emotionless, as we walked past the old ruined Roman wall, crumbling apart like my marriage. "I just cannot be expected to tolerate your tantrums, your rudeness, your mood swings any longer. I've simply had enough. What happened yesterday was completely unforgivable! Denise expects an apology from you – and quite frankly, so do I! She is very upset about the way you behaved towards her!" His pompous conceit seemed to have found an ally at last – in Denise and her histrionic ravings.

It was ever more absurd. "Paul, I really think it's me who deserves an apology from you and her – not the other way round!" My desperation was turning to cold anger. Unjust didn't come close to describing how I was feeling.

"No, Lesley! You were very rude!" he continued. On and on. Shouting, and shouting. Turning, as usual, everything around so that it appeared to be me who was at fault, me who was a half-crazed hypersensitive semi-lunatic. "She is going to sue you!" he declared throwing his arms up into the air.

"What on earth for?" Even more ridiculous. But he just carried on shouting at me. Provoking. Tormenting. Absolutely determined to make me upset and imprison me in grief forever.

Six weeks later I received two things in the early morning post. An air mail letter addressed to me in thick, black ink – and divorce papers from Paul.

William was devastated. "You cannot do this! You can't divorce! You can't break up our family!" He sobbed uncontrollably. "I won't let you!" Hitting out against the wall in anguish. His cry was like a knife striking me right through the heart.

I tried to reassure him. Tried to comfort him. Distract him, cheer him up. All the time knowing that a massive arsenal of greed was gathering and was marshalling its total force to overpower me completely. "This is crazy Paul. We can work things out surely. After all this time. Please at least think of Will," I pleaded with him. In return, I was met with rebuff and refusal that was complete and emphatic. Uncompromising. "What did Denise mean when she said you wanted to be rid of me? How long have you been planning all this?" I asked. But of course, I knew the answer in part. This was my ultimate punishment for being brave enough to stand up to Paul when I went to see Dr McKenzie and reported his abuse. Bringing into the open things Paul wanted to remain hidden. Why couldn't I see, even then, that it was I who should have run away? Far away. A long, long time ago. But we do what we think is right at the time. Programmed to put the needs of our families, our mothers, our fathers, our sisters, brothers and children, before our own. Not to be selfish. And I didn't run away, because I couldn't. Paul had managed to successfully isolate me. Convince me that I could never ever survive without him, or be able to manage alone.

And now that my self-esteem was achingly low, I really believed it was true. As terrible as his treatment of me had been at times – what was I going to do without him? I picked up the air mail letter. "Dear Lesley, I hope you are alright, and that you have managed to sort out things with Paul – once and for all! Divorce has been finalised today. Strange feeling. Decree Absolute came through the post this morning. You're the first to know! It's boiling hot down here at the moment. Temperatures are in the 30s. The beach is the best bet! I'm getting so used to barbecued steak I think I'm beginning to consider beans on toast a luxury! How's the job going? Bet you'll be entering the designer of the year contest soon! How's Will? All is well, I hope. Listen, Lesley – not much of a letter writer unlike you. Taken me ages to write what I have already, and I'm running out of ink…" Then he'd drawn a little character, a picture of an Aborigine man in felt tips, winking and sticking out his tongue simultaneously Beneath it he had written, in rapidly fading ink… "Seen enough of Sydney. Heading off to Ayers Rock, Great Barrier Reef and the Outback – all that stuff. Oh, what joy! Free at last! Catch you later, Les!"

He had signed it in his large swirly handwriting – love Ainsley – and one big kiss.

Chapter Twenty-Two

"Don't bother getting any legal advice, Lesley! Don't waste your money and time!" Paul directed. I didn't know where to turn for help. Paul's father had passed away suddenly, two years before. My mother was in a state of delayed shock and colossal denial about the divorce. It wasn't exactly what she had dreamed of for the free-spirited little girl who still had the desire to trek across the beach searching for pretty shells and passionate pirates! I just wanted to be allowed to do that. Instead, it was left up to me to sort out the tortured tangled aftermath of complete betrayal.

"That is ridiculous, Paul, and you know it. Things have to be agreed upon properly. Mutually with the help of a lawyer. Division of assets. All that stuff. And our house."

He rustled some papers in his hands and put them back inside his black leather briefcase. "Let's go down to the pub and the park for a drink and a chat while we're walking along shall we?" suggested Paul. It sounded reasonable enough.

"OK," I agreed to go along with him. We needed to talk, and we did, at first. Then just as I thought we were beginning to speak the same language at last, here it came again. The taunts the threats. Accusation. Paul's opinion of me. What a terrible person I was. How everything that had happened had been my fault. "OK, I've not come here to listen to your insults all over again. We need to talk properly about money," I said.

"Don't think you're getting anything from me!" he shouted, thumping the table with his fist, making the glasses shudder. "The house is mine! I am keeping it! It belongs to me! And my pension – don't think you're getting any of that! And I have no savings! You have your own pension – so I am entitled to half of that. And the Court will expect you to pay off all my debts – and so do I!"

"Debts?" I was alarmed. "What debts?"

"£60,000 – and rising!" He was exultant, almost. I was bewildered and frustrated. We had never even had a joint bank account or credit cards. I had no kind of debt. I had not run up bills in his name. It wasn't me who had sent him to the brink of bankruptcy. I tried to make some kind of coherent argument that he would listen to. But he didn't want to listen. The families sitting beside us at the next table looked uncomfortable, moving slightly away from the edge of the wooden bench seat. Even the swans ducked their heads down and floated off down the side of the pond, as quickly as they could.

"What about me and Will, where do you expect us to live?" I couldn't believe he was making me ask these things. Where was the loyalty – trust? Respect?

"I don't care! It's not my problem any longer!" He was triumphant. "You chose to bite the hand that fed you, Lesley. You! That's your choice – and you must therefore live with the consequences. And your attitude! It's simply intolerable behaviour and it's no wonder that I am divorcing you after the way you have behaved!" He stomped off angrily in his baggy beige Bermuda shorts, as the geese fled from his tramping feet, arms swinging backwards and forward by his side. Filled with self-importance. Filled with disgust.

I had to go to the County Court with my solicitor. Paul had chosen to represent himself. Standing at the front row of oak chairs, in front of the Judge, next to my legal representative, who had been asked to remove her wig and robes in this case. Before a Judge who sat under a Coat of Arms pinned to golden oak wooden panelled walls. 'Honi soit qui mal y pense'. Lion and unicorn protecting the Royal shield. Shafts of pale sunlight through stained glass. The smell of ruined lives and failure. Paul's pile of papers was huge. Perry Mason did not walk into a Court room with that many files. The whole procedure pandered to his conceit, snobbery and egotism. If he had been appearing in a soap opera on TV he couldn't have enjoyed it more. I was besieged by the vanity of others. I was ordered to sit behind him. I felt like I was in *Alice in Wonderland* and had entered the land where I was suddenly only two inches tall and everyone else was a giant. I had been persuaded by my solicitor to cross-petition Paul on the grounds of his behaviour. "But we don't want to go down that path," said my lady lawyer. "We really don't want to rock any boats, and it will only make matters worse. Best to forget all about that side of things," she told me brusquely. I had never felt so lonely.

Paul on the other hand had come up with some pretty imaginative fairy tales of his own. That I didn't do any housework and had friends he didn't approve of me spending time with. Like Ainsley. "Are you accusing your wife of adultery?" asked the Judge pointedly regarding Paul over the top of half-rimmed gold glasses.

"No," replied Paul in a flat voice. "I know that hasn't happened."

In the Judge's summing up, which was pretty swift, he told us we were both equally to blame. "Unreasonable behaviour is the reason for the breakdown of your marriage." Yet Paul was managing to make me feel as if it was all my fault. And the judicial system I had been hauled unwillingly into was succeeding in making me feel dirty, ashamed, soiled, cheap and sordid. I stood in the dock used for criminals. With the Holy Bible in my hand, swearing to tell the truth, the whole truth and nothing but... only they were gagging me, preventing me from telling the whole truth. It felt like someone had superglued my mouth and stuffed my tiny hands into enormous steel handcuffs behind my back. No fearless, lawless pirate or highwayman could have complained – but I could! I had committed no crime – done nothing wrong! Only to walk down the aisle in a pretty country church clutching pink roses and make my vows solemnly before God. Promise faithfully to love, honour and cherish till death us do part. And Paul had made exactly the same promises to me. To protect me. My dad had not handed me over carelessly. He had trusted Paul to look after me as he had always done. So had I. Now twenty-four years of my life had been extinguished into a pile of ashes that lay with the daily dust on the Courtroom floor.

"The Decree Nisi is granted," said the Judge, quashing his hand hard on a black embossing stamp. Trampling, crushing. Complete. "Do you understand what that means?" I nodded, half in disbelief. Numb.

Just like that. My marriage. Wiped out. Finished. Obliterated and ended as if it had never been there in the first place. "Paul?" He pushed his papers swiftly together, stuffing them into his lever arch file.

"Yes. Yes!" he replied, slamming the lid shut.

"All rise!" ordered the Court attendant.

I was in no doubt that Paul would disrupt my whole life in order to get what he wanted. Euripides said so long ago, "Marry and it may go well. But when a marriage fails, then those who marry live at home – in hell." Nothing has changed.

"The house belongs to me!" his voice thundered relentless as a ferocious and menacing storm. Paul's words lashed over me like sheets of icy rain.

"No, Paul. It doesn't. It's in joint names…" But every time I tried to reason, he would dig in his heels even more tightly. Till the inevitable arguments became even more protracted and spiteful.

Divorce, like the other scourge of our times – cancer, eats right through the human body and spirit, attempting to destroy the deepest part of your soul, right into every nook and cranny of existence. Every waking thought. Every sleepless night. Tearing every single shred of your life to bits, turning fine silk into grimy tatters of rags. It's not the overwhelming pain of losing a loved one. Death is final. No betrayal. Your dreams are left intact because they had no choice but to leave you. Dreams are left undisturbed, your pride. Your self-respect. And memories to cherish forever more like some kind of silken pillow to lay your head upon. They loved you and only you – till the day they died. But divorce is the demon riding with the four horsemen of the Apocalypse. Swathed in cloaks of black swirling decay, surrounding every deadly move that transfers abundant wealth to the lawyers, the Judges, the barristers and even estate agents. Slicing through lives like sticks of salami and tossing ordinary lives upside down, inside out. Pain spirals out of control as legal bills increase and tensions rise like the mercury in an angry thermometer that is red hot. Abandon hope – all who enter here.

I felt a kind of hurt that just couldn't be put right with any kind of painkiller or medicine. TV programmes became moving wallpaper. I just could not concentrate on any plot. Nothing made sense any more. Every magazine I looked at in WH Smith's seemed to have a headline about somebody famous being divorced. Shopping for food became tense. How would I pay the bills and put food on the table? Just how was I going to survive financially with no help from Paul whatsoever and a job that paid peanuts? And every single second it seemed I was on the phone or writing letters or receiving letters – from solicitors. I was made to fill in so many forms detailing my income, my savings, my lifestyle expenses and even how much I paid for my Estee Lauder make-up, I thought I would go nuts. And worst of all was the thought that Denise was cunningly working her way through everything I declared and signed. Enabling and encouraging Paul to demolish me.

The sheer volume of papers that passed into my hands, out of my hands, through my hands and then to the solicitor, on to Paul's solicitors and the Court, and back again in a never-ending circle, plus injunctions and documents, made me feel giddy, as if I was literally living in the middle of an earthquake zone. I dreaded the postman coming down my drive each morning. And when the weeping eventually stopped – I never thought it would – and my face began to look some way normal instead of a misshapen sore mess with bags so deep they sagged half way down my cheeks, and I couldn't even put on make-up because my face stung so much with the weight of thousands of tears, the self-imposed guilt trip took over. With a vengeance. The blame. Paul kept telling me it was all my fault. So maybe he was right. Maybe it was. But if I wasn't the contemptuous person he kept describing, where had I actually gone? I felt like I had completely disappeared. I didn't even know who I was any more. Every second he was in my sight he would goad me, incite me to lose my temper, provoking an argument for no other reason but to upset me and drive me eventually beyond the edge of reason. I couldn't understand why he was behaving in such a callous way.

"Just look in the mirror, Lesley! What a mess you are! Look at you!" And I did. And I was. Alana's attempt to cheer me up was knocked down flat just like skittles in a bowling alley by Paul.

"Come out to the local Italian with me tonight. We'll eat bowls of pasta and get fat! My treat!" she said. "Wear something cheerful! And for goodness' sake put some make-up on. It will make you feel much better." I pulled a face. "Honestly, Lesley – I'm telling you. Just do it – you'll soon see I'm right!" I put on a new white trouser suit I had purchased in the High Street and a little cream crochet top that I'd got in the January sale.

It looked surprisingly good. "You look lovely, Mum!" complimented Will. I put make-up on as Alana had suggested. And she was right. The moment I started to apply pastel-coloured sticks of eye shadow and soft peach blusher suddenly it was an altogether different reflection that was staring back at me from the dressing table mirror. I had a lovely time with Alana. A real girls' night out. We ate plates piled high with delicious pasta and creamy sauces. Drenched chunks of fresh ciabatta bread with pungent olive oil laced with fresh basil and oregano. Drank glasses of Chianti from wine glasses like goblets. Laughed with the Neapolitan waiters who flirted with us, and I felt some kind of energy draining back into the decreasing slim-line version of me that just couldn't eat properly lately.

When I got home Paul was furious. Striding right up towards me and confronting me like a member of the Gestapo, he put his hands on his hips and looked me straight in the eyes with a crazed glazed expression that looked remarkably like hatred from where I was standing. "Who the hell do you think you are?!" he began to shout. Loudly. "Just what do you think you look like and what do you think you are doing – going out dressed like that?" Anyone listening to Paul could have been mistaken in thinking I had just ridden bareback and stark naked through the local park like Lady Godiva. Yet my legs started to tremble.

I pushed my way past him into the bedroom. I looked back at the reflection in the mirrored wardrobe door. But my child-like joy had been erased in a second. Leaving me wasted and empty inside. Depression clung to me now like a dense freezing fog that just refused to go away. "You need counselling! There is definitely something seriously wrong with you! You are sick! You need some kind of professional help!" he would yell at me, constantly. And I would pull the duvet cover up over my ears so that I could drown out the sound of his voice. But I could still hear him. Even after he had gone to bed. His voice was constantly there – right inside my head. And I couldn't make it stop.

So relentless was the assault on each and every one of my senses that I began to feel sick. Eventually, I was sick. Unable to stand up. I could not walk. Or do anything. I was told by Dr McKenzie that a viral infection of my inner ears had gotten much worse because of the constant stress and trauma that I was going through. He gave me pills. He told me I could be suffering from Meniere's Disease, which affects the balance mechanism in the ear making people constantly dizzy. I felt like I was dying. Unable to stand up and being violently sick. "You have been, and still are, under such intense emotional stress, we cannot really tell what's causing this. What is wrong?" a kind young Indian doctor at the local hospital explained to me. I had been sent to the ear nose and throat section for special investigation. "Till you get things sorted out you just need to try to relax. Stress can be the trigger for so many illnesses and other things you know?"

Yes I knew. I went from chair to chair, having all kinds of tests. They took blood and they stuck instruments inside my ears. I thought this is the end. At that point, I could see no light at all at the end of my long dark tunnel. Was this going to be it from now on? Coming backwards and forward to dreaded hospital corridors for the rest of my life? I was so afraid. I sat there holding my mother's hand, trying to look brave and nonchalant. It didn't work of course. Those things never do work on mothers. I couldn't put one foot in front of the other. Could not even make it to the local shops. Alana had told me to rest. "Come back when you feel able. Don't worry. I'll keep your job open for you, Lesley. I don't want to lose someone like you. Take as long as you need. I'll still be here."

Alana still thought I was 'human' at least!

Meanwhile, Paul and his lawyers, together with the fanatical assistance of Denise, who had all the determination of a Rottweiler about to destroy a rabbit, tearing it limb from limb and tossing the bits aside in a bloody and filthy mess, had begun to concoct a convoluted collection of lies, deceit and corrupt misuse of authority to cover up the appalling state Paul had made of his finances. His income. And his debts. Paul kept repeating incessantly that, "You must pay them!"

I shook my head. "No way, Paul. I am not prepared to do that. I don't think you should expect me to. They are your debts. You are stripping everything from me. You must be responsible for your own debts." Thus we were perilously impaled on the horrendous ugly merry-go-round of immoral 'legality'. Sucked into the maelstrom of the judicial system. I didn't know it at the time, but the system hadn't even got into first gear yet.

Without Denise at the helm orchestrating his every move, Paul would have floundered quickly, falling at the first fence. His knowledge of the Law had always been minuscule. But I was also beginning to realise they had another sinister ally.

A policeman that Paul had been friendly with years ago, who I thought was still in Cornwall where Paul had first met him. He wasn't. I tried to reason with Paul still. A common-sense down to earth attempt at surviving this. Compromise. For the sake of all of us. He had an altogether more deadly agenda. A straightforward divorce was never what Paul intended. He would listen to my words. Then not answer me straight away. Rushing off to make contact on the mobile phone or somewhere in the dark places he met up with Denise and Robert, his PC.

When he returned his face was deadly dark and fury was etched across its furrows. And then the threats would begin all over again. Thick and fast as a building being demolished; his commands flying like broken bricks ferociously through the air.

And I would end up crying once more. Consumed by despair. Paul and Denise had devised a master plan and they were not about to let anyone stand in their way. Especially me. Their complete devotion and determination to cripple me completely was becoming insurmountable. And I was feeling increasingly abandoned – unprotected by the Law.

"What about Denise's husband?" I asked. "Does he know what she's doing? Doesn't he care? How's his health these days?"

Paul's reply was sarcastic. "Why don't you ring him up and ask him yourself?" I didn't. I wasn't prepared to put anyone else through what I was having to deal with. I could not live with that on my conscience. Let that be one for Paul and Denise to deal with. Not me. Enough had already been laid slap bang and uninvited at my door.

"Don't let him make you lose your temper!" Alana begged me urgently, so many times I lost count. On the phone, when she dropped in for coffee or a salad for lunch. "I know it's very hard. But try to walk away. Don't take the bait. Walk into another room. Pretend you cannot hear what he is saying. I don't know why on earth you try to talk to him anyway – he only upsets you every time you do!" And yet I still believed we had a chance of resolving things financially, to find some answers. Reason. "Reason with him?!" Alana shook her head vigorously. "With other men, maybe. But with Paul – never! Lesley, he will never ever listen. You of all people must know that. He's always got to be the winner. Always got to be right. You'll only end up hurting yourself! Walk away, Lesley. Walk away!"

I could hear echoes of Ainsley's voice warning me years ago about banging my head on the wall and not denting the wall, but ending up with an almighty headache. Yet still, I tried. I really, really tried. And how, I now realise, that must have driven Paul nuts. For that wasn't in his script. Not compromise. Not a fair settlement. Not at all.

But eventually even the best pirate captains get pushed to the very brink. Abandoning reason as they end up precariously walking the plank which propels them from a firm wooden foothold and plunges them deep into the turbulent ocean beneath. Devoted Black Bess carried Dick Turpin all the way from London to York without stopping. To save his life. Carrying him faithfully to safety. The shiny jet black mare made the ultimate sacrifice. She collapsed on arrival. And died right in front of him. Eventually Dick ended up swinging from a gallows.

And what lessons could I learn from these wayward heroes from days long gone?

I was swinging up and down on a dangerous pendulum of a legal see-saw with Paul on one end and me on the other, still trying desperately to hold on tight to my precious pirate's flag of freedom. My liberty. My life. Not long after that, I got arrested for 'Attempted murder'!

Chapter Twenty-Three

Humidity hung thickly in air consumed by summer storm clouds gathering on the horizon. Glasses of mineral water that I kept in plastic bottles lined up in the fridge were the only things that cooled me down. I tried to sit quietly in the conservatory, to rid myself of a thudding headache that was sticking to me like superglue. All week long Paul's fury had been festering, barely suffused, as the incoming thunder and lightning.

I knew by the time eight o'clock came that an early night was going to be the only sensible cure. I would just lie down on the bed quiet and still, until the raging storm passed over. I got ready for bed and went into the kitchen. William had generously tidied up the place, unasked, and was delighted with brand new handles that he had carefully fixed onto the kitchen cupboard doors for me, replacing the old broken ones. "They look lovely, darling!" I told him.

That's when Paul came hurtling through the front door, bellowing at the top of his voice. "What do you think you've done! That's wanton criminal damage!" I stared at him in disbelief as he carried on ranting and raving.

"What on earth are you talking about, Paul? It's not damaged the door in any way. They are new handles. Yes, indeed they are. I gave Will the money for them this morning after he'd been down to Homebase to buy them. They are my kitchen cupboards as well you know!" This was too absurd.

"We'll see about this!" he dashed off, returning minutes later from the garage, in a ferocious temper. Paul, brutishly armed with a huge metal hammer, began to smash lovely new wooden handles that William had so methodically and carefully crafted onto the pine door.

Paul was relentlessly hitting them with all his force, smashing them onto the clean kitchen work top, leaving the cupboard doors splintered and shattered, strands of wood everywhere as the doors were left dangling and twisted like hanged highwaymen in mid-air. "Stop it, Paul!" I put my arm out to restrain him. Immediately he grabbed hold of my injured right arm, and pushed me hard, with all his mighty weight behind him. So that I felt myself being flung backwards across the kitchen floor. I slid on the slippery surface, lost my balance and tumbled over a chair as I fell.

Will was alarmed. "Don't, Dad!" he put his hand out to stop Paul from hitting me again. That's when Paul pulled the phone out from his back trousers pocket and swiftly dialled – 999.

"Police? I need immediate assistance!" I heard him calling triumphantly into the tiny receiver. "My wife and son are attacking me – and I am in fear! You must come at once!"

Within what seemed like seconds, two uniformed policemen knocked on my front door. I let them in. "Look, there's been a mistake here…" I started to say.

"Well, it was your husband who called us," they replied curtly, pushing past me and striding into my kitchen where Paul was standing alongside the broken cupboards he had just smashed to bits. "We'll talk to you both separately."

My kitchen door was unceremoniously slammed shut in my face. They stayed with Paul for a long time. Finally, they returned to the lounge to speak with me. "This is absolutely ridiculous!" I told them. "We are in the middle of a divorce and my husband is making all this fuss because he wants the house – and everything else. It's as simple as that!"

"Why don't you leave?" asked the policeman bluntly.

"Because it's my home!" I replied, unable to believe he was actually asking me to leave it.

He repeated the question, saying, "This isn't a home any longer – it's a battleground. Why don't you leave?" My head was really thumping. I appreciated the fact that this man had a job to do and had do doubt he had been fully trained in dealing with what the Police refer to as 'a domestic'. But I had no faith in his reasoning. I was irritated. I was already in my nightdress, he could see I was about to go to bed for goodness' sake.

"It's my house." I tried to sound calm. "I have been told I must remain here," I replied evenly.

"By who?" he demanded.

"By everyone," I replied. "My solicitor, my friends, my family. They have all insisted to me that this is my home and I have a perfect right to be here – to stay here. And I must do so. I have nowhere else to go!"

"What do you think should happen then?" he continued.

"I think if anyone should be asked to leave then it should be Paul. After all, he's the one who's causing all the trouble and behaving in a violent way – not me and my son!" I told him.

"Well, we've already asked him. He refuses to go anywhere. He says he will not budge because it is you who is violent!" I looked back at him squarely. Where was the logic in this? Paul was over six foot two and, whereas my weight was diminishing by the second, his was tipping the scales in the opposite direction. The svelte twenty-something I had married had turned into a mid-life monster as broad as he was tall. All sixteen stone of him. I was speechless. Paul had just propelled me across the kitchen floor using all of his strength. I had fallen over. Me. I was the one who was hurt. Not Paul! There were no marks or bruises on him. He hadn't been injured at all.

The policeman handed me a card with a telephone number on it. I glanced down at it – 'Domestic Violence Helpline'. Here we go again. I placed it on the dining room table. "I'm getting a divorce," I said flatly. What more did these people want of me?

What use was a wretched help line to me – especially now? "Well, this won't be the last time we see you!" he maintained with an air of certainty as he turned to leave.

"What do you mean?" Instant chill gripped me like a vice.

"Well, it's quite common in cases like this. Divorce – all that. Things only get worse, not better – sometimes even ending up in murder!" This was so far-fetched and preposterous.

"Goodnight," was all I said as I closed my front door behind them.

I had never seen Will so distressed. "I'll get a criminal record!" he choked back sobs.

"Don't be silly, of course you won't! You've done nothing wrong!" I tried in vain to reassure him.

"They took my name and address." I took his hand and held it.

"They have to do that for their records," I replied. But although outside I tried to appear to be calm, inside I was furious with Paul for putting us through all this, to mercilessly get his own way. To take absolutely everything away from us.

"I'm going over to the Park!" cried Will.

"Oh no! You're not going anywhere. It's too late. I'll make you a milkshake and you can go up to your room and watch some television," I said. He did. His teenage face ashen and emotionally exhausted.

I walked back into the lounge. My head felt like it was being sliced in two with a sword. Splitting with pain. I could hardly focus But I knew I had to confront Paul about this. He had stretched himself out on the leather sofa, surrounded by ivory coloured cushions that I had bought from one of Alana's specialist suppliers. His personal computer was laying in his lap. He appeared to be concentrating on some papers. Oblivious. Unconcerned. As if nothing at all had just taken place in our home. "How could you?" I said. He carried on ignoring me, looking down his long nose with disdain at me as if I were some insect or lower life form that had crawled out of the skirting in order to get his attention.

"What game are you playing?" I asked. He looked up, peering at me over the top of his newly-acquired steel-framed glasses.

"Have the courtesy to be quiet – I'm busy!" His tone was imperious, condescending.

"But how could you do that? Calling the Police – upsetting Will – how could you?"

He made a clicking sound with his mouth. "William had criminally damaged the kitchen cupboards – and you were both assaulting me, being violent and abusive. I told this to the Police.

And I have simply had enough – I am not about to tolerate your violent behaviour any longer – and that goes for both of you!"

I froze with fury. "What?!!" I shouted at him.

"You see! You are unable to keep your temper! Unable to keep quiet! I've had years of this, Lesley, and that is why I am divorcing you! Now please leave! Get out!"

I picked up my wedding photographs, so lovingly framed in silver, still so precious to me. I slid them silently out of the glass protecting them. Almost unconsciously, I tore them in half. Paul on one side, me the other. Then I threw them into the fire place. All over – at last. Just like that. Nearly twenty-four years up in smoke, up the chimney – ashes to ashes, dust to dust. Paul didn't even look up from his laptop. I went back into the kitchen, reached into the medicine cabinet and took out some strong painkillers. I dissolved two in a glass of water. Then, remembering what a young TV nurse had once told me – "If you have a bad headache always have something sweet", I took out the honey pot and went to the bread bin to cut some bread and make a honey sandwich. The bread knife was in my hand.

I walked back into the lounge. Still Paul appeared to be focusing all his attention on the laptop, which was still strategically placed across his lower body, he adjusted it as I came towards him. The coffee table was between us. I stared across at him. Fuming. "Get out of my house!" I cried. "I could kill you for what you have put us through – all that you have done to us!" My reflex response, like a wounded animal attempting to target his assailant by making him aware of how terribly hurt and afraid he was, it was an impassioned outpouring of pent up grief and anguished emotional torment.

"Put the knife down, Lesley," Paul kept repeating it over and over again like a mantra. I couldn't make sense of that. Why keep referring to the knife? I wasn't doing anything with it. And it was nowhere near him. But provocation was making me even more angry and I stood there looking at the knife in my hand.

"If I were a pirate I could slice through your heart – if you even had a heart!" I yelled. Immobilised suddenly, like a frozen statue made of crystal cut ice. White light seemed to engulf me. And I realised with complete and utter certainty that I had only one course of action left open to me. There was no point in any of this. Paul would never change. With clear cut and absolutely rational insight I realised one thing – no one on earth should be allowed to make me feel like this. This pain. This despair.

And it had to stop. Paul's persistent and unremitting attempts to push me completely beyond the boundaries of reason had failed. I wasn't going to fall over the edge into the abyss. It was probably one of the most honest moments of my whole life. "You have no heart, Paul!" I repeated as I turned round, walked slowly back into the kitchen, replacing the knife into the breadbin as usual. Took a glass of water up to bed with me.

The stifling heat was beginning to cool a little. A tiny draught blew through the open bedroom window, rustling the curtains. I heard the front door slam. Paul had apparently gone out. Probably as upset as I was, I thought through the blur of my stinging headache, and stomach cramps.

Maybe he needed some fresh air, a walk round the park, perhaps at long last it had taken this kind of argument to make him realise what he had done to me – to us. Trying to push me beyond the point of self-control into a world plagued by demons. The painkillers kicked in and I drifted off into some kind of sleep.

Voices were loud, oddly disjointed, seeming to come from far away breaking through my semi-conscious state like waves onto a pebbled beach. One was female. Loud. Aggressive. Demanding. "Lesley! Lesley! Get up!" Rapping out a staccato command. Confusion. Someone was pulling pale peach bed sheets from my body.

Shaking me violently awake. My bleary eyes started to focus. Seven uniformed policemen and a policewoman had burst into my bedroom. It was midnight. They stood surrounding my bed, armed with batons and accusations. "What's going on?" I rubbed my eyes trying to comprehend what was confronting me. Then I started to shake. And to cry. "It's Paul isn't it? He's had some kind of accident hasn't he – my husband?"

"No," they replied. Moving in closer, tapping the batons between their hands.

"Oh my goodness – it's not my son William is it?" Then I looked across the landing where Will was following a policeman out of his bedroom. All I could see were white shirts, covered in bright luminous yellow overjackets, hats, epaulettes with gold and blue on them, badges, black batons, total chaos And what on earth were they doing in the very sanctuary of my secluded home – my own bedroom?

"Lesley – we are arresting you for attempted murder!" the policewoman's voice was harsh, brutal.

"What?" I couldn't believe what I was hearing. Complete and utter madness had forced its way into my life. Paul and Denise had just gone too far this time. "No! This is absolutely crazy! There's been some terrible mistake!" I cried.

"Get dressed, we'd like you to accompany us to the police station!"

"No!" I heard myself saying "I'm not going anywhere with you! I haven't done anything wrong! This can all be explained quite simply!" I was surely sleep walking. Awake but slap bang in the middle of a ghoulish nightmare. I would wake up in a minute, and realise I had dreamed of something macabre, that wasn't real. Only I didn't wake up. As I pulled open the wardrobe doors, dragging on trousers and a warm sweater, I could see Paul, hovering on the stairs next to the policemen who seemed to be crawling all over my home like marauding, poisonous ants. I'd never seen that look on anybody's face before in my life. At that moment I didn't even recognise Paul. For he looked insane.

"We have to warn you, Lesley, that you don't have to say anything. Anything you do say can be used in evidence against you and it could harm your defence in Court…" Words, words, spilling out like I'd heard a million times in the films I had worked on and watched, the television series about cops and robbers: *Starsky and Hutch* to *The Bill*, but this was real. This was serious. In my own bedroom. My own sacred sanctuary. My private place that belonged to me and only me.

"I don't understand any of this," I told them as I was being led downstairs, out to the waiting squad cars lined up in the street with flashing blue lights and sirens on top. They were talking on hand-sets, a commotion.

I saw Will climb into his own car. "I'm coming with you, Mum!" he called across to me.

"How did you get into my house?" I asked the policeman sitting beside me.

"We were let in," he replied. "Your husband came down to the station about an hour ago. He played us a tape recording of an argument that he says took place earlier this evening. He maintains it was you and him arguing and we have no reason to disbelieve him.

He says you made threats against his life and tried to kill him. He says he was terribly afraid." Was I the one going mad?

"Tape recording?" I echoed. "Where was the tape recorder?"

Beneath Paul's laptop – hidden like a deadly snake. Now I understood why he kept repeating over and over again, "Put down the knife, Lesley!" Provoking a response from me that he knew would make me lose my temper with him. But surely the whole point was that I had shouted. Certainly, I had an argument. Said stupid words, so dramatic they were laughable. But I didn't touch him! At all. There were no marks on him. I was the one with the migraine headache and period pain, I was the one with a searing pain in my shoulder. Not Paul. And I had been such a terrible threat to Paul that I had simply – gone to bed! Surely if I had it in mind to kill him I would have made a better job of it and would at least have run away? I sat speechless in the back of the squad car like a criminal. They didn't put handcuffs on me at least. The policewoman looked like she wanted to. But the policemen saw the expression in my face and that seemed to convince them that I was not a wildly out of control threat to anyone. The young policeman sitting beside me had gone into impassive expression facial mode. Blank. He didn't look much older than Will. Just a boy. Like the thousands of young soldiers conscripted and sent off to fight for their country in the blood sodden battlefields of the Somme. Goodness – they were hardly even ready to shave the smooth tender skin on their faces. What did they know of life? What experience? Just sent out to do a job. Like an automated Action Man toy that repeated commands like a recorded message, without the necessary built-in equipment to think for itself.

As we drove along in convoy, I looked out of the police car windows at shops I had been into so often to buy shoes, or pieces of fabric for Alana. When I led a normal life. Before I had been unwittingly thrust into this three-ring circus, orchestrated by the craziest and most dangerous circus clown of all – my husband – Paul Pearson. Will followed all the way to the police station, in his own car. When we got there it was midnight. Freezing cold. The desk sergeant was aggressive, treating me with disdain. And I could only think – how dare he regard me like this, what right did he have to do so when I had not been found guilty of committing any crime? The police were apportioning the same degree of contempt they would dish out to a wino sleeping rough in the streets, a heroin pusher or a prostitute, a real thief or a murderer. Yet you have to play the game the moment you are incarcerated inside the walls of this institution. Don't answer back. Don't say anything. Just stand there like a person condemned to the gallows. A person you are not. Innocent before proven guilty? Huh! Rubbish. They were taking Paul's word against mine. Listening like children behind the bike sheds to some tacky little tape that he had recorded of an argument I wasn't even being allowed to hear. Words I had shouted. I didn't even know I was being taped. That had been done in secrecy. A domestic argument. A foolish and personal exchange between a man and his wife who had been together for nearly twenty-five years. It was embarrassing, mortifying. What kind of a mentality does it take for someone to do such a thing? I couldn't equate it with the way I had treated Paul over the years. I couldn't believe he could put me through all this. I was ordered to put my leather handbag onto the counter. My best one, that Will had bought me for my birthday. Empty out all the contents.

They tipped out everything, itemising it and examining it one by one. "What are these?" demanded the sergeant holding aloft my little white cardboard box of tablets from Dr McKenzie.

"They're for Meniere's Disease – to stop me from being dizzy." I replied. He confiscated them as if they had been hard drugs. And my money. There was a lot of cash in my bag which my mother had generously pressed into my unwilling hands earlier that day for me to get food for William and me. In another life. A few hours ago. "There is quite a lot of cash there, I know. I haven't robbed a Bank or anything," I ventured.

He glanced at me with an indifferent expression. "Take off your shoes!" commanded the policewoman like someone from the Gestapo.

I walked bare-footed along the cold stone corridor. Either side of it were cells. She marched me to the very end of the corridor. Huge bunch of keys dangling from a chain in her hands. She flung open the door. It was pitch black. Like a dungeon.

"Go in!" she demanded. The only times I had ever walked down a corridor had been when I was shown into a room in four-star hotels. Or Disneyland.

"I can't – I get claustrophobia! I cannot go in there – please don't make me!" I begged her. She roughly pushed me in. Then I heard the 'clank!' of the heavy metal door clanging shut behind me. No light. A bench made of stone. Painted some hideous colour either bottle green or blue, it was too dark to tell. The metal door had a tiny hatch on it – which you could lift and rattle if you wanted someone to come and the window was a minute skylight with coloured glass, high above my head. I couldn't reach it and I couldn't see out. I had been wantonly abandoned in hell.

A shiver ran through my whole body as I shuddered with fear. The stone floor was very cold. I sat down on the hard bench, feeling numb. I realise now that I look back I was in total and complete shock.

I could dimly make out something wet and slimy slithering down the corner of the cell, running and dripping across the stagnating flagged floor. This cell's previous occupant had been so fearful he had urinated up the wall and let it go, and go…

I felt giddy, I felt sick, and terribly, terribly afraid. Why oh why had Paul done this to me? How could he even begin to think that I would attempt to murder him or kill him? My husband, the father of my only son, who had been beside me all these years. Mr and Mrs... and all that stood for. Me, of all people. Had he really been so in fear of me that he would go running off to the Police in the middle of the night? Things like this just didn't happen to decent people like me! Was he attempting to completely terrorise me? He was doing an excellent job of it. I found a small round bell by the hatch, and I pressed it. And then I pressed it harder once again. A policewoman came along, peering through it to look at me and see what I wanted.

"I need to go to the toilet," I told her.

"I'll have to come with you," she said. I asked her if she could get something from my handbag for me. Feminine protection. There were no doors, steel walls surrounded a steel toilet. The policewoman stood watching me, right by my side. My humiliation, shame and degradation was complete and absolute. Paul had turned my very existence, my very being, into someone I could no longer even recognise. Certainly someone I didn't wish to be. I tried to hold on to my dignity, knowing at that moment I felt as if I had been stripped of my whole self.

And as I sat there huddled in the darkness, isolated. So many thoughts went in and out of my head. I knew he was trying to frighten me – this was the ultimate threat. But surely even Paul must back down from this terrible trajectory?

Surely he must see reason, the senselessness of pursuing this. We still had our son to consider for one thing. The hours went by. And I sat there. Completely alone. And the slow tick-tock of time still went staggering slowly onwards. At about three o'clock in the morning the door was abruptly flung open. "We need to take a statement from you," said the two policemen confronting me.

"I want legal advice," I replied. I was marched straight back to the cell. Told to wait there, in the dark.

"The duty solicitor has a cold," I was eventually told. Too ill to come along to the police station especially at such a late hour. So

I had to be content with speaking to him on the telephone. He was as helpful as he could be given the circumstances. Snuffling woolly advice down the other end of the phone. But screaming inside my head was the feeling that I should simply have somebody here with me to represent me, not miles away at the other end of the phone. I needed someone beside me. Helping me. Telling me what to do. Protecting me.

I had never felt so absolutely alone. "Where's my son?" I asked the policewoman with the built-in frown.

"He's in the car park," she fired back her reply. Short. Sharp.

"Can someone please look after him? Give him a drink, or something. Tell him that I'm OK?" I asked her.

"He's old enough to look after himself!" she retorted scornfully. I stared up at the white police boards shining in the reflected light hanging over the desk sergeant's head. There was a list of that night's crimes, scribbled upon it in thick black magic marker. And then I saw it right at the bottom of the disjointed ugly list – 'Pearson – Threats to Kill'! I shuddered. Icy coldness shooting down my spine. I felt light-headed as if I was drunk. The pain up the back of my neck and across my temples was intense. Throbbing like swords entering my whole body.

'Threats to Kill…' what did those awful words have to do with me? My life? I felt strangely unconnected to this asylum I'd been slung into. Then, through the fog of incomprehension that was holding me captive in its vice-like grip, one single rational thought managed to fight its way through to my racing brain. For whatever reason, the Police had decided, despite Paul's terrible and grisly allegations, that it wasn't 'Attempted Murder' that was scrawled haphazardly on the notice board in careless letters. Instead, it was 'Threats to Kill'. Still pretty gruesome to look at, but not what Paul had wanted me charged with. Not what he had wanted – at all.

They took me back to the cell once more. "Would you like a cup of tea?" asked the young Policeman.

"Thank you – yes I would, please. Can you see if my son's alright and take him a cup too?" I asked him.

"I'll see what I can do," he replied. Suddenly a terrible sound emanated from the cell next to mine. Male, hysterically shouting abusive obscene swear words. Rattling the metal plate on the door like a wild caged creature, until the echoes of the tormented soul inside reverberated off the walls and all the way down the corridor. It was a ghostly, ghastly, chilling sound that shook me with fear and made my blood run cold.

I sat on the bench, pulling my legs up beneath me so that they didn't come into contact with the filthy floor. Trying so hard to come to terms with what Paul was crudely, cruelly subjecting me to. All the faithful years I had shared with him. Stood by him, no matter what. I had tried so hard. His betrayal was complete and absolute and I had no way of comprehending how and why he could do this to me and his only son. And just like all prisoners and captives before me – I simply could not think of a way out.

I knew that Paul and Denise had cooked up this whole scheme down to the very last detail. I was also beginning to wonder if Paul's policeman friend was also somehow involved. I had been stitched up, set up. Framed by a hidden tape recorder designed to rob me of my very reason. Would I have to be locked up in jail forever? My whole life had been brutally, indiscriminately smashed and swiped from me in swift, ugly strokes of a policeman's pen and a concealed micro tape. I knelt on the bench, staring up at the tiny skylight, trying to see something – anything. Knowing that William was sitting outside in the dark, somewhere in that lonely car park. Waiting for me. Afraid for me. But waiting I did the only thing that I could do. The only thing now left to me. I knelt down on the cold stone bench, put my hands tightly together – and prayed.

Chapter Twenty-Four

At around 5.00 am the door was thrown back again by two policemen. It made a heavy, grating, scraping sound. "We need to take a statement," they told me in a matter of fact tone. I followed them bleakly into a white painted room filled with recording equipment and some plastic chairs and a desk. My 'Rights' were read to me once more. "Do you understand?" they repeated.

No. I didn't understand any of it. Only that I was sick and tired and exhausted and weary and worried and I just wanted to get out of this dreadful place once and for all. And the only way to do it appeared to be giving a statement to the Police. My mind was whirring – slowly – but nevertheless, whirring. What was Paul playing at, this deadly vicious game? It would have been pointless me denying we had an argument, and in any case why would I say it hadn't taken place? I was an honest person wasn't I? A reasonable person. I had nothing to hide, did I? If Paul had indeed played a tape recording to the Police that night, accusing me of trying to murder him – well, surely common sense would prevail and they would realise that it was simply not true. Or was this all mixed up with Paul's paranoia? That the merest hint of disagreement with him, resisting him, every perceived 'slight' was magnified a million times over. Blown out of all proportion. I knew this about Paul. I also realised Denise's personality was a histrionic version of his. No wonder they got on so well. They were the soul mates Paul and I could never be. It was Denise who had threatened to sue someone at the office for allegedly touching her bottom standing next to her at the photocopying machine. She who had persuaded Paul to take his previous partner to Court and sue them for damages. She who bragged of 'friends in high places in the legal profession'.

Run-around-and-Sue I had nicknamed the pair of them privately. They had even sent a solicitor's letter and threatened to sue me and my mother – for no reason at all. But how on earth do you attempt to explain all that to two still wet-behind-the-ears police officers in the wee small hours of the morning. When you have spent all night long in a police cell, feeling sick with fear. When your head is thumping, when your eyes are so tired you can hardly force them open any longer. When your son is patiently and worriedly waiting in the car park outside. Paul was a monster, certainly, yet I apparently the accused.

"This is all about our house!" I told them. They looked perplexed.

"I don't understand," said the older of the two, with a bald head like a bowling ball, and stubbly shoots of hair attempting to break free.

"We are going through a divorce. I have already told you this. My husband insists our home belongs to him and he is absolutely determined to hang on to it at any any cost. He doesn't care how he gets it!" I started to cry then. Hopeless tears of grief and utter frustration. They stopped the tape. Brought me some tissues. Deep inside I had come to the horrifying realisation during that long night all alone in the cell, that Paul was prepared to put me in one of two 'secure' places to ensure that he would be able to retain our house and everything we owned, lock stock and smoking chimney. He obviously intended to have me committed to a prison cell or a mental institution. Either way he thought he was now safely rid of me. And that I would be unable to live my life without him.

Even after all the years sharing the same home and everything else, Paul did not know me. Not the real me. I was not about to toss away my liberty so carelessly or lightly.

But I also knew he had landed me in deep trouble of the very worst kind. And I had to keep a level head in order to fight my way out of it. "If Paul wants the house – let him have it!" I told the policeman. "I will put it on the market – immediately."

He peered back at me. "But last night you told me that no way would you leave your home! You were most emphatic about that."

"That's right. I was," I replied.

"What made you change it?"

"A night locked up inside one of your cells!" I told him. Salty tears were in my eyes now, spilling down my cheeks and running down the side of my nose till they fell into my mouth.

"That's some change of mind isn't it?" he continued. "I mean to change it so quickly," he clicked his fingers in the air. "Jut like that! It's amazing!"

Yes, I thought. Amazing. That intimidation, strong-arm tactics and blackmail can still be used so ruthlessly and effectively by the powerful against the powerless. And so they carried on and on recording two whole tapes full of so-called 'evidence'.

"Was your husband in fear?" they eventually asked me.

I gave a wry laugh. "My husband has never been in fear of anyone in his entire life! Least of all me! He knows me very well and that I could never harm him. He is the father of my only son."

The PC bent his flat bald head a little lower. "Did he ask you to approach him with a bread knife, and threaten to kill him?!" It was an overly dramatic and brutal description of what had taken place in our lounge.

"No," I replied wearily.

"Say that again?" they persisted.

"No – look I had a bread knife in my hand. That's true. When you are a woman you walk around the house with a lot of different things in your hands. Depending on where you are and what you are doing at the time. But you don't intend to use them to harm someone. I don't know anyone – married or single for that matter – who has not turned round to someone they love at some point in their lives and said the words, 'I could kill you!'. They are words we all shout at each other in the heat of the moment. In temper. And we say things to hurt and wound the other person because we have been so hurt by them. And for just a moment we want them to realise what they have done to us. How we feel. Nothing more than that!" This was barmy beyond belief. I knew people who had thrown crockery, plates of food, glasses of wine, even a knife which impaled itself in a wooden door, during domestic disagreements. In the intense heat of a difficult divorce when temperatures are soaring, mitigating circumstances abound by the barrel load. But they weren't listening to any of the explanations I was attempting to give them. They had already made up their minds – been got at – by Paul. And maybe they were as intimidated and afraid of him as everyone else could be at times.

"You were angry!" they kept repeating.

"No I wasn't angry."

"You must have been angry – you had just cut up your wedding photographs, you already told us that. You must have been very angry! Angry enough to kill him!"

"I wasn't angry – I was upset!" I carried on defending my corner like a boxer without gloves.

"Did you say anything to your husband about his heart?" The bald cop glanced sideways at his notebook, then straight back up at me.

"I remember telling him he doesn't have one," I replied. He merely bent his head forward then, scribbling down something on the crumpled pages.

"Yes," he said. "I remember that bit."

Soon after that, they took me back to the sergeant's desk. I stood completely still as I was formally charged with 'Threats to Kill'.

I had my photograph taken just like Hugh Grant did when caught with a prostitute having oral sex in a car in Beverly Hills. They took my finger prints, coating my small hands with thick black ink and pressing them onto glaring white sheets of paper. The youngest of the two police officers helped me to wipe off all the goo from my hands with tissues and told me he had given a drink of some kind to William. "He's a nice lad," he said.

"Yes – I know. I wouldn't have got by without him," I said.

Now the sergeant was arrogantly reading out my 'bail' conditions. "You must not go anywhere near Paul Pearson! You must not attempt to return to your house or within a radius of five kilometres. You must not interfere with Paul Pearson in any way, he must not suffer harassment of any kind…" The words were a jumbled blur of an excuse of legal junk draped in deceit. Paul had got what he was after at last. Oh – what a sweet victory for him and Denise. How they must be rejoicing, laughing their heads off with glee at my expense. "You have to attend the Magistrates Court on Friday. If you break the terms of bail in any way whatsoever, then you will be re-arrested and go straight back to prison. You must stay at your mother's home. You must sleep there each night. You are not allowed to sleep anywhere else overnight. You cannot go away. You must report back to your mother's home every night. You must not return even to pick up clothes or personal items. Your son must get them if you need anything. Do you understand? Lesley – do you understand?!"

Oh yes, I understood all right. I was led out into the early morning summer sunshine, escorted by the policeman. The fresh air had never smelled so sweet to me. The sky looked impossibly pale blue and wide open – I was still alive. I was outside of that terrible hell hole of a dungeon.

Will ran over to me, clasping my arm tightly. "Mum!" He kissed me. "Are you alright?!" I nodded.

"Yes," I was too choked to speak.

"It's so sad it had to happen this way," the policeman was saying. "It could have been either one of you walking out here beside me this morning. It's just your rotten luck it turned out to be you." It had nothing to do with luck – rotten or otherwise. But I was too exhausted to disagree or attempt any further explicit clarification. I just needed to be with Will. "Think of this as the beginning," said the PC. "The first day of the rest of your new life – with your son."

***

Some experiences are so horrifying that while you are enduring them you are numb. Like someone lopping off their big toe with a lawnmower and not even feeling the pain until later. I was traumatised with disbelief, shock and an overwhelming sense of fear and foreboding. My mother became unexpectedly strong. William was simply my champion.

I was ordered to appear at the Magistrates Court on Friday morning. On Thursday afternoon my legs would hardly support my weight as I attempted to navigate a trolley round the local branch of Tescos. I was completely terrified by the thought of being made to go back inside the prison cell. The Police had informed me in no uncertain terms that I had no choice what-soever. Either I agreed to stay at my mother's house or I would be re-arrested and locked up inside the cell once more. I would have taken off to the Moon in a solar-powered bucket if they had told me to. I felt woozy and dizzy, completely galvanised by frozen fear that was locked deep inside me. I had never ex-perienced anything like this in my whole life.

While my mother searched vaguely for cartons of fresh ap-ple juice and bunches of bananas I scoured the shelves of the pharmacy section searching for packets of extra strength Disprin and paracetamol. I bought two large boxes while my mother was preoccupied with frozen peas. Unceremoniously stuffing them into the pockets of my jeans before she returned. At that moment I felt truly desperate. I felt I had been left with no choice. I could not free my mind from the vice-like grip of terror that consumed me. I could not face the gruesome prospect of ever being locked up inside a cell again as long as I lived. I knew if I was told by the Courts that I would have to go to prison, I would take both lots of painkillers, I thought. I would have a way out of this crippling well of horror that I had been viciously kicked down into. At that moment, I was too afraid not to. I felt I just could not carry on any longer. I was finished. I stared up at the ceiling from my bed, unable to sleep. Lying very still. My mother's voice drifted over towards me. Commanding. From what seemed far, far away. "Think of William, Lesley," she said. "You're all he has." Then she turned out the lights.

Before going through the legal proceedings involved in my divorce from Paul, I had never set foot inside a Court room. I didn't know the difference between High Court, County Court,

Magistrates Court, or even the difference between a solicitor and a Barrister. I had never been anywhere near one. Ever. Friday morning dawned, hot and sunny and humid. I am reliably informed that it used to be referred to as 'The Cop Shop Court'. The local Magistrates Court was alarmingly surreal. For beneath the actual Courts are the cells. And in those cells, they keep hardened criminals who are locked up until they are ordered to appear. No bail for these 'heavies'.

In the morning they are accompanied by armed guards to the open-plan top floor where the Courts are situated. From rooms with iron bars bolted across the windows to glass that you can actually see out across the rooftops of the City spread out like a toy town below. "Lesley Pearson." I gave my name to the woman sitting at the reception desk. She was wearing a long black gown. And a grey wig slightly askance on her blonde page boy haircut. She looked carefully down the long typed list.

"Who are you representing?" she asked me smiling. I explained that I was the one being represented by someone else – my barrister – Amy Franklin, who had told me she would meet me at the Court. "Oh." She referred back to the list. The expression on her face altogether different now, or was it me imagining it? I felt different. Like someone had just clicked their fingers and magicked away the 'real' me the 'honest law abiding citizen' me and suddenly turned me into an alien from another planet. Not a nice person any longer. Not respectable. Not me at all. Then she looked back at me through the dusty glass. "Are you pleading guilty – or not guilty?" I just shook my head. "Fill in these forms, please and return them when you have done so." She thrust a handful of papers through the slit at the bottom. I didn't think I could stand any more degradation. I walked slowly past scruffily clad youths with knitted woolly hats, pulled low on their foreheads down to their eyes. Some in cuffs with their probation officers. Some looked angry and belligerent. Some just looked plain scared. Two teenage girls with bright pink miniskirts slit to their waists and heaps of junk jewellery slung carelessly around their necks. On the game. Arrested for selling their bodies. But so many women do just that, all over the world, every day of their lives. Disguised to cover the disgrace and deceit like a shroud – it's called 'marriage'.

I slid onto a seat. Amy appeared before me. Short, sweet and armed with such an enormous bundle of files and folders I thought for a moment she would lose her balance and topple over falling flat on her little elfin face. She didn't. What Amy Franklin lacked in inches was more than compensated for. She was erudite, enlightened and willing to do for me what none of the legal professionals who were supposed to protect and help me had done so far – quite simply – Amy Franklin was prepared to fight for me. Amy was young and ambitious and bright but without the trappings of self-satisfaction and self-appointed superiority that so often cling to the mantles of solicitors and barristers like superglue. Judges that I had dealt with recently throughout my divorce and the wheeling and dealings hovered above like venomous vultures overseeing the spread of a rampant disease that was rotten and decaying. Dickensian and out of touch and elitist. Amy was quite simply a breath of fresh air in the middle of the stench. Open-minded, fresh-faced and determined.

Taking my arm she said, "Come with me – you look all wrong sitting there! You shouldn't be sitting out here with this lot. We'll find a room where we can talk – properly."

The burly Court Attendant scowled disapprovingly as Amy swept past her, brushing protestation aside. She found a little room. Tiny, quiet and peaceful, mercifully away from the hubbub outside. With a pine desk. Three wooden chairs with faded cushions surrounded it. And a coffee machine was right outside the door. She half dropped the files onto the desk, spreading the papers out all over it. "Now," she said, crossing her arms on the table and leaning forwards towards me. "Would you like to tell me exactly what has happened?"

I did. And as I opened up to Amy the floodgates burst. Torrents of tears, which threatened never to stop, the deluge was so enormous. Like a dam bursting. Like a tropical storm raining down on me through the mid-summer heat. I didn't just confess what had happened that night. It was a confirmation and affirmation of all that had gone so tragically wrong in my once 'perfect marriage'. To the wrong man. "I am so sorry," I apologised, wiping my nose, pushing away salty tears that welled in my eyes and rolled down my burning cheeks, splashing onto my new notepad below.

"It's alright." She patted my hands as she pulled her own chair even closer. "It's the shock. You've been in shock, Lesley. And now it's all coming out. That's all!" I looked up at her. Yes, that was it. Simple. I hadn't been able to put it into words before. "It's a delayed reaction to all that has happened to you in the last few days. Let it come out. Don't be afraid to cry. You'll feel better! I'll ask the Court to list your hearing for later. You'll be able to face it more when you're not so upset. More composed." Amy then asked if I minded if she attended to one of 'her boys' first. "It's not his first time! He's a real tearaway. Now – he really is guilty, I'm afraid!" She disappeared.

I sipped coffee from a paper cup. Didn't really taste of anything. But it was warm. It helped to settle my trembling, tangled thoughts momentarily. When Amy re-appeared she listened intently to everything I told her. Writing brief notes in the margin of her sheaf of papers. "I've seen this so many times!" she said, clenching her small fist on the table. "It really makes my blood boil! Domestic Violence! And it's the men who are in most cases the perpetrators, yet always the women who end up in trouble! Don't get me started on that one – we'll be here all day long. Suffice to say that I work with abused women a lot. It is always so unfair. Like scales out of balance. We females are expected to be the nurturing ones, the protectors, and therefore it's the women who try so hard to keep the family together, to cover things up – until everything just gets worse and worse, eventually spiralling out of control."

I squashed the tear-stained handkerchief between my fingers. "I realise now that I should have walked away from all these years ago. It's all my fault. I feel so guilty!" I sobbed.

"No!" she replied firmly putting a restraining hand on top of my damp clenched ones. "It isn't! I have spoken to so many women about these things. Working with specialist domestic violence units. If you could have left you would have left at the time. But there were reasons why you didn't. There are always reasons. And if there were reasons then you couldn't have done it before. For heaven's sake, Lesley – Don't blame yourself! It's not you! There are enough people laying all the blame at your door and accusing you of things! There are plenty of people out there telling you it's all your fault – don't be one of them! Now, let's go and see what the Magistrates have to say. Oh – and don't forget, Lesley – chin up! When they ask you just reply in a clear voice. Your plea is NOT GUILTY!"

The seven hours that we hung around inside the Magistrates Court that day seemed like an eternity. The courtroom was as I'd seen on TV so many times. Three magistrates, two men and one woman sat behind a long wooden bench. Behind them on the wall was the Coat of Arms. Anyone can be a magistrate, I am told. No special legal training is necessary. But the three people confronting me at that moment didn't feel like just 'anyone'. I was ushered to a chair by the lady in charge of the courtroom. "All rise!" We stood.

Paul's representative had been appointed by the Crown Prosecution Service. He stood up immediately and in an accent brimming with privilege read out the charge against me. "The Crown…" The Crown? Paul had abused both me and Will physically and subjected us to verbal violence for years. And yet here he was, being represented by, protected by, cowering like a coward behind the 'defence' of the Crown. Injudicious hypocrisy. I wondered if the Queen was aware of what slid by like daily sewage down the drains of Windsor Castle in the Law Courts, in her name? I started to shake involuntarily from head to toe and couldn't stop. I collapsed. A Court orderly came over to me and handed me a beaker of cold water.

Amy approached the Bench. Then she asked me to wait outside, while she checked some points of Law. Eventually, she reappeared. "They are prepared to change the terms of Bail and the Court Hearing will be in six weeks' time," she told me.

I was called back once more to hear what the Magistrates had decided. They read out my amended terms of bail conditions in monotone voices. This time I was allowed to return to my home in order to collect clothes, and personal items, as long as I was accompanied by two police officers. Paul had to agree on the date and time in advance. I wasn't allowed to speak to Paul or to contact him at all. I was still not allowed to go anywhere near my own home. I was given permission to take Will on a short holiday that I had booked the day before this had all blown up in my face. The magistrate in a grey suit smiled at me when he announced that I could go away.

"With my son?" I said. He nodded in agreement and fidgeted with the frame of his glasses. Finally, I took Amy's last piece of sincere advice.

"Which Court have you elected to be tried in?" asked the Magistrate, holding a long black pen in his hand.

"The Crown Court," I replied evenly. He nodded as he wrote that down in long swift strokes.

Everyone in this country has the right to be tried by Jury, Amy told me. Twelve good men and women and true. I was prepared to be judged by my peers. My equals. Amy shook my hand vigorously. "We did well! See you in six weeks' time! Enjoy the holiday with your son!" She smiled.

Summertime blues descended all around me like a thick blanket of darkness. Filled with sorrow and gloom and continued delayed shock as the full and sickening realisation of all that had taken place engulfed me. I woke in the middle of the night drenched in sweat and shaking from head to foot like an out-of-control jelly; I was still so terrified. Consumed by fear. Reliving every single moment over and over again in my head like an old cine film that just wouldn't stop and yearned for the plug to be pulled on it. Feeling sick. I walked along river banks and across corn fields of gold, but wherever I went I found no peace of mind. No resting place. No hiding place. I was completely exhausted. Devoured. I had never had my freedom obliterated before. It was emotionally harrowing and incomprehensible. I was on the brink. Paul could go wherever he wanted and do as he pleased with who he wanted to. He had started to entertain Denise in our home, flaunting their affair. And Alan Parkinson, his policeman friend, was a regular Sunday lunch guest and beer swilling comrade. No manacle of iron secured around my ankle could have bolted me more firmly to terra firma. Paul had pushed me to a place where resistance had proved to be futile. Suddenly I could appreciate with clear vision how the Jews must have felt in Nazi Germany, Anne Frank in Amsterdam, ordinary Russians under Stalin's rule. Or anyone living in a police state, indecorously robbed of their own home, their own possessions, their own passport and bank books – their whole life in fact.

'Threats to kill'. *I could kill you for what you have done!* Careless words tossed into the air like a pancake yet I was being forced to reside in this hell, because I had uttered them in the heat of an argument during this deadly divorce I was sailing recklessly through the centre of on a terrible voyage into the bowels of perdition.

I picked up a dandelion and blew the flared bits off of the ends, watching as they flew off like dusty moths into the evening sun that was fading hot red on the horizon. Why do people kill anyway? I had always imagined murderers must either be insane or wickedly cruel beyond belief and help. Certainly not worthy of anybody's pity. Yet now I was even beginning to question that. Why do people kill? Why does an animal kill? Because they are maybe propelled into a situation that they can tolerate no longer and find no way out of, pushed beyond the point of reason, and they end up so complexly afraid that they believe for a moment that no other choice is left. And I came to the conclusion, as I watched the sun fall down like a guillotine beyond the cornfields, that fear has the potential to make killers of us all.

Emotional pain used utter shame as its unwilling dance partner. I felt humiliated. Out of touch with any reality that I had known or perceived. I felt like I'd sunk to the very bottom of the ocean, without a trace. Grotesquely grounded, unable to fight my way back up to the daylight at the surface. A kind of non-person. Plundered and paralysed. Everything I held dear was brutally stripped from me. Only it hadn't been. For I also knew that the most priceless treasure of all was still with me. William. It was his choice to be with me. And everyone else had cautioned, "We would advise William to stay with you – for his own safety." Police, solicitors, magistrates, friends – so who was the threat – exactly? And who was on bail – exactly?

Chapter Twenty-Five

Evening sunshine was flickering through the windows when the phone started to ring. "Lesley – how are you?" It was Lucy. I told her – everything. I cried a lot. she understood. Lucy being Lucy. She was graphic in her choice of colourful superlatives and expletives and went into cringing details of what she would like to do to Paul. Which made me laugh out loud for what seemed the first time in years. Finally, she admitted something I'd often wondered about, but never dared put into actual words. "It's not just you, Lesley. I had a lot of trouble with Trey. That's why we ended up getting divorced. That and his alcohol problem. He was a bully, too. Not quite like Paul – but a bully nevertheless."

I felt awkward, retrospectively disloyal. I should have been there for my best friend when she needed me. "You never told me about it," I half whispered.

"How were you to know? And let's face it – it's not something you want to talk about at the time – when you're slap bang in the middle of it and trying to cope – is it?" she said firmly. "And, Lesley – when I lost the baby? Well, I've never actually told anyone this. I didn't fall off that chair. Trey and I had a terrible row, he had been drinking a lot that night. He pushed and shoved me and – well, you know?"

Yes, I did now. Only too well. Sweet-natured Lucy, full of confidence, full of life, stuck with a misfit of a man who couldn't fulfil his promises either and tried to push all the blame onto her shoulders instead of taking responsibility for his own actions. "Let's have lunch and a real talk!" she suggested. I agreed to meet her on Sunday for lunch at the Watermill.

Two days later I received a text message on my mobile phone. At first, I couldn't make head or tail of it. My mind was obsessed with Court proceedings, legal jargon, and fretting about every passing police car. I had even convinced myself that the Police helicopters circling overhead near the local aerodrome were actually watching with me with long-distance binoculars.

I squinted into the small screen as the bright sunshine reflected back at me from it, and started to read what somebody had sent to me. "Complete disaster. Mock, crock shock! Back from the outback in from the cold. When R U free 4 lunch?" At the bottom, it said – "The Wizard of Oz!" What was this rubbish somebody was sending me, some kind of sick joke? A crackpot from the police station with a Judy Garland fixation, who had mysteriously managed to get hold of my mobile phone number?

I looked back at the screen again. Re-read it. Then I looked at the number. I knew this number. It was Ainsley's number! I couldn't believe it. Ainsley had come back home. And I was instantly so glad. I replied to his message straight away, sitting cross-legged on the grass in my mother's garden, warm sunshine massaging my bare shoulders. "Out of jail – on bail – at mum's," I tapped in carefully. Moments later the telephone in my hand started to vibrate, playing the tune I had programmed into it, Bizet's 'Toreador's song', from *Carmen*.

"Lesley?" his voice was like smooth silk, warm and reassuring. "What have you been up to? What's all this about?" And as relief started to engulf my body like a tidal wave, my bones began to feel soft like dough, not brittle like rock candy. Easing the terrible pain inside of me and lifting momentarily the tremendous weight from my back.

"Oh, Ainsley!" His voice truly was at the end of my phone. Connected. At last.

"I'm listening," he said. "I've got plenty of time. Tell me all about it."

And so I did. He listened silently while I poured out my heart to him. Then when I'd told him everything he gave a hugely audible sigh. "You're still speaking to me then?" I tested his reaction half-jokingly. Only half sure what he would think of me now, I'd changed. Not the girl he'd known.

"Yes! Of course, I'm still speaking to you! I'd still be speaking to you even if you had actually killed him! But don't do it, Lesley! Please!" He laughed. There was mitigation in Ainsley's laughter. "Don't go anywhere near him – or the house! Don't give him any opportunity. Just keep well away from him. He'll only try to get you into trouble again!" I couldn't have agreed with him more.

"I came close to nearly ending it all. I bought two big boxes of Disprin and paracetamol." I felt ashamed as I confessed to him like a schoolgirl to a Priest.

"Well, I don't know quite what you thought that would achieve, exactly! I suppose you wouldn't have had a headache for a week or two!" His tone was stern now, fatherly almost. "There are too many people who care too much about you to even think of doing anything like that," he told me.

That's when I started to weep silently. "When are you free for lunch then?" he asked, lifting the gloom and transferring the weight of expectation.

"Next Tuesday?" I replied.

"OK – I'll see you then. Oh, and just one other thing, Lesley?"

"What?"

"Don't' bring your police escort with you!"

I laughed feeling freedom embrace me.

"What about you, Ainsley – what's happened?"

"Oh, disaster, Lesley – complete disaster. Don't worry I'll tell you all about it when we have lunch next week. See you later!"

I felt overwhelmingly cheered up. Optimism filling my thoughts after long hot dismal weeks of depressing negativity and fear. I filled a glass with fruit juice and gazed up at the vivid yellow sunshine bursting from the dazzling blue sky. What a beautiful day it had turned out to be!

We met down by the river, as usual. A gorgeous summer suddenly, warm breezes softly blowing across the rippling water. Everyone was kitted out in shorts and brilliantly coloured sundresses and miniskirts of pink, orange, lime and white. It was one of those days with a 'buzz' in the air that you only get in England when the sun decides to come out in all its glory. Holiday atmosphere, a rising tide of eau de cologne and ambre solaire scenting the steaming, sweating streets. I saw Ainsley in the distance straight away. Unmistakable still, the way he stood leaning nonchalantly against the pale grey brick wall, with one long leg loosely crossed in front of the other, running his fingers idly through his long black shining fringe. Wearing a white T-shirt and dark navy jeans. He put his hand up to half-shield his eyes from the glare of the dazzling mid-day sunshine. He had already seen me approaching. Holding out his hands at arm's length in front of his lithe body. "Don't! Don't do it, Lesley! I'm an unarmed man!" he called out. "Oh, by the way – you're looking ridiculously cheerful for a fugitive!" I chuckled, swiping his elbow with my hand.

"Very funny – Now tell me why you've decided to come home so soon? What's been happening to you on the other side of the world?" He lowered his right arm very slowly, that's when I first caught sight of it. Carved deep beneath his flawless high right cheek bone, a livid bruise and a crooked deep purple slash. Ainsley's perfectly tanned, perfectly handsome face, had been irreversibly mutilated. "Ainsley!" My voice was a kind of strangled sob. "Oh – good heavens above – whatever has happened to you?!" I reached out involuntarily to touch his face. He winced, flinching backwards. Awkwardly away from me. Trying to smile. A half-hearted attempt that distorted his face, twisting it sideways as the scars slid down his face like acid on magnesium.

I bit my bottom lip so hard I could taste the salt of blood and then I burst into tears and started to cry. "It's alright, Lesley – don't get upset." He patted my hands.

"Why didn't you tell me, Ainsley? Why?!" I found myself pumping his forearm up and down, like someone trying to draw water from a deep well. I don't quite know what I thought that would achieve, exactly. I just felt a compulsion to hold onto him, to make physical contact with him. His black hair was now streaked with grey, I could see close up. He had dark blue Oakland glasses enveloping his eyes. "What's behind these?"

I reached up to slide them carefully from his lacerated face. He stared back at me, swollen, dusky circles of mauve and indigo and magenta edged with sickly yellows, like the wounds of a warrior. His chocolate brown eyes were bleary beneath drooping, weary lids. "Oh, Ainsley!" I put my arms around him and hugged him tightly. This time he didn't try to stop me.

We found seats right by the water's edge. The mid-day heat shone from the flowing river, glinting silvery sparks of reflections shooting along beside us like arrows. Timber tables roasted as we inhaled the piquant smell of beer-stained wood. We both had an awful lot to talk about as we shared chilled Chablis and warm chicken salads. I swiftly brought Ainsley up to date with my troubles, sharing them with him and watching his mobile features react the way they always did. With pity, shock, and finally, pain. I wasn't being selfish. I reasoned that if I talked first it would give him a chance to relax enough to feel comfortable with me once again. Even though the face looking at me from across the table was no longer the face I had known all these years. Yet in a comfortingly familiar, rational way – it still was. And as I talked, and he listened intently, I realised it didn't matter what he looked like.

Ainsley was still Ainsley, and always would be. He was my best friend and always had been. And he must be in such agony. His beautiful classic features, battered, and half-broken. I tried not to focus on the terrible mess down the right-hand side of his lop-sided cheeks. But I only half managed to convince both of us that everything was still as it had been. "Are you going to tell me then?" I gulped a large mouthful of cool wine, leaning on the table with my arms folded in front of me. "I'll shut up now. It's your turn to talk!"

And so he told me. How he had departed from Sydney early one spring morning and met up with some English kids from Essex, Molly, Sam and Tracy, who had left good jobs in the City to go trekking in Australia. How they had first of all headed to the Gold Coast, which was spectacular and full of brand-new condominiums. Moving on up northwards, to the Great Barrier

Reef, and then he had left his young companions enjoying the coral and the surf and the amazing beaches, to set off alone, go walk-about to discover the fundamental centre of Australia and the innermost part of himself. The 'real free true spirit' locked up inside both of them. With a guide called Gus. Who sounded like a complete idiot. But it was not time for misgivings and regrets. Just as my temporary lapse of judgement had left me in chaos with the Law, it was too late for Ainsley to turn back time any more than I could. What had happened, had already happened and there was nothing either of us could do to change it. "He asked if I wanted to go and see the places where the crocodiles congregate." Ainsley was talking in hushed tones now. "And you know, I thought, that sounds cool – like…"

"Like *Crocodile Dundee* in the movie?" I said it for him.

"Yes, yes." He looked a little sheepish, perspiration dripping through his fringe as he brushed it aside.

"But unlike the movies, this was for real. They were proper crocodiles for sure – not fibre glass models! Gus was an alright kind of bloke, you know one of the lads, but he was also a bit brainless when it came to taking proper safety precautions with the kind of 'hands-on' Safari trips into the Bush. Anyway, we went out on this expedition together, just the two of us, and this sounds so daft that this could happen, I can hardly bring myself to tell you about it. One moment I was standing on the edge of the river bank in boiling hot sunshine, the next I heard Gus shout, 'Watch out for the crocs!' And when I looked across to the middle of the water sure enough there it was – I could actually see it – a real crocodile, half out of the water and heading straight for me. I think it was a baby one probably, but it looked pretty big and pretty fierce to me, I can tell you. I must have reacted so quickly at the sight of it, I lost my foothold and fell over. Flat on my face. Probably fell over my own feet it all happened so fast; I'll never know for sure. Anyway, there was a rusty little boat that we were supposed to get into in order to paddle down stream to see the crocodiles. That had been the plan. There was a big piece of jagged metal attached to the corroded craft and –

to cut a long story drastically short – there was a rapid change of plan. Instead of ending up sitting safe and sound in the little boat, I was impaled on the outside of it – with the piece of metal sticking out of my face, like a sword."

I tried to keep a sense of proportion, not to show my alarm. "So it wasn't a crocodile that did it?"

His smile was lop-sided. "No, Lesley! It was – as I said in the text – a mock crock shock! There were definitely crocodiles in that river, of that I have no doubt. I saw one. But it didn't mug me. I did that all by myself." Then he picked up a glass and swigged back the remaining wine in one, draining his glass till it was empty.

He allowed himself a short dry ironic laugh. "But as you can see for yourself – it's ruined my good looks – forever!" I stroked the back of his hand with my fingers.

"Will it get better?" I asked him. Knowing the answer already, seeing the state of him. But asking anyway. "I'll always have the scar and some disfigurement on that side of my face. So the doctors in Australia tell me," he replied. Then he downed what was left in the bottle in one swift gulp.

I went to get another bottle of Chablis. When I returned, Ainsley was slumped, unusually, with his head forward on his arms. Dark silky hair shone in the sunshine as it cascaded onto the back of his neck, smooth as sable. And how I wanted to just lean over and stroke it. I put the glass down on the table, filling them up once more.

"Thanks, Les." He raised his head up slowly. "Do you hate Paul?" he asked.

"No," I replied honestly. "I don't hate him. I hate what he has done. I am afraid of him. And I hate what he has proved himself to be capable of. That chills me to the core. Terrifies me. Makes me angry. To think he could have put me in prison like that – robbed me of my freedom. It's a terrible price to pay for over twenty years of marriage isn't it? I never realised before just what it feels like to lose your liberty. It's a fundamental right, isn't it? Freedom. To say what you want, believe what you want, think what you want and to go wherever you want. To be able to live in your own home, to have the things that you have bought around you. Not to be locked out of it. To be restricted, restrained and treated like a prisoner or a refugee. I don't know how to stand it any longer, Ainsley. Not me," I told him sadly. He nodded. "But also I know that if I give vent to my feelings and end up hating the person I once loved, then Paul has won. He will have succeeded in making me somebody I am not. He will have destroyed the very essence deep inside of me that makes me who I am. And I'm not going to let him do that. I've paid a high enough price. He's done enough to disrupt my life and despoil me already." I picked up the glass which was forming condensation on the outside as the chill of the Chablis melted in the warmth of the sunshine. I drank some. "Sorry – I'm getting a bit dramatic!"

"No – no, not at all. It's understandable." Unequivocal support and perception was something I had silently craved. Ainsley, despite his own terrible ordeal, was still prepared to provide it in generous bucket loads.

"Do you hate the bloke with the crocodiles – Gus, or all that happened with Emma?" I asked him.

He drank some more wine. Then pushed himself back into the wooden seat, crossing one long leg over the other, thoughtful, contemplative. Taking time to answer. Choosing his words with care as if he was walking barefoot across a pebbled beach. He explained to me how he felt. "How can I hate him, Lesley? I don't even know him! What happened was an accident. Like you, I hate what happened to me. I wish with all my heart it hadn't. But it did happen. That's an indisputable fact and I have to live with that – the same as you do. But in different ways. My injuries are visible as well – yours cannot be seen by outsiders. I can say to you – what if I had stayed with the guys from Essex? What if I'd stayed behind working in a wine bar in Sydney and painting in my spare time in the studio apartment I was renting? What if I hadn't had such a wild and passionate desire to explore all on my own and see the 'real' Australia – find the 'real' me? What if I had a bona fide guide who knew what he was doing, not a dopey twit like Gus. Any of these choices could have left me 'safe'. But all of these avenues of thought lead us nowhere in the end. Only to a wall of stone. It's pointless to have regrets. You cannot think like that. Because at the end of the day it doesn't make a bit of difference. None of us can put back time. We can't replay our lives like a video tape, editing it constantly, wiping out all the bad bits and superimposing them with something wonderful. What happens to us happens to us, and we have to deal with it. It's the same for you Lesley. Say you had gone straight to bed, not picked up the bread knife to make a sandwich, not been drawn into an argument with Paul? What if Paul hadn't been secretly tape-recording that argument? What if the Police had been older and wiser and listened to your version of the truth instead of Paul's histrionic ravings? What if you had actually used the knife and not replaced it in the breadbin? It's no use, Lesley. It doesn't provide solutions. No answers." He looked at me earnestly, willing me somehow to understand him.

"While I was away in the East I experimented with many things. People, ideas, philosophies, ideologies – all kinds of things, trying to make some kind of sense of life, as we all must do. One of the things I discovered was Buddhism. And I am a practising Buddhist now. From the Tibetan school – like Richard Gere – nothing too heavy! And I won't be giving away all my worldly goods or anything like that! Whether you would call it a religion or philosophy is open to debate. It's certainly a way of life, a completely different way of thinking. But all I know is that whatever we believe, we keep on learning as we travel through our lives, attempting to become enlightened, in so many ways. To make sense of the senseless! Organised religion has never really appealed to me, but there is something so basically pure and spiritual about the teaching of the Buddha, that, I don't know, Les – although the suggestions might not at first appear to be very 'deep', may even appear naïve and simplistic, it does have a fundamental clear cut truth which speaks to me."

He leaned towards me across the table, looking deep into my eyes, until I imagined I would dissolve under the intensity of his complete attention. "I will tell you a story." He smiled as if he were Schehezerade herself about to unfurl magical words of wisdom. "Written down by Shakyamuni the Buddha – one of the truly enlightened ones! I didn't make this up! He says this, 'If one comes across a person who has been shot by an arrow, one does not spend time wondering about where the arrow came from, or the caste of the individual who shot it, or analysing what type of wood the shaft is made of, or the manner in which the arrowhead was fashioned. Rather, one should focus on immediately pulling out the arrow.'"

I stared straight back at him, transfixed by his gentle story, touched by the clarity of what was truly genuine. Moved beyond words by his handsome, disfigured, fabulous face. "Does that make any sense?" he asked me.

"Yes. Perfect sense!" I replied, smiling. And at long last – it did.

Chapter Twenty-Six

Six weeks after my stint in 'jail' I returned to face the Magistrates once more. Amy told me it was to re-address terms of bail, enabling me to have more freedom to move around, not to be forced to spend every night at my mother's house or to have to attend the local police station to ask for a police escort to accompany me whenever I wanted or needed to go to my own home in order to collect clothes, shoes, all my own things. Which were all still locked inside my house, held hostage by Paul. Furniture I had purchased, chairs, ornaments, cut glass, fitted wardrobes, bushes full of roses, garden statues, even my passport and jewellery, all locked inside it in order to give Paul and Denise the 'absolute right of occupancy' and the opportunity to raid all my belongings, clothes – everything. Living their lives in complete and absolute freedom. Coming and going wherever they pleased, whenever they wanted. Will went home on August Bank Holiday to collect some clothes, with a friend, only to find Paul and Denise cuddling together on my sofa, watching a DVD on my TV. Drinking fine wine from my glasses. I continued to feel so giddy I could not even stand up most of the time. The last time I had visited the house to pick up personal items, I had found most of my clothes unceremoniously dumped at the bottom of the wardrobes, in black plastic bin liners. I could never have treated Paul with such utter disregard and malicious contempt.

"You're finding all this very hard to handle, aren't you?" the policewoman with a Liverpudlian accent noted. It was a hot Saturday morning. I had gone round with my mother to pick up summer clothes, and retrieve a precious porcelain ornament that my parents had bought us back from Majorca, before my dad had died. Paul stood by the doorway, arms folded across his chest like a massive burglar, watching everything I took with me, saying 'yes' or 'no' to the police when they asked if it was OK for me to take what belonged one hundred per cent to me and me alone. I was ordered to fling all my things in higgledly piggledy heaps by my own front door. The wooden Tudor door I had chosen together with Paul at the local hardware superstore when we moved into our brand new home all those years ago when William was a baby.

"Yes, I am!" I burst into tears. "Wouldn't you?!" Paul did not even look at me. He had cropped his hair violently short like a member of the National Front. His body language filled with suppressed fury, menace and ill-disguised hatred. I didn't recognise him any longer. It was a weird lonely feeling.

I arrived early at the Crown Court, which was plush, smelling faintly of polish, covered with soft beige coloured carpet. Only to be informed that I was not supposed to be there at all. I was to report to the Magistrates Court across the Square for referral first. That was apparently, 'the procedure'. Lucy had pluckily volunteered to come along with me. "You can't go there all alone, Lesley!" she warned. "I'll be there – I promise!" But I had turned her down. My mother came with me. So did William. It was, after all, a family affair, and it needed to be dealt with carefully and discreetly by the family. That's how I felt anyway. I didn't want to impose on Lucy's generosity or let my mum believe I didn't trust her enough to come into the Court with me.

Ainsley offered to speak for me. "If you need a character witness I'll be one!" he had assured me. I didn't even have to ask him. "Whatever you need, Lesley, I'll do it for you. As long as Paul doesn't try to somehow turn it around and use it against you in some way, implying there is something improper going on between the two of us. You know what he is like! I'll be there for you, Lesley. All you have to do is tell me when and where." My two oldest and very dearest friends had come back to me, rallying around me, after all these years, joining up the circle once again. I was completely overwhelmed by their kindness and quiet confidence in my ability to get through this no matter what – just when I needed their support most of all. I would never ever forget that.

So, I sat in the waiting room at the Magistrates Court once more. Only this time I had Will beside me. I'd put on make-up and was wearing a new jacket, bought when the only clothes I had at my mother's were summer skirts and Tshirts. And I wasn't in tears of grief and shock this time. "Focus!" I kept reminding myself. Dignified was what I aimed to be, at all costs. Amy turned up right on time. Armloads of files tucked under her tiny hands, wearing a warm smile of encouragement.

"You look better today!" she said, approvingly, taking me in from head to toe in one sweeping movement of the eyes.

"Yes – thanks." I introduced her to William, who politely shook her by the outstretched hand that she offered to him. I had agonised over the decision of whether or not to let him come with me. Eventually conceding that it was really the only way to ensure that the truth was acknowledged, and to show him exactly what Paul had landed us in. And not least to impress upon him the dreadful consequences he would face if ever he stood up against his bullying tyrannical father.

I still did not know the correct medical term for the personality disorder that by now I was certain Paul obviously suffered from since those early childhood 'tests with the psychologist' that he had whispered about on the top of Richmond Hill a million light years ago. I tried desperately to explain the condition – the symptoms – to Amy. To give her the background of the kind of man we were up against. But now I know exactly what it is. I have found that out, at last.

I thought I would have to stand in the box with iron grilles around it. Instead of the three magistrates beckoned me forwards. I stood at the side of rows and rows of wooden benches, clasping my hands around the notebook I clutched like a Bible trying to stop myself from trembling. Amy sat down surrounded by all of her files, next to the man representing the Crown Prosecution Service, acting for Paul. The charges were read out once more.

Then they told me I could sit down. I watched Amy as she referred to copious notes removing her reading glasses from time to time, looking the Magistrates squarely in the eye whenever she had a vital point to make. Telling them the truth.

When the time came for the CPS to produce Paul's illicit tape recording, and papers they said that they had a problem. "We will have to adjourn," replied the Magistrate in the centre of the Bench. We dutifully trooped out of the Court like soldiers, reassembling outside in the waiting room. Will squeezed my hand tight and gave me a watery smile. My mum was confused. Didn't understand what was happening. "Is it all over?" she asked.

Amy explained to us, "They cannot find the tapes or the correct paperwork, they have requested an adjournment for another maybe six months' time." I was horrified. "Don't worry – I've said no!" she replied firmly. Good for Amy! "Are you prepared to be patient and maybe stay here all day if necessary?" she asked me. Oh yes indeed – I was learning to be very patient these days! I thought of Ainsley and the Buddha and took a deep breath.

At 11.00 we were summoned back into the Court by the attendant in a long flowing black gown. The CPS could not find the papers, we were told. Amy had overheard the Prosecutor on the phone frantically demanding that they be located immediately. "I'm in trouble here – I need them – now!"

Would we mind waiting a little longer? asked the Magistrate.

"No," we replied. We sat drinking coffee in the canteen, chewing stale shortbread biscuits. We'd eaten real shortbread in Scotland – on holiday, climbing mountains – when we were a family. When I was free. Two prostitutes sat down at the next table, wearing black plastic miniskirts and big white dangling earrings like gob-stoppers. Will gave me the kind of look only a seventeen-year-old boy can do effectively.

At noon we were asked to go back inside the Courtroom. Still, the papers had not been found. "The Crown seeks an adjournment!" Paul's prosecutor's decibel level was getting higher pitched, and much louder. I could sense what Amy had already. The three magistrates were becoming increasingly irritated by the prosecutor's complete inability to produce the relevant paperwork. All summer long they had been afforded the luxury of time to get the documents prepared.

"No." replied Amy firmly. "That's not acceptable."

Paul's prosecutor's face became more inflamed above the collar of his striped shirt. He spoke now at full volume. Amy's voice, in contrast, was soft. But determined. "We'll give you until lunchtime," said the Magistrate. Shuffling his papers. Just before one o'clock, we were called back inside once again. Told to reassemble finally at two. I was tired.

When confronted with situations of such magnitude you either panic completely or go into 'switch off automatic pilot this isn't really happening to me mode'. I had gone into the latter. I needed some fresh air. "Have some lunch, then come back," Amy advised us.

William was flagging fast. His face was ashen. "Do you need him anymore? Can he go back to school?" I asked Amy.

"Yes, of course, he can," she assured me. "The magistrates have seen him, I pointed out to them that he was here all the time. They've noted all that down. Don't worry. Let him go now – he'll be fine." Will returned to have lunch with the boys.

At two o'clock we sat outside waiting once again for the final summing up. The verdict. Amy looked at me, earnestly. "I haven't been doing this for a very long time, Lesley. And I so much want you to win this case. If you feel you would be better off with someone older, someone more experienced, a more senior barrister – a man to represent you, perhaps – all you have to do is say so."

I looked back at her, tiny in her brown suit. She had believed in me all along. There was no doubt in my mind whatsoever. I reached out and took her arm firmly. "I trust you, Amy. I trust you to fight for me, and I am putting my faith in you. I know that you can do this. You know it too. So come on – we'll do it together. Call it girl power!" Then I quickly hugged her.

"OK!" her eyes sparkled with tears at the edges behind her glasses. She straightened her jacket and smoothed her hair. "Let's go!" I followed her as we marched back inside the Courtroom.

My legs were shaking, my heart was indeed pounding. I had a headache. Nevertheless, I stood straight and as calmly as I could manage, while the Magistrates addressed me one more time.

I still could not believe that all this happened just because of a domestic argument in the furnace of tempestuous, inflamed heat of a low down dirty divorce, fuelled by the greed of others. Incredible. That I had been set up I was in no doubt. I was also in no doubt that there was no way on earth I was prepared to go back inside that prison cell for all the treasure in the Tower of London. So I played the game. Did as I had been told. Saying nothing. Still, Paul's prosecutor had failed to produce the necessary paperwork even though he had been toiling all through lunch. Amy stood up straight. Looking so tiny beside her mammoth male adversary. Speaking softly, yet determined and decisive. All the things I had told her suddenly condensed into legal language and a coherent structured argument to be set before the Magistrates – my defence.

When she had finished summing up she folded the papers together in her small hands and replaced them firmly onto the desk in front of her. Still looking straightforward. They turned away from her, bending heads together as they earnestly whispered to each other, nodding, expressing opinions, confirming my fate. It seemed like hours. Of course, it was only minutes. Then they all looked up. Two gazes were directed straight at me. One looked away to the right. I could read nothing in their expressions. The man sitting in the centre wearing a dark grey suit and glasses was speaking and I couldn't hear what he was saying. Then he announced in clear well-modulated tones, words I will never ever forget. "The charges against you are dismissed. You are free to go!"

Tears sprang into my eyes, and I was choked with emotion. "Oh – thank you – thank you!" I cried. Amy took my arm swiftly, propelling me out of the Courtroom. I'd probably overstepped some kind of legal Court protocol rule that says you're not supposed to address the Bench directly or something. But I didn't care! I was free! Free!

Wings took hold of my heels as I floated through the door. I flung my arms around her hugging her tiny frame so tightly, like a little china doll. "You've given me my life back!" I wept. Tears of unrestrained joy. "I don't know how to thank you!" We sat down in a small side room to gather our thoughts.

"There's just a small chance that Paul could re-bring the charges," said Amy. "Because of the way it was dismissed and the lack of paperwork from the prosecutor. But I've never ever known it to happen. It is very rare. I just have to tell you that though!" I felt like I'd just won the jackpot on the National Lottery.

The first thing I did was go around to meet Will from school. As the lads came tumbling out across the grass they hugged me in turn, shook my hands and kissed me. "We're so glad you're free! We knew you would be!" they chorused. Grinning. So thrilled. "Will's been so worried, especially this afternoon," they confided. "So quiet in class – not like him at all!" Then he appeared, walking through the school entrance doorway. My son. I waved to him, and immediately he knew everything was alright.

"I'm free! Case dismissed!" I told him. We hugged each other so securely I felt I never ever wanted to let go of him again!

That evening, I rang Lucy and Alana to pass on the good news. But first of all, I rang Ainsley. "Lesley! I couldn't be more pleased if it had been me that had just been set free! Well done, Lesley! Great news! Fantastic. But listen, Les, don't get carried away. You know just what that evil bastard is capable of now. Don't attempt to go back home!"

"But, they said I can!" I was delirious with delight.

"Not yet, Lesley. Not tonight especially! For heaven's sake listen to me. And not even tomorrow. There's plenty of time for all that. Let things sink in – sort them out first. For goodness sake, Lesley – you've only just been let off! Don't give him another chance to hurt you and put you right back to square one – even worse – straight back in jail again! Lesley! Are you listening to me, Lesley?!" he was actually yelling quite loudly down the phone.

"Yes!" But I was on Cloud Nine – and your auditory perception diminishes almost completely when you're flying that high.

Chapter Twenty-Seven

"You must go home, Lesley!" said my mother. "Now!"

"I'll go home tomorrow," I replied. She was not pleased. Not pleased at all.

"It's your house, Lesley. You should be there. Not Paul with that woman or all on his own in your house!" But in my mind, although I had always obeyed my mother's instructions, I could hear Ainsley's words of warning – words of caution. And Lucy too.

"Don't rush back, Lesley. There's plenty of time. Stay safe!" they had both implored me. The next morning I rang my solicitor. Early.

"That's marvellous news, Lesley!" she gaily pronounced. "This puts us in a very strong position now! Go back home – straight away!"

"Do I need any paperwork, injunctions against Paul – anything of any kind?" I asked her.

"No. I'll talk to Paul's solicitor and make a mutual agreement, don't worry about that! I'll tell him you're prepared to stay out of Paul's way. After all, it's a big house! You've been together for over twenty years. Just go home, Lesley – as swiftly as possible! Don't worry about a thing!"

So instead of heeding the words of the wise, my two oldest and most trusted of allies, I listened to my seventy-eight-year-old mother, and the edict of my duplicitous divorce lawyer. I bought a special meal for William and me to have a modest homecoming celebration. Fresh salmon with lemon dressing and a bottle of bubbly.

Our first night back together again in our own home. I was ecstatic. I bought bunches of fresh yellow gerberas with flat petals that stuck out like the sun and the softest sherbet-coloured spray carnations with gypsophila of pale white. I went into my bedroom, placing make-up back carefully in the drawers of my dressing table. Lipstick and perfume that had been previously tipped out on the floor in front of the police.

My toothbrush and flannel I put back in the bathroom cabinet. Hung up my clothes in my own wardrobes again. I was home. At last. I was free. Not on bail. Not living out of suitcases and boxes made of cardboard and plastic.

I visited the physiotherapist at the local clinic to have my back manipulated and felt better. I got back in time to meet William from school. He was simply over the moon. The boys all came back with him. Andy, John and Charlie. They had all faithfully stuck by us when the going got really tough. And they had been such a positive force of strength. I made chocolate milkshakes for me and Will and his best friend, Andy. The others went off to pass on the good news to their own mums.

"Did you hear something?" Will asked me, clutching my sleeve.

"No" I replied.

"I think it's someone in the garage – listening behind the door. Maybe Dad!" he said.

"What on earth would he be doing in there?" I asked.

We carried on making frothy shakes, squirting thick cream on top. Andy and Will disappeared into the lounge to launch themselves into the latest Playstation game. I went upstairs, sat on the bed and phoned my mum. "Yes, it's wonderful to be home!" I reassured her. "Everything's fine!" And as I sat there on the bed crossing my legs in front of me, something appeared in the corner of my vision that made me suddenly freeze. Will and Andy were both standing bolt upright by the bedroom door, looks of dismay strewn across their young faces, which only seconds ago had been filled with boyish laughter.

"Mum," Will attempted to say something, and then I saw them, deja-vu – two uniformed police officers standing armed like terrorists on my stairs, on my landing, in my own home once again.

"Lesley Pearson? We are arresting you…"

"Whoa! Just a minute – now you hang on!" I cried. "You've made a terrible mistake. You have no business being here at all. I went to Court yesterday and the charge against me was dismissed." But they weren't listening to me. Not at all. They were flapping pieces of white A4 paper in my face. Rapping out orders like a machine gun.

Then I saw Paul, cowering behind them on the stairs, a spineless, grotesque conniving cowardly excuse for a man. Foreboding, his eyes filled with evil intent. One of the policemen folded his arms decisively across his chest, blocking my access down my own hallway. "You must leave here – immediately!" he demanded.

"No," I said.

"You have to, otherwise you will be re-arrested and put back in jail!" he threatened.

Will and I gazed at each other across the kitchen. Shattered. Shell shocked. "I'm ringing my solicitor," I told them. I dialled her number with trembling fingers as they thrust grubby papers with attached 'Power of Arrest' stapled to the edge of it like a warped merit badge. A cheap trick.

"You must leave immediately, Lesley or you'll be re-arrested," my solicitor was now shouting at me down the other end of the phone.

"But I don't understand any of this! You told me it was perfectly safe to come home. You told me everything would be alright. There would be no need for injunctions on either side – nothing!"

She was sounding annoyed. She didn't like being questioned or challenged. "That's right," she repeated.

"But how can this be happening? The case was dismissed yesterday. You know that!" I was distraught.

"I'm telling you, Lesley – you must leave now!" I still couldn't grasp any of it. "You will be arrested; if you don't like it get yourself another lawyer!" She slammed down the receiver. I was beginning to shake. Sweat began to pour down my face. I was angry and confused, deep fear held me captive in a bubble of iron grip once again.

This was a recurring nightmare from which there was no escape. I had been lassoed by the law whose tentacles were reaching into every crevice of my being and sticking to me like superglue. I couldn't shake them off of me. No matter how hard I fought back. My solicitor rang. "Paul took himself off to the local Court this afternoon ex parte," she started to explain. "He has obviously managed to convince the Judge that you are such a threat to him he has granted an immediate injunction barring you from the house, and with the attached Power of Arrest." I was stunned into complete numbness.

And then suddenly Andy's kind and sensitive mum, Lauren from New Zealand, was standing there beside me. Holding me. Wrapping her arms around me like a comforting cloak of reason. "You'll be alright, Lesley. You've had a terrible shock. You'll be alright. Just keep calm." She kept repeating the words, in a calm soft voice, like a mantra. Then she turned to Paul. "Why are you doing this to them?" His snarling curled lip sneer and mad-person's crazed gaze answered the question without the need for words. Then he ran back to hide behind one of the policemen in an attempt to impress upon them 'how afraid' he was. I felt sick.

Lauren helped me to gather some things, and my fresh salmon steaks still wrapped in the plastic bag and the bunch of gerberas, now depressingly hanging limp heads that had earlier looked so proud and happy to be alive. Then she took my arm and held me safe and took me to her house to make me mugs of hot sweet tea. I couldn't stop shaking. I felt like I was having a nervous breakdown of some kind. I'd lost it. "He's pushed you right to the limit, Lesley. And you cannot go any further. But although he's shoved you to the very edge of reason – you won't succumb to that! Don't let him succeed in doing it! There are things inside that house – OK. They're just things. They are not you! A house is just a pile of bricks. And you've got the most precious thing that was ever inside that house – William! What's more important?"

I just looked at her and we both smiled. "Don't even have to ask!" we both said the words together, then hugged each other.

I wrapped my icy cold hands around the comforting mug painted with pale pink flowers and filled with hot tea. And I began to sob. I don't know how it can be that in the middle of chaos and the depths of personal hell when you are confronted by absolute and complete evil and wickedness perpetrated by someone you once loved with all your heart, an oasis of tranquillity appears like a small miracle. Lauren had done just that for me. With words of comfort, intuitive understanding and old-fashioned wisdom she sat there rubbing the life back slowly into the ice cube sticks that my fingers had turned into. And the feeling stayed with me long after that dreadful night had passed. Sense and reason filtered slowly and shakily back into my bruised, wounded body and tortured soul, like freshly percolated coffee in a jug.

When I returned to my mother's house she was upset and angry. Arguing with me. Refusing to understand. Demanding that I went back home immediately as in her opinion, this: "Just isn't right! Your solicitor said you must go home! You've got to go straight back!" And at that point, I really felt as if I was being dragged back to the very brink of reason once more. I knew I couldn't stand this any longer. I flung open the street door and strode off into the darkness. I went for a long walk, although it was approaching midnight. The air was still warm in the midsummer heatwave we were having. Will followed, running behind me till he caught up.

And we walked – fast. And we talked – fast. And our pace slowed as we began to find comfort and answers in the shared hysterical version of reality that had been brutally enforced upon us like a gigantic festering muzzle. "It'll be alright," we told each other. Holding hands tightly in the damp night air that was now turning cooler.

"What did I tell you, Lesley! Do you ever listen to a single word that I say?!" Ainsley was obviously very upset with me. I had known that he would be. And no matter how many times I had argued with Paul – I mean really argued – somehow I just couldn't stand it when Ainsley was annoyed with me. But I had to tell him. "What are you going to do now?" he asked.

All I knew for certain was that I had to find a way of getting back inside my own home. "My solicitor says I have to go to Court again. To try to get the injunction reversed," I said forlornly down the phone, attempting a half-hearted explanation. Feeling sad. Worn out.

"Well, if it's the only way then go for it, Les. But I still think you're crazy. And I also think you should shoot your bloody stupid solicitor!" I couldn't handle all this. Not now, not on top of everything. I needed his unquestioning assurance and I needed him on my side. And yet, hadn't he always been totally on my side? It had never been any other way. He had never betrayed me as Paul had. Of all the people I had recently doubted Ainsley would never be one of them.

"Come with me?" I pleaded. Knowing it was the wrong thing to ask him.

"No," he replied flatly.

"Why?"

"Because I just don't think that would help at the moment." Then he paused, sighing deeply. "You know I'm always here for you, Lesley." I was becoming a proverbial pain, leaning too much. I didn't like myself very much right now. I had to stop doing it, step away, or I would risk losing him forever. And my other dearest friends. I couldn't keep dumping all this in their laps like unwanted garbage. I had to take control. It was my life. I had to be the one to do it. Once and for all.

So I bravely went to Court the following Friday. We sat there stoney faced staring at each other across the dented pine table, like gladiators. "I don't have time to hear this today. We'll have to adjourn till next week," the Judge wearily told us. Then he swiftly gathered together his papers, dashing through the huge wooden doors like lightning. No doubt heading off for a weekend away with friends and his family.

A week later, on another Friday morning, we took our seats inside Courtroom number four, on the third floor once again. Still, no decision was reached. "But I do give an order for the house to be sold. I think under the circumstances that's the only answer don't you?" He peered at me over steel-rimmed glasses, as I nodded agreement. Paul actually spluttered. Protesting wildly, nearly falling from his chair, as he looked around incensed at his legal representative, Mr Wolfe. Who just shrugged his shoulders and scribbled something onto a piece of folded paper.

"We'll have to go back to Court for a two-day hearing in October," my lawyer, Cynthia Hudson, told me crisply. "It will be like a mini-trial of all that occurred in the summer. All about – your conduct! Your behaviour!"

I was dismayed. "My behaviour?! No way!" I cried. "I cannot handle any more either physically or mentally. Surely you can see that? I have been through enough already, and I cannot keep going over this again and again. I just cannot!" But once more my hands were tied fiercely behind my back in metaphorical chains. I'd have taken my chances with Captain Jack and his gang of Caribbean pirates, or any highwayman worth his salt for that matter, rather than be coerced into putting my life on the line in the creepy crawling hands of these legitimised embezzlers.

Not for the first time, and not for the last, I felt utterly powerless as I wretchedly took part in the perilous journey through the morass yet again. And as time passed, I wasn't just trying to mend my totally broken heart, I was pitifully depressed and I could hardly stand up. The doctor prescribed tablets – I felt light-headed and dizzy constantly.

"You're under an incredible amount of stress," he told me as he typed up notes which appeared on his computer screen. "Divorce – very stressed." Yes, I knew that actually. But the worst thing of all was that I was beginning to believe the vicious taunts that Paul and Denise had chanted over and over like ugly pantomime dames. That I really was useless. That I was the 'sad old cow' she had described. That I was actually some kind of inferior being. Not good enough. All that I had done to please Paul had meant nothing to him. It was like going through a bereavement. But the person you were grieving over was still alive. I felt like a box of broken biscuits. Sub-standard. And so I took myself off to bed early. Snuggled up and cried myself into a restless sort of semi-sleep. Tossing and turning all night long because I just could not clear my mind of all that had happened. My life had been crushed, stolen and put on a roller coaster ride that would rival anything at Disneyland or Alton Towers – absolutely guaranteed to make you throw up – every time you set foot on it.

And yet again I was expected to appear in Court. And I went. And I tried so hard to get back into my own house. For the last time. Paul was accompanied by Mr Wolfe, and his barrister, Mr Seed. A grotesque apparition, he could have easily been assembled in the Hammer House of Horror movie workshop.

A latter-day Uriah Heep character, wearing an ill-fitting grubby grey suit with a black knitted kipper tie widely knotted, and a multi-coloured friendship bracelet made out of ageing thread on his right wrist. Though how on earth this malformed foul-mouthed monster had possibly been able to acquire any friends at all in his life was completely unfathomable. I decided he must have picked it up from somewhere and stuck it on his own wrist!

I looked across the room at Paul. Pleading with my eyes and my answers. To just stop this. For Will's sake, if nothing else. We could then all start to get on with the rest of our lives. Time is so precious. But he stubbornly, obstinately refused. For Paul didn't want justice. He craved revenge – for something I hadn't even done. This greedy glutton wanted me to be completely, utterly broken. Like a little rag doll stripped of its arms, legs and clothes, and discarded onto the rubbish heap. Mr Seed's voice was a low droning noise – like a pneumatic nasal rotary tool. Pounding relentlessly into my head. "But… Mrs Pearson… Mrs Pearson… You said you could kill your husband, threatened to kill him, kill him…" boring into my brain like a dentist's drill. All I wanted to do was make it all stop. Pull the switch, get up and run far, far away. But I couldn't.

I stared out of the window at the grey flags suspended from a nearby building. Drooping sullenly, refusing to fly even in the smallest breeze. Dead. They had given up the fight for life already.

William's 18th Birthday, one day before the hearing, had ensured that, according to the ruling of Judge Adams, he was termed 'legally irrelevant'. By twenty-four hours.

"But he's still at school! Where do you expect us to live?" I cried out in exasperation.

My protestations were swept aside like a pile of dust. "You know the Law!" he reprimanded my solicitor pointedly, tapping his pen on the top of the table and slicing through my survival tactics with swooping superiority. Mr Seed started up once again, like a monotonous motorised and frighteningly aggressive robot. Rude. Abusive. Surely he could not be allowed to say such things to me, deeply personal, crushing insults, assassinating my character, my integrity, my whole life – me, in swift, sharp, savage blows. This was surely not allowable in a Court of Law before a County Judge? But he got away with it. And the more I squirmed and suffered, the more Paul's smile was smugly smothered with self-satisfaction.

Once more Paul had succeeded ruthlessly as he had done so often in the past. Twisting everything around to suit his purpose. Lying over and over again. Contemptuous of the truth. "I don't know who to believe," said Judge Adams looking nonplussed. My goodness, there was only one person in the whole room actually prepared to tell the truth and she was 'on trial' – how could this dopey relic from another century not be able to tell who was 'telling the truth'. I had begun to understand only too well that the truth and the Law share merely a passing acquaintance with each other.

On the second day of the Court hearing, Judge Adams leaned forward across the huge desk separating us. It was just before lunch. Shafts of sunlight were trying to glimmer through the smeary windows. They didn't get very far. "What would you like to happen, Mrs Pearson?" he asked me quietly.

"I would like to be able to go back and live in my own house again – with my son," I replied. Then looking straight back at him, I confirmed. "That – is my dearest wish."

My face after two days on the rack inside the Courtroom was red, bloated and disfigured by trails of tears that had engulfed me like a midsummer thunderstorm. "We'll adjourn till two o'clock," said Judge Adams, as he got up. Disappeared in seconds.

"I think it's going well," said Cynthia during lunch. At two we re-convened. I felt hot and my throat tight, as if it was the beginning of a cold or the flu. Judge Adams started to read sternly from his summing-up notes. And I knew. From the first moment that he started to read stiltedly. There was no way that this County Court Judge was going to overrule his previous decision. No way he was prepared to stand up and tackle the truth. No way he was going to back down and admit he had made a mistake and let me retain my rights to live in my own property. To return to reside once more in the house that I owned jointly with Paul. That I had helped to pay for. That I had lived in for eighteen years. I had been summarily locked out – just as I had been locked up – like a refugee. An asylum seeker from a far-off land would have more chance of a home of their own. "Have you thought of applying for a Council flat?" drawled Cynthia, attempting an upper-class accent. I don't know who she thought she was trying to impress.

"No," I replied flatly. Then as the final summarisation was still taking place, everything started to swirl around me, sliding out of focus. I felt sick, everything went dim and gauzy. And I passed out.

***

I could not face the fearful prospect of going to Court anymore. So I withdrew applications for maintenance and financial as-sistance from Paul. I decided to change my lawyer and apply for Legal Aid. Up till this moment, I had been lumbered with paying Paul's astronomical Court costs.

All the time he was refusing to pay money for William and me, he was pouring every pound of his annual income into joint accounts held by him and Denise. I decided on one final desperate attempt to salvage something, make a financial deal of some kind with Paul to bring some kind of resolution. A full stop. I decided to meet up with Paul in a local restaurant. "You're stark raving mad, Lesley! Do you expect him to be reasonable?!" Ainsley exploded down the phone.

"I have to try," I replied. Lucy threatened to stop being my friend – forever.

"You're nuts, Lesley! With anyone else, perhaps, you could reason with them. But not Paul! Not after all that he's done to you. No way! Never!" But I went along anyway. At first, the familiarity that we'd accepted over the years was shared. But suddenly soured, as if someone had pulled an invisible switch in the darkness. Paul lurched into, 'I hate you, Lesley' mode.

I poured out my heart, at first. Asking questions. Suggesting solutions. Short-term and long-term compromises. Fifty-fifty splits. Some kind of 'all-inclusive package deal' that we could jointly take to our lawyers for approval. He was having no part of it. Denise and his copper friend had done their homework avidly. Primed him well. Taught him his script, off by heart, so he was 'parrot perfect'. "I'm in debt for £60,000 and rising. I expect you to settle these debts!" he announced imperiously like a King to a jester.

"No way – they are your debts. You are more than happy to share everything else with Denise these days – I suggest you share them with her too!" That's when I confronted him with the knowledge that I had found out her husband had died at Christmas time. That's when I asked him, "Why did you put me through all that in Court? Why be so vicious?" His voice was uncomfortably high as he waved a barbequed spare rib smothered in hot sauce towards me like a dagger.

"My solicitor – unlike yours – did what I paid him to do!" Then he leered at me. "And you have a criminal record – you won't be getting anything at all!" He beamed.

"But I don't, Paul. I don't have any kind of criminal record," I replied. Trying to stop my voice from wobbling.

"Yes!" he screeched. "You do! And that means you are not entitled to half of the house! You are not entitled to a penny!" He was jubilant. Acting like an escaped lunatic.

A sudden hush descended around us like the aftermath of an atomic explosion. "So let me get this straight," I repeated. "You were prepared to go to such lengths – to get me arrested, convicted of something I didn't do – to give me a criminal re-cord – just so that you could have my share of the house, and everything else as well?!" He was nodding his head vigorously up and down like Mr Punch in a fairground show. "You're sick!" I retorted.

He got up to walk away at that moment. "We have nothing to say to each other – I'll see you in Court!" One more final threat.

I watched as he flounced out of the door like a dame with his large nose actually sticking up into the air like a duck's beak. Out of my life. I asked the waiter for a cafetiere of hot Pico Duarte. And I sat alone quietly drinking it, savouring it, for a long time, before I went back to my mother and William waiting patiently for me to tell them what had happened.

Chapter Twenty-Eight

"How did it go?" Ainsley was talking to me at the other end of the phone. After I told him there was a long silence. Finally, he spoke. "I just don't believe all this! You cannot be trying hard enough, Lesley! How on earth can they possibly believe Paul all the time, and not listen to your side of things? I bet he came across as being very credible, a respectable businessman, sanctimonious?"

I mumbled back, "Yes." My voice felt like lead. "And he's changed the locks so I cannot get back inside the house even if I wanted to," I started to tell him.

"But he cannot do all these things, Lesley! It just isn't right! It cannot be legal!" Frustration and weariness flooded my whole body and soul.

"Well, it appears that he is getting away with it, Ainsley! And it's my home! I'm the one who should be upset – how do you think I feel?!" I had never really had a proper argument with him. Not really. But this time I just let rip and finally cried like a petulant little child. "I don't think we have anything to say to each other again – ever!"

"Fine," I heard him say. Then I slammed the phone down hard into the receiver, making it shake.

Ainsley bloody Logan – what the heck did he know about anything anyway? I steamed off into the garden feeling pleased that I'd told him exactly how I felt. Elated that I'd made my grievance clear as glass. Deflated. Consumed with remorse. I went and made a cup of tea, floating the tea bag around like a flag on a wonky wand. "If there is anything you need to know about divorce or indeed lots of other things, then all you have to do is look it up on the Internet," Ainsley had told me this so many times, I'd lost count.

The time had come – to surf the information superhighway and find out everything I could. "Knowledge is power!" my dad used to insist. OK – well it was about time I got some power of my own right now. I logged on to Will's computer. I knew that he wouldn't mind me using it. It was after all in a good cause – a quest of discovery for the truth just like a crew member of *Star Trek* boldly setting foot where no man had been before. I typed in 'keywords', like 'divorce', 'pension sharing', and 'division of matrimonial home'. And like the maze at Hampton Court itself, one site led to another and then another. An endless stream of legal advice, explanation and exploration. Was everyone in the whole wide world getting divorced? I started to print off the results of my investigations methodically, like a private detective, onto clean white crisp sheets of A4. I could have contributed to a dictionary of divorce law. Some were relevant, some not. But I hungrily devoured it anyway. That's when I found the website run by a colour supplement of a leading national newspaper. 'Getting Divorced – All you Need to Know!' it said. In bold letters. I did need to know – all. So I sat there sipping Quick Brew and scrolling down the pages. Reams and reams of stuff. That's when I saw it. Something that made me stop quite still. I highlighted the words, started to read, and read on – tortured letters of torment from women on the brink of absolute despair, words of comfort from those who had encountered it too, been there done that and escaped – like prisoners of war grasping for their freedom. Three words – and suddenly all the unanswered questions that had been locked away inside me, that had been veiled behind walls of 'professional confidentiality and secrecy', 'moral obligation' stared back at me as naked and as unpretentious as a newborn baby.

Like a bright beacon shining on top of a lighthouse reaching out to me telling me I had found what I'd been searching for. 'Paranoid Personality Disorder.' Passages taken from an American manual of mental disorders from the American Psychiatric Association 1994. Case studies. The disease perspective. I was grounded. Fascinated. Compulsion tugged like a moth to the flame as I read in complete silence.

'Sufferers –Suspect, without sufficient basis that others are exploiting, harming or deceiving them. That they are reluctant to confide in others because of the unwarranted fear that the information will be used maliciously against them. Read hidden, demeaning or threatening meanings into benign remarks or events, persistently bear grudges, are unforgiving of insults, injuries or slights. Perceive attacks on their character or reputation that are not apparent to others and are quick to react angrily or to counter-attack. Have recurrent suspicions without justification regarding fidelity of spouse or sexual partner.'

I was transfixed. If someone had asked me to put pen to paper and describe Paul's character in a thumbnail sketch it could not have been more accurate. I read on.

'Special Effects – Hypersensitivity, hypervigilance, fearfulness, suspiciousness, persecutory anxiety, quiet hostility, emotional aloofness and restraint, coldness, tenseness, seriousness.' I continued to read on, 'Behaviour – Under-achievement at school, social anxiety, solitariness, difficulty in handling stress, conflict with superiors, unwillingness to compromise, argumentativeness, stubbornness, defensiveness, deviousness, deceptions, disloyalty, maliciousness, litigiousness.' On and on I kept going till I reached the bit written by a man called Theodore Millon.

'Links: Hypersensitive – Because persons with paranoid personality disorder are hyperalert they notice any slight and may take offence where none is intended. As a result, they tend to be defensive and antagonistic. When they are at fault they cannot accept blame, not even mild criticism. Yet they are highly critical of others. Other people may say that these individuals make "mountains out of molehills". They have difficulty expressing warm emotions and tolerating feeling anything that is being dependent upon another person.'

And as the light started to grow dim outside sending warm golden shafts of evening sunlight shooting straight across my desk like a spotlight, I continued to be mesmerised, instinct driving me to unravel the truth the whole truth and nothing but.

'Histrionic Personality Disorder Criteria – High neuroticism, exaggerated, shallow emotions, enthusiasm, anger, boredom, hysteria, jealousy, disappointment, fear. Motives – desire to coerce, manipulate and deceive others into giving help and to establish and maintain dependency. Behaviour – overly dramatic, reactive, intensely expressive behaviour, strident and superficial emotionally. Emotional storms, constant attention seeking, sexually seductive behaviour, histrionics, ruthless wilfulness, affectation, overreaction, emotional manipulation.' Denise! Two magnets being drawn together – like to like. If opposites had attracted Paul and I, then pushed us poles apart, neurotic navigation of a demented kind was steering his uncharted course right now.

Finally, I came to the part that made me freeze as I came face to face with the absolute. At last. 'Sadistic Personality Disorder' it stated, in thick black letters.

'The Diagnostic and Statistical Manual of Mental Disorders – Third Edition 1987, for research purposes describes – "Sadistic Personality Disorder" as a pervasive pattern of cruel, demeaning and aggressive behaviour, beginning by early adulthood, as indicated by the repeated occurrence of at least four of the following.' I grimly read on. 'Has used physical cruelty or violence for the purpose of establishing dominance in a relationship (not merely to achieve some personal goal, such as striking someone in order to rob him or her). Humiliates or demeans people in the presence of others. Has treated or disciplined someone under his or her control unusually harshly (eg a child). Is amused by, or takes pleasure in, the psychological or physical suffering of others. Has lied for the purpose of harming or inflicting pain on others (not merely to achieve some other goal). Gets other people to do what he or she wants by frightening them (through intimidation or terror). Restricts the autonomy of people with whom he or she has a close relationship. Is fascinated by violence, weapons, martial arts, injury or torture.' Four? I'd just ticked the lot.

On and on it went and still I couldn't stop myself. Peeling layers from an onion of secrets that had made tears stream down my face like a waterfall of despair for so long. Outside it was dark and still. I switched on the little golden lamp I used for my design work. Will was out playing football with the lads. 'High

Extraversion – inappropriate attempts to dominate or control others. Low agreeableness, exploitive and manipulative, lying, rude and inconsiderate manner alienates friends. Inflated and grandiose sense of self – arrogance!' Yes, this was Paul certainly. And the Behaviour Perspective – 'Motivations – Wants to gain power and control over self and over outside objects. A driving need to dominate. Wants to have an impact on others. Wants to gain validation of his own being, his importance and his powers – by hurting and dominating others.'

I took out my luminous yellow highlighter pen, sliding it across the next bit. 'Cognitive Effects – I need power over others. I must dominate. Power is the most important thing in life. It's always the objective that counts. Whatever means are expedient are justified.'

I had my answers, it seemed. Yet I was compelled to keep on reading as my eyes grew tired with concentration. Letters from women struggling to keep their everyday lives in some kind of symmetry. Janice from Essex, 'Rainbow Cloud' from Surrey and Heather from Edinburgh. Desperate words, pleas for help. Battling to keep their families together despite the overwhelming odds. Empathy, solicitude and compassionate responses from the experienced, who had already been there and lived through it. "How hard it is to stay with men like this," said one. "If you think you are strong enough to cope with it, every day of the rest of your life, then you are brave to stay. If not – you have a choice – walk away."

Fragile, sensitive, strong, beautiful women, intelligent women – feeling anxious, inferior, defeated, depleted, engulfed and plagued by a terrible incurable disease they didn't even know the name of. All had been successfully brainwashed. It was they who had the problem – not the men in their lives! So the men kept reminding them. An overwhelming feeling of guilt and shame, that it was all their fault was disturbingly, scarily familiar. But the burden of blame had been given the green light to go. Up, up and away, out of my conscience now forever. My mind was filled with facts, reasons and explanations. Like Melpomene the muse of tragedy, I sat silently reflecting, in the still of the warm evening, as the north star shone brightly in the inky dark skies outside. More level-headed than I had ever been. And one joyous realisation was staring straight back at me – it wasn't just me!

I had discovered an invisible thread of connection to people I hadn't even met. I was not alone any longer. As my eyes were becoming so bleary I could barely focus, I came across some extracts from a US reference book about PPD. I wrote down the words methodically in navy blue ink. 'Don't expect them to change,' it began.

'They will get much worse as they get older. How can you recognise the paranoia? One way is by the remarks a person makes, that really cut into a sensitive person's inner being. And are never forgotten. The reason they come out with such cruelty is that they have met with resistance. The only way to get along with a PPD is to agree with them. The PPD has an inability to be aware of the feelings of others. If a similar remark is made to a paranoid – watch out! They flare up, feel hurt, and strike back, tossing insults about They are tremendously sensitive, but have no sensitivity to others. Paranoids are money and possessions mad. Paranoid thinking is based not on something that happens – it is based on the suspicion that it will.

'Beware the female paranoid! She wants to control all individuals and situations in her circle. Manipulates, puppets on a string. Causes tension and hostility. Thrives on putting people down. Wants to control. Attacks those around her if they disagree. Fault-finding, controlling, suspicious, hostile.

'What do you do if you live with a paranoid? Agree with them – over everything! Unconditionally. Otherwise, there is constant friction, there is no middle ground. Everything is black and white. If you live with one, be careful to keep the peace and allow him to be the leader, steer clear of him if you can and if you don't agree he will turn on you – viciously.

'Paranoia increases with age. We build patterns of behaviour and as we get older they will become ingrown. We form patterns of thinking as well. PPD often blooms when there's a death in the family (to do with money). Age does not mellow with the paranoid. Experience tells us that a PPD does not come full bloom from a happy, comfortable family as a rule. There are paranoid elements in the parents that show up in minor ways, coming to full fruition in later years – usually in the 40s and 50s.'

I switched off the computer, turned off the light, rubbed my weary eyes, picked up all the papers carefully, placing them in a blue box file. Feeling at long last that my pirate ship had managed to manoeuvre the way through murderous, savage and violent seas. Surviving the turbulence of the storm and the cyclones of vicious, stinging, piercingly raw winds that had bitten right down to my very soul. My battered battleship was safe at last, it seemed, in settled, still quiet waters. She'd found a storm-free harbour. It was time now for me to work side by side with the turning tide and make sure it stayed turned – forever.

I sat in the darkness, looking out at the stars for a long, long time. Much later, I picked up the phone. "Ainsley? I'm sorry. I took your advice today. I've found out lots of things… Are we still friends?"

"We've always been friends." His reply was a little muffled. Probably he was in bed – half asleep. But we were still friends! That was all I needed to know right now.

"Night, Ains!"

"Night, Les."

Chapter Twenty-Nine

We pin our dreams on people, just as we hang gaudy baubles on an overburdened Christmas tree, challenging it to collapse under the sheer stress and weight of expectation. Somehow someone else will make all our dreams come true. Because we want them to – so much. Because we have chosen them to be 'the special one'.

And that's when we often decide to overlook the simple things that matter the most. The only things that matter. Kindness, generosity of spirit, everlasting and true friendship, understanding, tolerance, patience, shared laughter and the knowledge that someone cares enough to be there beside you holding your hand when you are sick, or worried – or frightened. Knowing that another person understands you completely and accepts you unreservedly for who you really are, and wants you despite your flaws and weaknesses. No matter what misfortune or adversity has befallen you.

I've learned from Ainsley that Buddhists live and appreciate and enjoy every single moment of every single day. I've learned to really look at a sea shell or pale pink rock, marvelling at its colour, texture and smell. I've learned to stand still every so often, stop rushing around at full speed – see nature. Really see it. I've learned that to be free is the most wonderful, natural, precious gift that no one should be allowed to steal from you – ever. It is priceless. It should never be carelessly tossed away. Or taken for granted.

I've learned to treasure simple pleasures, taking the course of each day at a slower pace – one step at a time. Like a little child learning to walk again. And I've also learned not to worry too much about the future. No one can plan it.

We marry – 'for better or worse' – take the 'safe path'. The traditional path – is guaranteed to lead us to happiness and security. Perhaps sometimes that path is the right path to take. I've discovered 'the road less travelled' can perhaps be even better.

For it may not be 'safe' and it may be unpredictable, but so is life. And no one has the right to rob us of ourselves. No one is entitled to make us feel inferior, or useless or afraid. Life isn't something to run away from – even when it becomes calamitous.

The transient belief that you cannot carry on is never justified. I have learned never to take life for granted. Your life is yours – no one else has the right to determine what happens to you. If you have to learn to bend and nearly break, trying to force yourself to be someone you are not in order to please somebody else – you will eventually come to grief. I have learned that true and honest friends accept you for who you are and what you are, and are happy with that! Anything less is too high a ransom to pay. I've learned that nothing, and nobody, is perfect! I've learned that the only way I know how to – the hard way!

***

I have to meet some people at the station at lunchtime. I get up from the sturdy rust-coloured rock, brushing crumbling bits of shingle from my skirt, and walk back across the beaming beach. The sun's beginning to come out.

It's probably not changed very much since Hercule Poirot's day, yet the dinky Devon station is oddly comforting. No big shiny platforms and soulless stainless steel bridges and escalators. Just ice cream-painted wood and cinnamon brown benches. Even a little old-fashioned vivid red pillar box and a poster advertising 'Fry's Chocolate'. Like stepping back languorously in time to a far more gentle age. The warmth of the sunshine is beginning to filter through the awnings overhead and the breeze is now a soft warmth drifting down the platform. "What time does the train from Victoria arrive?" I ask the guardsman, feeling like one of *The Railway Children*. I put my arm up to shelter my eyes as the sunlight bursting through the clouds becomes even more startling.

"At mid-day!" How very appropriate and proper! Not 12 – not 12.30 – but mid-day! High noon! I have fifteen minutes to wait before the train arrives. I sit down on the wooden bench, straightening my pale lemon T-shirt and smoothing my floral-printed cotton skirt.

I peer down the track. The sun is warm now on my bare legs, caressing my cold toes in their brightly coloured strappy summer sandals. I watch as the signals go up and down. Watch as the guard comes out to blow his whistle, smelling the soft sweet perfume of poppy-coloured petunias spilling over from the hanging baskets dangling about randomly from gleaming black-painted wrought iron lamp posts.

In the distance, I see a train rumbling at last towards me. I squint into the sunshine as I continue to look down the railway line. And strangely, my heart seems to skip a beat. It actually can do that! Like the cha-cha! I feel lightheaded and carefree as if this is only the beginning of a whole new wonderful adventure. And for the first time in my life, I have no idea where I'm going or who with – and it doesn't matter!

I keep watching till the silver grey and yellow train comes closer and closer. Slowing, slowing, until it eventually comes to a standstill. People cascade, tumbling out like skittles or acrobats. Little boys and girls with buckets and spades in red and yellow gaudy plastic, gaily coloured hats, men in suits, women carrying babies, and cases, and bulging handbags or Sainsbury's bags – or a combination of all three. Jumbling, fumbling, disorganised and happily chaotic.

And my eyes start to search wildly through the sea of strange faces now. I cannot recognise anyone. And I start to panic – a bit. And feel disappointment start to sink down into my stomach. Maybe a last-minute change of heart? Maybe he missed the train for some reason? And then I look up again and I can see him, smiling straight at me. Striding down the track carrying two massive, fully-filled deep blue satchel-type cases. Wearing well-worn faded blue denims, and a battered brown Australian bush hat. Which he raises with his right hand. "Hello, Lesley!" And he's standing in front of me. Deep brown of the scarred lop-sided cheek jarred against the paler tan of the rest of his perfectly chiselled cheekbones. He shoves his sunglasses into his open shirt pocket. I throw my arms around him, hugging him so tight. Just like a little girl would.

"Oh, Ainsley!" I don't know how long we stand there in the middle of the platform. Me hugging him, and he just stood, accepting, not quite knowing where to put his hands. Then I feel something tugging at my arm.

"Mum! He...ll...o!" I spin around and there is Will. Deep green trendy sunshades pushed high onto the top of his newly spiked haircut and wearing a blue T-shirt with rude writing on it. I let go of Ainsley and throw my arms around Will. Holding him so close I think for a moment I'll crush him. "Alright, Mum – steady on!" He clears his throat and stands back a little. Laughing, the merry chuckling sound I've missed so much. "Look who's here as well – this is Emily!"

And I turn around, and there she is, standing on the side of the platform. The most exquisite creature. Quite lovely. Colt-like legs and long silky jet black shining hair swinging down her back. She reminds me instantly of a wild Andalusian pony. She's holding a tiny embroidered bag spangled with sequins which sparkles in the sunlight, and a vivaciously printed silk scarf is slung low around her hipster jeans. She's shy. Of course, she would be.

I walk over to her, slowly. Smiling. So this was the little girl that Ainsley had described to me joyously so long ago with shining eyes, as 'the light of my life!' I could see why. And now she was all grown up.

"I'm, Lesley." I offer her my hand. She instantly takes hold of both of mine, squeezing them together.

"I know." Her voice is soft, well-spoken and easy. Emily's eyes are as deeply brown as ever Ainsley's had been. And look lost.

"Would you like some lunch?" I suggest a place down by the harbour, and she looks relieved. We pile all the cases into my brilliant red 4 x 4. When we reach the harbour it is bustling with new-found life. Yachts in dazzling white and azure with silver trim, the tinkling sound as the masts clink together, ruffled by the breeze. The sun is blazing hot now.

Sea spray and salt and Ambre Solaire drift through the balmy air like mist in a sauna. Smelling of summer. We sit outside, ordering huge jugs of ruby Sangria with bits of fruit floating around on top and all kinds of seafood salad, and warm freshly baked ciabatta bread. With special exotic oils and dressings for us to dip into. Ainsley wanders off for a while and leans on the white railing, looking out at the boats. It seems odd to see him by the seaside, I've never seen him outside in the fresh air by the coast or even in a field! It feels completely natural.

I watch as he bends his head forward and lights a cigarette. That's new. I see something twinkling in his left ear. Two tiny silver filigree earrings with turquoise gems. They are new too. Emily strolls over, standing beside him. He drapes his arm loosely and amiably across her shoulders like a much-loved well-worn scarf.

Meanwhile, Will is eager to chat. Telling me all his news in a continuous non-stop volley. All about University. And exams. And girlfriends. Then he sees me glance across at Emily. "She's nice, Mum. We were talking to each other on the train all the way here. She's so easy to talk to. Not like a lot of the girls who have nothing interesting to say and have silly conversations half the time. I haven't known her long have I? Yet I feel I could talk to her about absolutely anything!" I smile back at him. "Do you know what I mean, Mum?"

"Yes," I reply "I do know!"

When we at last finish our leisurely lunch, Will decides to take Emily for a wild ride on the red and white speedboat – Atlantis. Then they disappear. "We're off to the beach afterwards!" they trill in unison.

"Looks like it's just you and me then!" Ainsley smiles, leaning his face on his hand as he rests his elbow on the table.

His face has healed from when I saw it last. And the swollen black eyes have gone. But the ragged, jagged scar was vividly visible and his face still was not symmetrically aligned. I put my hand up to feel it, very lightly. This time he doesn't flinch away. He just sits still. "Does it hurt a lot?" I ask him.

"All the time. I try not to think about it! Especially on a lovely day like today!"

His smile is still the same. Filling the warm deep brown eyes I know so well. So honest and trusting. Like the reindeer in Richmond Park had been. He pushes his fringe back in the old familiar way. Leaning forward on the table we begin once more to chat like conspirators. "So come on, Lesley. What's this big cloak and dagger surprise you're so eager to share with me? I'm intrigued! I was trying to work it out all the way here on the train. You've kept me guessing since you rang last week and asked me to meet you in Deepest Devon. Have you got a secret lover stashed away down here in a smuggler's cave or something?"

I smile back at him. "Come with me. I've got something very important to show you!" I take his hand and it just feels so right. We stroll back to my flame-red Freelander.

"Let's take the top off!" says Ainsley. "The car I mean – not yours!" And as we drive fresh air feels warm on our faces, so much better than being cooped up inside the vehicle on such a hot sunny day. I climb into the driving seat, set off driving determinedly round the harbour, then up the narrow twisting cobbled alleyways smelling of fish and salt and brine, up past crowds of noisy, clattering holidaymakers, up to the very top of the cliffs where the air is sweet, fresh and pure. I switch off the ignition, shoving the keys into my yellow canvas handbag with a bright pink handle. Ainsley jumps out, pulling his hat lower across his wounded face. We walk arm in arm across tufty turf that now appears to be the most radiant shade of green. Then I share with him my secret.

"That's it!" I wave my arm into space. Behind us is a whitewashed 18th century villa with apricot tiles on the pitched roof and aquamarine-painted shutters blowing gently back and forth in the benign breeze.

Ainsley gasps. Pushes open the door. Steps inside. It's cool. "Lesley – it's – it's – it's an empty building!" he proclaims, simultaneously laughing out loud and bending forward clutching his stomach as he grins at me.

"I know! I know it's empty at the moment," I confess. "But it won't always be empty! It's going to be filled -up – with the most wonderful paintings from brand new artists and sculptors, and unknown designers who make unforgettable impressions! I'm turning it into a working studio, Ainsley. Where I can design things – all kinds of things Make things Sell things even! And it will be mine! Paid for it with the money I got from the divorce settlement from Paul when the house was eventually sold. I didn't think he would ever be made to agree to anything at all. But in the end, the solicitor and barrister who acted for me just made him get on with everything. When I finally got the money I decided to do something I never ever would have dreamed of doing for real. I came down here to be by myself. To get over everything. To work out what happened and why and I am climbing slowly out of the deep black pit that I thought I would never ever have a chance of getting out of. Fresh sea air. Recovery. I signed the papers last week – and this place is officially mine! And here I am!" He is, for once in his life, completely speechless. So I carry on. "And I'm calling it – 'Buccaneer'!"

He shakes out a cigarette from the packet tucked into his shirt pocket. Lights it, inhales deeply, thoughtfully, walks around with a critical eye surveying the wonky primrose plastered walls, looked up and down and then out of the bare window at the magnificent view of sparkling ocean spread out before us. Right across the whole of the bay as far as the eye can see and into infinity. He turns to me with a glimmer of something I haven't seen before in his eyes. "You're serious aren't you?"

I can't read his expression, for the first time ever. He is – incredulous, amazed – admiring? I need some help here. Come on Ainsley – "Say something!" I blurt out.

"Well, I'm flabbergasted! It's just so unlike you, Lesley! I mean, you've always been so careful, so sensible, going for what you thought was the safe option – not being a wild child – taking the traditional…" He stops full flow, acknowledging with a shake of his head the incongruity of his ill-chosen words. "I'm sorry, Lesley. That was insensitive of me. That wasn't what I meant to say to you at all. You don't deserve that. There was nothing 'safe' about the option you chose. I realise that! Not with a man like Paul. Not at the end of the day – was there? You'd have been better off in the jungle fighting the lions and deadly snakes! He led you and William one hell of a life and I cannot blame you one bit for wanting to change that – forever! Good luck to you, hon – I hope all your dreams come true!"

"Let's go outside," I say. We sit on the grass, gazing out to sea. It's very blue and very calm. The way the sea should always look on a lazy early summer afternoon. I pluck idly at grass blades. "It's taken me a lot of soul-searching, it's been a long and painful journey of self-discovery to reach this point," I admit to him.

He covers my hand with his long sensitive fingers and strokes it very gently. "I know. I know that," he says. "I'm still coming to terms with all that has happened to me and I just have to take it one step at a time. A bit like you I guess." He shakes his head till his fringe falls into his eyes. "Lesley, what you believed you had with Paul – your dreams – it was like a big beautiful solid piece of precious crystal. And Paul has smashed that completely to bits – shattered it into a million tiny pieces that can never ever be replaced or put back together again."

I stare back at him. "My goodness – Ainsley. You do understand, after all!"

He nods drawing again at his cigarette, smoke pluming into the space between us. "Of course," he states simply. Of course, he did. Why wouldn't he? He had known me nearly all my adult life.

"I'll never get married again!" I hear myself saying defensively. He smiles properly then, and it's like the old days when it reaches his eyes and makes them dance.

"Never say never!" he says.

"Oh yes! I can say never!" I reply quickly.

Then I feel the need to tell him why. But I guess he knows anyway. Ainsley knows everything about me. "I thought marriage meant respectability, dependability, loyalty, love, mutual respect – so many things – but it doesn't! It doesn't necessarily mean any of that at all! Getting married ended up turning me into a person who felt dirty, degraded, humiliated and ashamed and almost got me a criminal record. I was locked up inside a prison cell!" I gasp as the words start to tumble out so fast I feel I will fall over them. "Sorry, Ains – but – you know…" He nods once more.

"Well, I'm not even on speaking terms with Emma at the moment. She fleeced me for everything when it came to the final divorce settlement. My pension – she wanted absolutely the whole lot. All I had. And still, that doesn't seem to be enough! So – you're looking at a very unwealthy man – who is also very ugly!" He stubs out his cigarette, twisting it gently with his fingers to extinguish the flame. "Who would want a man like that?!"

"You're not ugly," I begin. He looks at me, with a lop-sided kind of half-smile, his earring glinting mysteriously in the evening sunlight.

"Oh right – well, I'm not Donny Osmond am I?"

I laugh back at him. "No, you're not! You never were! You're you, Ainsley. And that's enough. You are beautiful – inside and out!"

He looks embarrassed and pulls a comical face. Not as mobile as it once had been, but pretty effective nevertheless. "Oh, that's very Mills and Boon! But thank you for the compliment, and for being so kind!"

He bends forward and makes a mock bow, before kissing the back of my hand which is still impaled beneath his. "I meant it – I'm trying to be honest here!" I carry on. I have started this so I am determined to finish it. Because I know if I don't say it now I will never have the courage to say it again. "I don't care if you think it sounds daft, or slushy. I don't care if your face isn't perfect. Nobody's perfect! It's what's inside of people that matters. And that's all that matters. All the other stuff – comes – and it goes. Our dreams get shattered our lives get battered. We grow old. And we have to survive the storm somehow, Ainsley. Because life is all we have. And all that matters is the truth. To accept each other for who we genuinely are – not to have to keep up some morbid pretence, to impress anyone else or comply with everybody else's version of what is 'correct' or 'right'. Not to be forced to live in fear. Not to have to feel the despair of lies you tell when your husband is knocking you from here to kingdom come and you keep covering up constantly because you don't want the neighbours to know, you don't want your friends and family to know. You want to keep the 'image of perfection' that no one can match. And it's you who ends up feeling the shame at the end of the day. You who feels the pain and the hurt. You who hides away in the darkness crying. You who ends up locked up inside some morbid prison cell!" I've got his full attention now, and at least he's listening to me properly.

"I can't make you any promises, Lesley…" he finally says. Looking at me steadily from beneath the thick floppy fringe that I love so dearly. And I know if I have to go through the rest of my life and never see that fringe again, I would be very sad. And very lonely. And at last, I can admit that to myself.

"I don't want promises," I tell him. "I want what's real!"

That's when he really starts to laugh out loud, a vivid, warm chuckling sound that echoes and rumbles right across the cliff tops and out to sea like a fanfare. "You, Lesley! The Champion Dreamer of all time! Do you want what's real? You have always wanted the fairytale. The romance. The Highwayman – the Pirate Captains!"

And as I sit there listening to him in the glow of the gently fading golden evening sunlight, I see the silver gleaming in his ear-lobe, I see the black shining hair cascading onto his pale blue shirt collar, and I see the scar skidding across his tortured, tanned cheekbones, and I think – "What's so wrong with that?"

- The End -

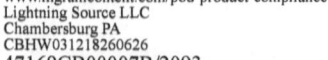